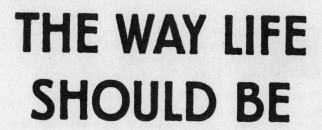

THE WAY LIFE SHOULD BE

TERRY SHAW

A TOUCHSTONE BOOK
PUBLISHED BY SIMON & SCHUSTER
New York   London   Toronto   Sydney

Touchstone
A Division of Simon & Schuster, Inc.
1230 Avenue of the Americas
New York, NY 10020

Copyright © 2007 by Terry Shaw

First Touchstone trade paperback edition September 2007

TOUCHSTONE and colophon are registered trademarks of Simon & Schuster, Inc.

For information about special discounts for bulk purchases, please contact Simon & Schuster Special Sales at 1-800-456-6798 or business@simonandschuster.com.

Designed by Mary Austin Speaker

Manufactured in the United States of America

10 9 8 7 6 5 4 3 2 1

Library of Congress Cataloging-in-Publication Data
Shaw, Terry.
    The way life should be / Terry Shaw.
       p.   cm.
    "A Touchstone Book."
    1. Fathers and sons—Fiction.   2. Politicians—Crimes against—Fiction.   3. Murder—Fiction.   4. Maine—Fiction.   I. Title.
PS3619.H3946W39   2007
813'.6—dc22   2007025418

ISBN-13: 978-1-4165-6312-9
ISBN-10:   1-4165-6312-1

For Beth

THE WAY LIFE
SHOULD BE

PROLOGUE

It was three a.m. and anything was possible—all he needed was a little luck. At least that's what Paul Stanwood tried to tell himself as he turned his Range Rover onto the wet, sandy road and its headlights bounced through the shadows and fir. He knew he shouldn't be there. He just couldn't help himself.

When the Rover began to stall on the ruts, Stanwood downshifted to let the tires grab hold, which seemed to do the trick. He was nervous but kept going until a sign on a steel gate read: "Sullivan Park Closed at Dusk. Violators Will be Prosecuted to the Fullest Extent Allowed by Law."

Whatever that meant.

He wasn't sure but was willing to take a chance, so he cut the ignition, got out, and began walking the footpath through the gently swaying spruce before reconsidering. He stopped and took a deep breath. The rot drifted up from the clam flats below and a full moon burned like a bare bulb off the dark water of Penobscot Bay.

The park was at the end of a long peninsula, a tangle of rock, surf and pine that had once been a saltwater farm. Now it was just a road through the woods, a small, unpaved parking lot and an oddly out-of-place pay phone. Past the clearing where he stood, a few scattered picnic tables and a cinderblock bathhouse completed the scene—not much, really, given the recent sensation. Of course, there was the boat launch.

"The only place in town to get off at low tide," according to John Quinn, who'd come home to run his family's newspaper. He said the park was an embarrassment and that grown men—no matter their sexual preference—should have a sense of decency.

Quinn had no idea what was at stake. After being gone a decade, he was clueless about the changes taking place in their hometown. Paul planned to tell him as much, once he was sure of everything himself, though he'd been warned against it. He shook his head at the thought, when something cracked behind him.

"Who's there?" he asked.

Nobody answered.

For a moment he listened to the waves lap the granite shore, the whole time wondering if those had been his own steps echoing in the darkness. He stopped and spun around. Damn. He couldn't believe how paranoid he'd become. He took another deep breath and tried to relax. Easy now, he told himself. The sun would be up in a few hours and everything would be safe and fresh with the new day.

Keeping that in mind, Paul walked toward the bathhouse and stepped inside. The place was a mess. He could make out overturned benches and a cracked toilet. The urinals reeked and it was hard to believe the spot had become the object of such fierce debate. Men were being arrested. The cops were under fire. Neither side would listen to reason and somehow Paul was caught in the middle. What was he supposed to do?

As he shuffled his sandals along the gritty concrete and lit a Camel, the flame shined briefly on a wall covered with crudely drawn slogans and promises that made him laugh out loud. The whole thing seemed suddenly absurd, and by the time he was halfway through the cigarette and beginning to relax, the gravelly sound of tires came from the road.

A car door slammed and someone began walking his way.

"Helllloo!" Stanwood's voice echoed off the low, flat ceiling.

"You alone?" came back.

"I was."

The other voice hesitated. "I thought I saw someone else poking around."

"That was just me, admiring the scenery."

"Glad to hear it." A figure appeared in the doorway. "I was hoping you'd be here."

"I'm flattered," Stanwood said once he recognized the voice. "But you're the last person I'd expect to turn up in a place like this."

"I wish I could say the same about you."

Stanwood ignored the shot and asked what he had in mind.

"A little surprise." The man reached into his nylon Windbreaker.

"So what's that?"

"This?" The man flicked on a steel Maglite the size of a nightstick and stepped toward him. "Why, it's the surprise."

Stanwood held up his hands to shield his eyes from the glare. "Look—I'm not here for what you think."

"Then what are you here for?"

He wasn't sure. "To tell you the truth, this whole deal has become a little too complicated."

"Maybe I can simplify things." The man swung the Mag

in a small, fast arc, catching Stanwood on the collarbone and sending him to the floor.

That knocked the wind out of him.

Stanwood forced himself to his hands and knees but the man swung again, connecting with the side of his skull and causing everything to blur. Stanwood rolled onto his back and tried to cover himself. The man swung a third time and shattered a forearm. Stanwood curled into the fetal position and tried to smother the pain. "Jesus Christ," he muttered before another *crack* sent him under.

"That's right," the man said, his breath heavy from the effort. "It's time to go home to Jesus."

He swung again and the light went out.

1.

Quinn snatched the phone on the first ring.

"John, it's Ginny Sewell."

He groaned, fell back onto his bed and waited for her to continue. He was used to calls at odd hours, but this was a little early, even for Ginny. "Well, what is it?" he asked when nothing else followed.

"It's Sarah," she finally managed.

"Is she all right?"

"No," Ginny said. "She's not."

Sarah was the police reporter at the *Stone Harbor Pilot* and Ginny was her mother. Since she was sobbing at the other end of the line, Quinn thought the worst—that her daughter had been in a horrible accident rushing to a crime scene or fire.

"Tell me what happened," he said slowly but firmly.

"She—she—she's been arrested."

Quinn relaxed. "That's it?"

"What do you mean, that's it?" Ginny couldn't believe his attitude.

"You made it sound like she was dead."

"Don't yell at me!" Ginny shouted.

"I'm not yelling at you!" he said, though suddenly he real-

5

ized he may have been. He had a temper and his heart was still racing from being jarred awake so early on a Sunday morning. The glowing numbers on his alarm clock read 6:00 a.m.

He took a deep breath as Ginny blew her nose into the receiver and tried to compose herself. "I'm sorry," she said. "I didn't know who else to call."

"Don't worry about it," Quinn said. "You just scared me. That's all."

"Well, I'm scared, too."

"I bet." During the next awkward moment, Quinn looked around the bedroom. His wife, Maria, was on the other side of the sheets, lying perfectly still in the early morning light, which could mean only one thing: she was pissed.

"John, you still there?" Ginny asked.

"Yeah. I was just thinking."

"About what?"

"Nothing important" was probably the wrong thing to say. By then it didn't matter. Anything he said could—and would—be used against him. He knew by the way his wife's whole body was stiffening beside him. "So what did Sarah do?" he asked Ginny.

"They charged her with disturbin' a crime scene," she said. "At Sullivan Park. It happened an hour ago."

"Jesus." Quinn could just imagine the call they'd answered. The park was the biggest pickup spot on the Maine coast and had been making headlines all summer. In the past month alone, twenty-three men had been charged with public lewdness as part of a police crackdown. Despite the arrests, they kept coming, up and down Route 1, from Belfast to Bath. Tourists, locals, it didn't matter.

"Don't you have anythin' else to say?" Ginny asked.

"I hope she was wearing rubber gloves."

"That isn't funny."

"I know." The full effect was beginning to hit him. "And I'm not laughing."

Neither was Ginny. "The police chief says she'll have a criminal record!"

"Oh, he's just trying to scare her. Trust me."

"He's serious!" she sobbed.

"Calm down. I'll be right there." Quinn hung up and shook his head.

"Where are you going?" his wife asked.

"The police station." He smiled and ran his hand along her soft, bare shoulder and down her arm. "But don't worry— this won't take long."

Maria turned on her side, away from him. "It's them again, isn't it?"

He didn't answer as he got up and pulled on a pair of shorts and a T-shirt. He couldn't just leave one of his reporters in jail, especially when she was only doing her job. It wasn't her fault she usually beat the cops on calls and they were tired of being embarrassed. Given her crap salary and the hours she worked, driving down to the station was the least Quinn could do. He was probably going to stop by the office later that morning anyway, which would make his wife just as mad. With the way things had been going, he really didn't have a choice.

Besides, no matter how much of a pain Sarah could be, he admired her. She was twenty-two and had worked her way up from part-time librarian to news clerk to reporter. She had real passion. She was always in a rush, always carrying a hand-held scanner and always running down fires and accidents and random police calls. The only drawback was she didn't have a license and her mother had to drive her everywhere.

The whole arrangement may have sounded strange to the uninitiated, but Ginny had a lot of time on her hands and didn't mind waiting around in her ancient Lincoln Continental, scoping out men, reading the racing form or working on a romance novel that had occupied her free time, on and off, for the past five years. That's how long she'd been on disability after ruining her wrists stitching moccasins at a local factory.

Driving in, Quinn went right past the place. Now converted into an outlet store, the building's brick exterior had been painted, polished and given newfound charm. As he descended into the lower part of town, the streets were quiet and empty, save the occasional shriek of a gull, with block after block of wooden frame homes, brick sidewalks and cluttered storefronts stacked on a waterfront dating to the seventeenth century.

Boats of every size filled the harbor, from Boston whalers and dories to the hulls of navy destroyers and the three historic schooners that tied up each summer at the maritime museum. It was a picturesque setting, one that made him feel like he was driving through a postcard, until he got to the police station and noticed television crews set up for a long siege on the front walk. Quinn cringed at the image viewers were getting at home, since one of the talking heads was already going at it.

"...and in a bizarre side note to this sensational story, a reporter has been arrested for..." The reporter paused, as though he couldn't quite remember. His cameraman mouthed the rest of the sentence and TV Boy delivered the line "disturbing a crime scene," as though the hitch had been deliberate.

Quinn couldn't wait for this to be over. The last thing Sarah needed was for her arrest to be blown even further out of proportion. He got out of his car and slammed the door.

Ginny was waiting in a bulging red dress, pacing and smoking frantically. She was a short, busty woman in her early forties and her face was flush with makeup and concern. "John, thank God you're here!" she said breathlessly as she clicked up the stairs in her high heels beside him. "We'll see what they have to say now."

He stopped halfway. "Maybe you better wait here."

"I've been waitin' more than an hour and don't think I should have to wait any longer."

"You're probably right," he said. "But let me handle this."

She crossed her arms and sighed.

He put a hand on her fleshy shoulder. "So tell me everything that happened," he said. "From the beginning."

"I guess it all started with Anthony Perkins."

"The actor?"

"Of course," she said, as if that were the numbest question she'd ever heard. "Just as he was stabbin' his first victim on the late, late show, a call came across the scanner about Sullivan Park. Since it's only a half mile from the trailer—if you go the back way—we took off. We were the first ones there and Sarah went right in."

"You let her go in alone?"

"I left the headlights on," Ginny insisted. "And the next thing I knew there was sirens and policemen and Sarah was under arrest."

He waited for Ginny to continue but she didn't.

"Then what happened?" he asked.

"I went home and changed outta my bathrobe," she said slyly, as if to tease him.

"Well, that explains it." Quinn wasn't fazed. He knew the Sewells had their own way of operating and let it go at that. He told her to wish him luck, then went inside.

The station was packed. A couple of powdered and puffed TV reporters milled about in suit jackets, ties and shorts, trying to act casual yet keeping a respectful distance from the department's two detectives, who along with a handful of patrolmen worked the phones. Every one of them was yakking, until they saw Quinn. He knew something serious had happened at the park when they all looked away rather than making eye contact.

That wasn't a problem with the chief. When Quinn stepped into his office and pulled up a chair, Al Sears sat staring behind his desk, 220 hard pounds on a square-shouldered, six-foot frame. He was tan and wore faded jeans and a tight red polo shirt. Despite the casual attire, he still had his blond flattop, a chip on his shoulder and a Glock 9 mm clipped to his belt.

Sears tried to look right through Quinn, something that usually worked with teenage delinquents but came across as silly to a grown man who was just as big, especially when that grown man had known him since the third grade. "Alvah," Quinn said in greeting.

The chief nodded and waited for Quinn to get to the point.

"Any particular reason you locked up Sarah?" Quinn asked.

Sears looked down at a report on his desk, then back at Quinn in his Bob Marley T-shirt, as though he couldn't decide which deserved more attention.

"Well?" Quinn pressed.

"She mucked up a crime scene," Sears finally answered.

"Can you be a little more specific?"

"It's a felony."

"It sounds like a stretch."

"I don't care what it sounds like," Sears said. "I put her tight little ass in jail and that's the end of it."

Quinn figured that was unlikely, given Sears's reputation with women. "Does her 'tight little ass' have anything to do with this?" he asked.

"I doubt it."

"Well, that's all you ever seem to think about." Quinn rolled the chair back from the desk to make himself more comfortable. "So does that mean I have to pay to get a lawyer out of bed on a Sunday morning?"

"Could be."

"Alvah, be reasonable."

"I have been." Sears hated to be called Alvah, a name only Quinn still used, now that the chief's mother was dead and buried.

For his part, Quinn couldn't believe what was happening.

"You think this whole thing's funny, don't you?" Sears asked.

"It's unusual, to say the least." Quinn stood up and leaned on the desk. "My God, you spent the whole summer bullying those poor bastards and now you have to bully Sarah."

"I'm not bullyin' anyone," Sears said. "She brought this on herself."

Quinn raised an eyebrow but didn't respond.

"And I s'pose you're an expert on this sorta thing," Sears said.

"I didn't say that," Quinn insisted, though he'd spent three years as a cop reporter at the *Miami Herald* and knew a thing or two about crime.

"Well, this isn't Miami," Sears said, as if reading his mind.

"I'll say." Quinn smiled and walked over to scan a wall lined with yellowed newspaper clippings of Sears as the school D.A.R.E. officer, as coach of a championship Little League team, as the most recent inductee into the Stone Harbor High School Football Hall of Fame. In addition, every stripe and medal he'd ever earned was framed and mounted, including a front-page *Pilot* story announcing his promotion to chief. But the spot of honor was reserved for the game ball from a 17–16 homecoming win over Westbrook.

"Now, if you're through gawkin'," Sears said, "I have work to do."

Quinn picked the football off the tee, tossed it in the air and caught it with a smack. "Well, it must be pretty important if it got you in here on a Sunday morning," Quinn said. "Especially when there's a favorable marine forecast."

Sears stopped what he was doing and turned to angrily face Quinn. "It just so happens a prominent member of this community was found beaten to death." Sears stepped forward and got a hand on his precious ball, which only caused Quinn to tighten his grip. "And I'm not gonna put up with any crap, no matter what cocksuckah got popped."

Quinn let go and watched Sears stumble backward a few steps. "Who's dead?"

Sears quickly regained his footing and stood back up to his full height. "The name isn't being released till the family's been notified," he said as he carefully set the football back in place.

"Come on!"

Sears hesitated. "Sure you can handle it?"

"Yes, I can handle it."

"Okay, then. Paul Stanwood was beaten to a bloody pulp in the Sullivan Park bathhouse. We found what was left a him this mornin'."

Quinn couldn't handle it. He felt like a granite block had fallen on his chest, and the only thing he could do was slump in the chair and stare at the ceiling as tears came and he struggled to make sense of it all. Paul was his best friend. How could he be dead? They'd just spoken the day before.

And what was he doing in Sullivan Park? He was married, had two children and was straight as an arrow. For God's sake, he'd been a jock and an Eagle Scout and legend had it he'd lost his virginity to their French teacher, Miss Racette, in ninth grade.

But Sullivan Park?

"So why was he there?" Quinn finally asked.

"That's not a question I'm prepared to answer on behalf of the deceased."

"Well, you better say something."

"I don't know," Sears said as the very beginning of a smile began to form on his face. "Seems like I already said too much."

"This isn't funny."

"I know it has to be tough." Sears reached for a pack of cigarettes on his desk and offered one to Quinn.

"I don't smoke."

"Relax."

"Don't tell me to relax!"

"I won't tell you again," Sears warned.

"You're twisting this all around." Quinn stood back up. "Paul was on the board of selectmen. I'm sure he was just checking out the situation."

"At three o'clock in the mornin'?"

Christ. The small-town speculation had already begun. "It's a homicide," Quinn said, "not an inquisition."

"It's a fact a life," Sears said. "So get used to it."

"You don't know what you're talking about."

"I'm afraid I do." Then Sears laughed like it was Christmas morning. "And for the sake of his wife and children, we're lucky we didn't find a dick up his ass."

"You know that isn't true!"

"Do I?" Sears asked. "I'm just looking for answers and don't want to make any assumptions."

Quinn stepped toward him and squared his shoulders. "I'm warning you, you sick son of a bitch. One more crack about Paul and I'll put you through that wall." Instead, Quinn kicked his chair across the tiled floor into the steel desk, where it crashed and tumbled over.

"That's enough." Actually, it was more than enough. Sears walked over and cracked the door. "*Sergeant!*" he called into the hall.

A woman in uniform stepped inside. "Yes, Chief?"

"Did you hear what this man just said?"

"Sure—everyone did."

"That's what I thought," Sears said. "Arrest him for threatenin' a police officah."

"Right, Chief."

Sears went back to the file cabinet, took out a folder and sat back down at his desk as though Quinn were already gone.

"I want a lawyer," Quinn said.

"Sure," Sears said absently before adding as an after-thought, "If you want, I'll even call a good psychiatrist."

That's when Quinn was led out of the office under the glare of the TV cameras.

2.

"AND THEN YOU KICKED a chair," his wife said.

"I guess."

"You guess?" She was standing with her hands on her hips and her dark eyebrows arched over a pair of Ray-Bans. "What do you mean, you guess? Are you telling me you can't remember?"

Quinn wasn't sure what he was telling her.

"Is that all you have to say for yourself?" she pressed.

He didn't answer. Hell, he didn't even know how she'd heard. She just showed up outside the police station after he'd finally been released. Quinn had no idea his name had been blasted across the Bangor and Portland television stations after nearly getting involved in a scuffle with the police chief over the investigation into the homicide of an "as yet un-named" local businessman.

"Well, how are you going to explain this?" she asked.

That was a very good question, one Quinn hadn't begun to consider as they stood on a sidewalk filled with joggers, dog walkers, couples out for bagels and a newspaper. "I was mad," he finally said. "He was baiting me."

"And you took it. Just like that."

Not exactly, Quinn started to say before reconsidering. A few doors down, an older crowd filed into the First Parish Church, which stood like an exclamation point on the town common. Beneath the wooden Gothic structure, the styles of the faithful hadn't changed in his lifetime: pastels, pearls and hats for the ladies; oxford shirts, khakis and blue blazers for the gentlemen. Of course, several had traded their penny loafers for sneakers.

Quinn eyed his wife, who would never be confused with one of the blue-hairs in her tiny white capris and short green top. He took a deep breath and tried to explain: "Things were a little more complicated than you think."

"Were they?" she asked, pulling off her glasses.

"Yes."

A dour-looking woman with a Scotty dog frowned at them for talking so loudly, though others slowed to hear more.

"He called Paul a fag!" Quinn told them all.

"I'm sure he'll get over it."

"I don't think so," Quinn said slowly, for emphasis, and that's when it hit him. "My God, you don't know," he said in a much lower voice.

"Know what?" Maria asked, even more loudly than before.

He held her arms in his hands and looked into her brown eyes. "They found Paul a couple hours ago in Sullivan Park," he whispered. "Beaten to death."

She blinked hard as her face fell flat in disbelief. "He was what?"

"He's dead," Quinn said. "Somebody killed him."

"But why would anyone want to hurt Paul?" she asked in a barely audible voice.

Quinn had no idea. His friend was always sticking up for others and it was hard to imagine him a victim, especially under the apparent circumstances. "None of it makes any sense."

"Not at all." She dropped to the curb, slouched forward and put a hand over her face to hide her tears. Not Paul. He was the guy who was always grinning. The guy who would do anything for you. The guy who never said a bad word about anyone.

Quinn put an arm around her and she leaned into him. The same thoughts had been running, over and over, in his own mind.

"Does Lizz know?" she asked.

"They were trying to notify the family. She has to know by now." And she had to be devastated.

"That poor woman," she said.

"Those poor kids."

Maria began to cry softly and he continued to hold her. She'd always liked Paul. He'd been the best man at their wedding, and years later, when they finally moved to Stone Harbor, both Paul and Lizz Stanwood went out of their way to make her feel at home among the Maine natives. That wasn't easy, considering Maria was dark and Cuban and living in a state that was 99.9 percent white, but they managed to pull it off. The Stanwoods had a way with people.

That's what made Paul's death so hard to believe.

"Everybody loved him," Maria said.

"I know," Quinn said. "Everybody did."

As she buried her face in his neck, Quinn slowly caressed her back. She was a tough little woman but she let everything out. Her chest rose and fell with each sob, and he wished there were a way to protect her from the pain they both felt.

He didn't know what else to say.

That was never a problem with Maria, and after a bit she pulled back from him, wiped her eyes with a tissue from her purse and stood up. "Lizz shouldn't be alone," she said, and that was that. "I have to get over there."

"What about Jack?"

"I left him with Mrs. Adams." She was a neighbor.

Their six-year-old presented another problem. "So what are we going to tell him?" Quinn asked, dreading the thought.

"Do we have to say anything?"

"Of course we do. Would you rather he heard it somewhere else?"

"I'd rather he didn't hear it at all," she said. "He's a little boy. He shouldn't have to hear any of this. I thought that's why we moved here—so he could have a chance to be a little boy."

"I'll talk to him."

"Right now, as upset as you are?"

"Soon," Quinn said, and left it at that.

She hesitated a moment but didn't ask the next question, since she already knew where he'd be. Instead, she kissed him on the cheek and held his shoulder a moment longer. "I'll meet you at home."

THEN THERE WAS SARAH. Quinn still hadn't seen the young reporter, so he decided to check on her, since the office was only a few blocks from the station and on the way. The *Stone Harbor Pilot* occupied a long, narrow brick building—

three stories tall and stained by time—that Quinn's great-grandfather had built in 1895, before television or radio, let alone the Internet. The *Pilot* anchored Front Street, or at least the two sagging buildings on either side: the Book Corner and the Laughing Gull Bar, whose sign offered the promise of "free beer tomorrow."

The original wooden newspaper building had burned during a terrible fire—along with much of the waterfront. The running joke was that it had been the last time the *Pilot* had done anything interesting. It's also when brick became the downtown building material of choice.

The Wellsen House across the street had been a restaurant and bar since the 1920s; Bliley's Newsstand, the Magic Muffin Bakery and Povich's Men's Store had stood nearly as long. Then there was the First National Bank on the corner. Built in 1929 of granite and marble, it opened the day before the stock market crashed, which was what being uppity in Stone Harbor got you.

Quinn often wondered how he ended up in the town where he'd been born and raised and spent his first eighteen years waiting to leave. Back then the place seemed boring. With the whole world to see, it drove him nuts to be stuck in a cold, empty corner of his own country. But after the University of Miami and a dozen years among misfits and losers at English-language newspapers throughout the Caribbean and Central America, he'd grown to appreciate Stone Harbor.

Now that he'd returned, older and wiser, he liked the fact that nothing much ever happened—or at least never had before today. With that in mind, he hopped the curb with his beat-up Volvo wagon, parked on the sidewalk, then took the steps three at a time. Once inside, he passed the mahogany front counter and went up the wide stairway that was punctuated by historic front pages:

"Peary Reaches Pole"

"Chase-Smith Blasts McCarthy"

"Kennedy Dead"

"Sox Lift Curse—Win Series"

At the top of the stairs, "Bush Wins" and "Bush Finally Wins" and "Bush Wins Again!" hung three in a row, the father and son with the Kennebunkport connection each flashing crooked grins. Quinn imagined the next day's front page and saw his friend, smiling in a shot from better days, along with another picture of the Sullivan Park bathhouse, surrounded by crime scene tape and cops.

As he continued on, his steps echoed on the bare landing and a voice called out, "Is that you, John?"

He looked down and saw Blythe McMichael, the paper's ancient society editor. Stooped from decades spent hunched over a typewriter, she still managed to project an understated authority in her calf-length floral dress, white hair and the round, thick glasses that seemed to magnify and expose the smallest details in anything she examined. In addition, she was the only employee who never had a problem speaking her mind in Quinn's presence, since she was also his aunt.

"Well, have you cooled off yet?" Blythe asked in that all too familiar, patient but slightly scolding tone. "Because from what I saw on television, you were pretty hot."

"Sure—I'm like ice." He looked at his feet as he spoke.

"You don't sound like ice."

"Well, to tell you the truth, I don't really feel like ice."

Quinn could see tears magnified behind her heavy lenses

and on her wrinkled cheeks. She reached out with small, fragile hands that felt weightless in his. As she slowly shook her head, everything he'd tried to block out for the past few hours washed over him—the hurt, the anger, the confusion—and he just let go with a flood of his own tears. He had nothing to hide from Blythe, who knew him better than anyone.

"I came as soon as Seth called me," she said, referring to his cousin, the newspaper's general manager. "I'm so sorry."

"I know. Everybody is. The early consensus is that he was a helluva guy. Only someone, for some reason, decided to bash his brains in."

That image hung in their minds and no amount of grief or regret could undo the harsh reality.

ONCE QUINN REGAINED HIS composure, they walked together into the second-floor newsroom, with its rows of desks, cubicles and his glass-walled office. Sarah had a phone cradled on her shoulder and was typing notes into a computer while a TV blared.

Ginny was nowhere in sight.

Quinn figured she must have suddenly found religion, since it was Sunday, the track was closed and she had plenty to pray about.

When Sarah noticed them she pointed toward the laser printer, and Quinn walked over and picked up her story.

CHAIRMAN FOUND DEAD IN PARK HAD BEEN AT ODDS WITH POLICE CHIEF

By Sarah Sewell
Pilot Staff

The chairman of the town's Board of Selectmen was beaten to death early yesterday at Sullivan Park—10 days after accusing police of harassing gay men there.

Paul Stanwood, 37, died from multiple blows to the head with a blunt instrument, according to Georges County Coroner Earl Canby. The body was discovered at 3:35 a.m. in the Sullivan Park bathhouse after an anonymous 911 call alerted police to the scene.

Chief Al Sears refused to say if there were any suspects. He did, however, warn the public to stay out of the park after hours. "Maybe this will serve as a wake-up call to those who didn't think that place posed a threat to public safety."

His department had been ordered by the Town Board to stop making arrests following a controversial crackdown on gay activity there. Before last weekend, Sears had undercover officers in the park 24 hours a day.

Since May, two dozen arrests have been made on charges ranging from public lewdness to sodomy.

The crackdown drew 300 residents to a board meeting June 3. That's when Stanwood, the board's chairman, in a blistering exchange with Sears, questioned the need for the arrests.

The chief called him a "meddling pantywaist."

"I'll have your badge before this is over," Stanwood responded.

A fellow selectman speculated Stanwood, the married

father of two, was in the park to get the views of the men who frequented it.

"It's unfortunate, but that's just the kind of thing he would do," said Selectman Bryan Bowen-Smythe, a political rival and frequent critic. "Even though he meant well, he didn't always listen to reason."

In a related matter, a *Pilot* reporter arrived at the scene shortly after the call went out from the dispatcher and was held briefly by police. Editor and Publisher John Quinn was also detained after threatening the chief.

No charges were filed.

"Everyone's a little too worked up," District Attorney Jeff McKenna said. "They just need some time to cool off."

Quinn looked from the copy to Sarah and considered her carefully: she was just a kid, really, in a tank top, bell-bottoms and flip-flops, with her brown hair yanked into a ponytail at the side of her head.

"I couldn't believe what I saw," she said quietly.

He stepped toward her. "You actually saw him?"

She turned away, as though trying to escape both the memory and the question. "I saw what was left of him. It was so bad I didn't know who he was till I heard at the station. But that took at least an hour."

Quinn felt like vomiting, but he was still a journalist and the questions kept coming. "How'd they ID him?"

"His wallet was still in his back pocket."

"Any money in it?" he asked.

"Four hundred dollars."

That surprised him. "I guess that rules out robbery."

"It rules out anything that makes sense," she said, sobbing. "John, it was the worst thing I've ever seen."

Quinn wasn't surprised. Sarah was a scanner hound who rolled on every call that came and went, but a homicide was something completely new for her—and the local cops who had to investigate it.

"They think it was someone who hated gays," she said, nearly swallowing the words as she struggled to get them out. "I mean, who else could it have been?"

"Paul wasn't gay."

"Whoever killed him didn't know that," Blythe said. She had a hand on Sarah's back and stood between her and Quinn.

"Well, I know it," Quinn said, his voice rising.

Blythe gave him a subtle tilt of her head to let him know his shouting was the last thing the kid needed to hear.

"I didn't mean anything," Sarah explained.

"I know," Quinn said quietly as his aunt glared at him. "I'm sorry," he added, as much for Blythe's benefit as Sarah's. Then he walked to the window and looked down on the street below. Scores of tourists were poking about, sticking their heads in the small shops and complaining that half the businesses hadn't opened yet, though it was already eleven o'clock.

"Just look at them," Quinn said. Making fun of visitors was a local obsession. They asked odd questions and took pictures of the strangest things: stacks of wire lobster pots, the sign at McGary's Drugstore, Danny Thibitout's old Ford truck. *Why not?* Quinn thought. It was a beautiful day. The sun was over the hills that edged the harbor, the sky was blue as far as the eye could see and it didn't matter to them that his friend was dead. Those people were on vacation, for chrissake, coming to a quiet coastal town to get away from it all.

"John?" Sarah asked, puzzled by his sudden silence.

He told her to relax, which was silly. Sarah never relaxed and never slowed down. At times she made him feel guilty. He owned the place, but she was the one on the clock, 24–7. She reminded Quinn of himself years earlier. Back then he'd been full of idealism. He didn't know what he was full of these days.

"Have you ever covered anything like this?" she asked.

"Never with anybody I knew."

She turned and started back toward her desk, then stopped, as if she sensed he wanted to ask another question.

He held up the printout of her story. "So why'd you use my name and not yours?"

"Channel Two already had it," she said. "I didn't want anyone to think we were covering something up."

"We aren't covering anything up," he said slowly, annoyed by the implication.

"So I can leave it in?"

"Fine."

"At least they haven't identified Paul yet." Sarah tossed her head toward the tube. Instead of a news break, the picture showed the regular Sunday morning fare: candlepin bowling.

"Any idea where the police are going with this?" Blythe asked.

"They're calling it a hate crime," Sarah said.

"What crime isn't?" Quinn wanted to know. He could never figure out the concept—one of many things he and Paul had argued about in recent weeks. They hadn't agreed on the police crackdown in the park or Quinn's handling of the news stories that followed. They'd bickered back and forth over the most foolish things, like whether to publish the names of the men accused of public indecency or if it was the selectmen's role to get involved with something as sleazy as an illicit pickup spot. And this was the end result?

It didn't help when Sarah said she was working on a sidebar on gay bashing. "That's all the cops were talking about. They said it showed why he made such a big deal about the park."

That set Quinn off. His face reddened and suddenly he was standing up. "Look, Paul was a lot of things . . . an idealist . . . a politician . . . a putz. But he wasn't gay, all right? He was just a do-gooder who was in the wrong place at the wrong time. Now he's dead. End of story."

"John, it's part of the story," Blythe said calmly. "That's what makes the most sense. Your friend was killed and you're upset. If this were someone you didn't know, you'd say we needed to write about it."

He thought about that. "You're right."

"So why does it bother you so much?" she asked.

"Because it isn't true," Quinn said. "Jesus, is that so hard to understand?"

Blythe wasn't sure.

Neither was Quinn. But no matter how he felt, they had to run the story. Adding to the mix, a prominent local artist and activist, Danny Sloan, kept insisting the beating death was the latest in a string of attacks targeting gays. He'd called the paper three times that morning before reaching Sarah and had probably called anyone else who would listen.

Sarah played the tape of the interview for them. In it, Sloan claimed that in the past month, a gay shipbuilder had been savagely wounded at Stone Harbor Shipyard and a gay Wellsen College student had his Audi sprayed with threatening graffiti. And finally, three dogs had been poisoned and their lesbian owners warned to leave a north-end neighborhood. Sloan said those and a half dozen other incidents had been reported to the Stone Harbor police over the summer and ignored. He found it equally troubling that the public wasn't made aware of the problem through the media—especially the local paper.

"How can people protect themselves when they don't even know they're in danger?" he'd asked. "The cops can deny it all they want, but everyone knows Paul Stanwood was killed because of his support of our community. He stood up for us and look where it got him."

Quinn, Sarah and Blythe hashed over his theory; none of them had an answer.

"How else can you explain the fact that a string of attacks hasn't generated a single arrest?" Sarah asked.

"The Stone Harbor cops have always been pretty incompetent," Quinn said.

Blythe considered this before adding that maybe they wanted it to come across that way.

Quinn looked oddly at her.

"I don't know, John," she said wearily, sounding every one of her seventy-five years. "I honestly don't know what to make of any of this. I just wanted to see how you were holding up. Call me later if you need to talk."

After Blythe left and Sarah filled Quinn in on the rest of the details, he decided to make a few calls of his own, which was usually the way things started when he stopped in the office for a few minutes.

HE GOT HOME AT eight o'clock that night.

Maria and Jack were curled on the couch watching the

Disney Channel—a safe bet, given the circumstances. Her eyes were red and swollen and she looked exhausted. Jack just stared at the television until he realized his father was home, then turned and smiled cautiously.

"Hey, Dad."

"Jackpot!" Quinn said, which was the way he always greeted his son. Then he picked him up and kissed Maria on the cheek. "Bedtime for this Bonzo," he added, which was another part of their nightly routine. Only this time Quinn gave Maria a questioning look.

"He knows," she said softly. "But there's no way he understands."

Jack was already in his SpongeBob SquarePants pajamas and for once didn't object as Quinn carried him upstairs. He just held on more tightly than ever. "We went to Pauly's," Jack said once Quinn deposited him in bed.

"That's what I hear."

"His dad's dead," Jack said matter-of-factly.

"I know." Quinn looked into his son's wide blue eyes and wondered how much he really understood.

"I never knew anyone that was dead." Jack considered that a moment, then asked, "Do you know what happened?"

"I know a little bit," Quinn said. "I also know there has to be a lot more to it than that."

"Tell me."

He didn't know where to begin. Quinn wasn't the type who believed in lying to a kid for his own good, so he told Jack what he could, without bothering to include every gruesome detail. Jack had no need to know Paul Sr.'s skull had been shattered or that most of the bones in his body had been broken. The generalities were bad enough. Still, Quinn didn't want his son confusing life with a dream world. He knew children were capable of dealing with worse things, but that didn't make it any easier when Jack asked why Uncle Paul had been in Sullivan Park.

"I don't know," Quinn admitted.

Jack looked at his father like he expected him to have all the answers, when the truth was he didn't have a clue.

"I don't think anyone knows what he was doing there," Quinn explained.

Jack thought about that. "Does that mean Uncle Paul was bad?" he asked.

"No," Quinn said. "It just means he wasn't very careful."

Jack put his small hand on his father's shoulder and pulled him closer. "Are you careful?" he asked, his lower lip trembling.

"Yes." Quinn hugged his son.

"What about Mom?"

"She's careful, too."

Jack considered this as his father held him tightly. "Are you gonna die?" he finally asked.

"Someday," Quinn answered. "But not for a long, long time."

"Uncle Paul died."

"It was a freak thing." Quinn tried to say this in a calm and reassuring tone, even if he didn't believe it himself.

"Somebody killed him."

"That's right."

"Do you know who?" Jack asked.

"Not yet," Quinn said.

"What if somebody else gets killed?"

"That won't happen," Quinn said.

"Are you sure?"

"Positive."

The little boy looked down at his hands. "It makes me scared."

"Sometimes it scares me, too, but you have to understand that everyone dies," Quinn said. "Uncle Paul just died a lot sooner than he was supposed to."

Jack took a moment to absorb this, then asked, "Is he in heaven?"

"Yes," Quinn said. At least that's what he hoped.

"Pauly doesn't think he's dead."

"It's probably hard for him to think of his father that way," Quinn said. "We all wish Uncle Paul were still here, but that can't change things. He's gone."

Jack still wouldn't look up. Quinn hugged him again. The boy felt small and fragile and Quinn wanted to protect him. He just didn't know how. "Now, this is going to be pretty hard for Pauly, so you're gonna have to be especially nice to him," Quinn said.

Jack nodded and kept his eyes locked on his father. "All right."

"Because that's what friends do when things get tough," Quinn said. "They have to be there for each other."

"Okay."

It didn't feel okay. Quinn was a realist but he was also angry. Paul was dead. He wasn't a story that had come and gone like yesterday's deadline. He'd been his closest friend for thirty years and when things had gotten tough, Quinn hadn't been there for him. What did that really say? Paul had been beaten beyond recognition, probably by someone they both knew, someone who walked away and left him to die on a filthy concrete floor with no more concern than if he'd been an insect. Quinn tried to imagine the final moments of his friend's life and shuddered. Yes, he was going to find out what happened. He was going to find out who killed Paul. And when he did, there would be hell to pay.

3.

STANWOOD LEAVES LEGACY OF
GOODWILL, ACTIVISM
By John Quinn
Pilot Staff

Paul Stanwood, a popular selectman, successful entrepreneur and committed environmentalist, was killed Sunday morning in an apparent homicide. He leaves behind a wife and two children, along with a legacy of grassroots activism stretching from this small coastal town to the nation's capital.

Stanwood founded the Friends of Georges Bay, initiated a statewide referendum that shut down the Marsh Flat nuclear power plant and testified before Congress on the effect Midwestern air pollution had on the Maine woods.

As a businessman, he embodied the spirit of Yankee ingenuity by guiding Rock Coast Outdoors, founded during a canoe trip to the Allagash River, into an international outfitting company.

"The whole idea came about because we couldn't find decent summer jobs," Stanwood once said. "My wife and I both had an interest in kayaking and whitewater rafting, and figured we could make a buck at it."

"It succeeded beyond our wildest dreams," Lizz Stanwood told *Down East* magazine in a profile that ran last fall.

The company now employs more than 200 people each summer and provides 35 year-round jobs. In addition to offering rafting trips and a paddling school, Rock Coast runs excursions to Labrador, Newfoundland, Costa Rica and New Zealand.

"He could have gone anywhere and done anything, but he chose to remain in Stone Harbor," said Selectman Bryan Bowen-Smythe. "We had our differences, but I'll be the first to admit this town is a better place because of him."

While Stanwood never held office beyond the local level, he was an influential member of the state Democratic Party. Last year he served as treasurer for U.S. Sen. Dale Woodlawn's election committee and played a key role in Woodlawn's upset of incumbent Regina Zaphris.

Born Sept. 23, 1969, in Stone Harbor, Stanwood was the son of Mary Ann and Angus Stanwood. In high school, he lettered in varsity football, basketball and baseball. During his junior and senior seasons, he led Stone Harbor Consolidated to state basketball championships. He attended Dartmouth College in Hanover, N.H., on a basketball scholarship.

He was predeceased by his mother. In addition to his wife, he is survived by their children, Diane, 15, and Paul Jr., 6, and by his father.

"At least you gave him a nice obituary," Lizz Stanwood said when she finally saw Quinn.

"I thought it would mean a lot."

"It didn't."

That stopped him cold. They were ten feet from Paul's closed casket and he didn't know quite how to respond. Lizz always had a way of blurting out what she was thinking, no matter the circumstances, but this was a bit much—even for her.

She realized it as soon as she'd spoken. "John, I'm sorry." She stepped forward, put her head on his shoulder and held him tightly. "That didn't come out the way I meant it."

"Don't worry. You were never one to pull any punches."

"That's true," she admitted. "But you were never one to walk right into them."

"Well, we've both had better days," he said, and suddenly he felt very awkward.

She looked at him like it didn't matter. They'd been friends too long to be bothered by dumb remarks. When they were younger, Paul, Lizz and Quinn had been known as the Three Amigos, inseparable from their early teens until the time Quinn left for Miami.

"Sorry it took me so long to show up," he said.

"That's okay. Maria's been a big help. And right now I really need my friends."

"We're here for you."

"I know." She pulled back and held him at arm's length. "Hey, I heard you made the big time," she said in a teasing voice. *"Action News at Noon."* Then she gave an exaggerated frown. "I also heard you didn't come off too well."

He held up his right hand as though taking an oath. "Guilty as charged."

"Only nobody's doing any charging," she said.

"They knew I had a strong case for insanity."

She shook her head, chuckling and crying a little at the same time. "Only you could make me laugh right now."

"If only it were intentional."

She squeezed his shoulder with one hand, as though she were trying to tell him something beyond words. Her green eyes locked on his—a little too deeply—and Quinn quickly looked away, embarrassed, from her to Paul's grinning portrait on top of the closed casket. That's when he realized dozens of mourners were still lined up to pay their respects, a task complicated by a gauntlet of elderly aunts and uncles who stood like fossils while a younger generation of cousins, Maria and Jack among them, hovered around the Stanwood children.

The father of the deceased stood at the end of the receiving line, an odd distance away. "Angus has been unbearable," Lizz said flatly.

Quinn glanced over. Angus Stanwood was a stout man who'd nearly broken Quinn's hand when he'd shaken it, almost as if he wanted to grip something that wasn't there. Maybe it hadn't been for a long time.

Angus had left Paul's mother during her first round of cancer, when Quinn and Paul were in junior high, and tried very hard ever since, yet there was always an unspoken distance between father and son. Still, Angus had a talent for making things seem like they weren't that bad. It came with the territory. The biggest car dealer in town had been making sales pitches all his life but wasn't able to put a happy spin on this. He was half in the bag and so blubbery it embarrassed Quinn. Despite Angus's flaws, Quinn considered him a friend, but after that initial encounter, he hoped to avoid another.

Keeping his back to the older man, Quinn asked Lizz how she was holding up.

"How do I look?"

"All things considered, great."

Compliments always made her smile, though she should

have been used to them. Lizz wasn't exactly beautiful but was fluid and willowy, and something about the way she moved or even stood with a hand on her hip had an effect on men. She stood that way then, but with a touch of weariness etched on her face. For the first time, he noticed the smile lines beneath her lightly tanned and freckled face. Looking over her shoulder in the direction of her father-in-law, Lizz said, "I need a break from all this."

"I'm not sure there is one." It had been a helluva two days. She was strong, hardened by years in the outdoors, but the strain was evident. A few feet away, Diane and Paul Jr. stood like zombies as Maria and Jack quietly greeted them. They were too young to have lost a father under any circumstances.

"It's even tougher when your husband goes out like that in a place like this," Lizz said.

"I understand."

Her expression drew sharper. "Do you?"

"Yes. Give me some credit," Quinn said. Her suddenly angry tone made him uncomfortable. "Look, people loved your husband."

"Somebody didn't." Before he could speak again, Lizz turned and embraced Maria, who had finally moved on from the children. After a moment, Lizz glanced over her shoulder at Quinn as he started to walk away. It was an almost desperate look, one that stayed with him as he went out into the soft summer night.

He couldn't help feeling oddly unnerved.

Outside, the air was cool and fresh, a contrast to the cramped viewing room, though the evening's embrace did little to lift his spirits. His mind was racing and as he waited in the parking lot for Maria and Jack to catch up, he felt overcome by events that, just a month earlier, had almost seemed comical—especially the afternoon his friend stormed through the newsroom and into his office, interrupting Quinn's brown-bag lunch.

"I CAN'T BELIEVE YOU PRINTED this!" Paul shoved the page 3 police blotter at him and pointed out the offending item: "Trio Arrested in Park Crackdown." Then he pulled it back and started to read aloud:

"Three local men have been charged with public indecency after they were caught masturbating each other in Sullivan Park yesterday afternoon.

"Arthur King, 73, of High Cliff Lane; Luther Snow, 68, of Rockland; and Jeremy Michael, 62, of Bowdoin Street, were released on their own recognizance and will appear later this month in District Court."

"So what's the big deal?" Quinn asked, his feet still up on his desk. "They were arrested. They were pulling each other's puds in a public park!"

"They shouldn't have been."

"That's why they were arrested."

"I meant they shouldn't have been arrested," Paul said, exasperated by the attitude. "They weren't hurting anyone. Nobody else uses that park."

Quinn was amused by his friend's indignation. "Well, how could they, with those old goats prowling the place?"

"When was the last time you cared about Sullivan Park?"

Quinn dismissed the question with a wave of his hand, then sat upright and put down the Italian sub he'd been eating. "We used to go there all the time in high school."

"Yeah—to drink and smoke dope."

"So what? We were kids."

"And the cops never bothered us." Paul slapped the desk for emphasis. "They didn't care what we did, as long as we kept it in the park."

"We only went there at night, when the place was empty." Quinn took a hard gulp of his Diet Pepsi, as if to keep from choking on the conversation. "Look, these guys were going at it in broad daylight," he quickly added, as if to make up for the pause. "And there were complaints. What were the cops supposed to do? Hose them down with ice water? My God, you'd think they'd have some sense of decency."

"I'd think you would."

"Please—since I've gained weight, I don't even like to do it with the lights on."

Paul looked at Quinn as though he were addressing a small child. "This isn't funny," he said slowly, for emphasis. "We're talking about people's lives."

"We're talking about grown men performing sex acts in a public park and how they were charged. We list every arrest—whether it's you, me or a bunch of old men who should have settled for shuffleboard."

Paul wasn't buying it. "As if they weren't going through enough without having their names in the paper," he said. "I understand you had to report what happened. But did you have to run the names? What about their families?"

"They should have considered that before they went in the park."

Paul slapped the paper open again. "Jesus—then everyone else got a hold of it."

That's because Arthur King was the retired president of Wellsen College, the town's snooty liberal arts college. Wellsen was always pushing for greater recognition and got its share that day, as Quinn later found out. The Associated Press picked up the item and ran it across New England. The *Boston Herald* played it on page 2 and the local television stations were even worse.

"So what was I supposed to do?" Quinn never expected the story to spread beyond the *Pilot*, which embarrassed him, since he probably underplayed it by running only a small police beat item.

"You need to show a little community sensitivity," Paul said, more pleading now than angry. "This isn't the *Miami Herald*. This is a small town. You just don't get it."

No, Quinn got it all right. In fact, he crushed the out-spread paper in his fist. "I hear what you're saying. I just don't agree with you."

"Your father never would have printed their names."

"Well, I'm not my father."

Paul crossed his arms and shook his head. "That's what people are starting to find out."

Quinn tossed the balled-up paper onto the desk. "What's that supposed to mean?"

"It means you need to tone it down a notch," Paul said, leaning forward and putting his palms flat on the desk. "You've been pushing too many buttons since you came back."

"Maybe those buttons need to be pushed."

"Some of them, sure."

Quinn was certain. That's why the paper had done stories on deadbeat dads and domestic violence and had recently begun to pay particularly close attention to the police blotter. Behind the lovely facade, the town had an underside. Plenty of drugs moved along the coast. Child abuse was underreported. And for every rich summer resident with a degree from Brown and a fourth-generation summer home, a thousand locals lived in the meanest poverty.

"You have to report the news," Paul said patiently. "I understand that. But this comes across as though you're preying on the misfortunes of others."

"You have to be kidding."

Paul gave his familiar grin and held open his hands. "I'm speaking to you as a friend."

"No, you're not. You're speaking to me as an uptight chamber-of-commerce fuck who wants to pretend nothing bad ever happens. That way you and the tourists can shut your eyes and believe the sign at the state line that says 'Welcome to Maine, the Way Life Should Be.'"

Paul's smile was gone. "Is that what you think?"

"Absolutely."

That's when Paul told him Arthur King, sitting at a desk that had belonged to his Quaker grandfather in a house his family had occupied for five generations, wrote a long and moving apology to his nine-year-old grandson, begging for his forgiveness and understanding.

Then he shot himself in the head.

Deflated, Quinn slowly digested the news. He'd known King casually. The guy may have been full of himself but had a good heart and founded the Midcoast Hospice. He'd also run an annual regatta that raised hundreds of thousands of dollars to benefit AIDS patients. Quinn looked up at Paul. "So you're telling me his death is my fault?"

"Who else publicly humiliated him?"

That was unfair. Quinn felt for King and his family, but that didn't mean he could pretend the arrest never happened. That wasn't his job and he couldn't be blamed for the suicide.

Paul had a different opinion.

• • •

QUINN COULDN'T GET OVER that as he waited outside
the funeral home for Maria and Jack. Didn't he deserve the
benefit of the doubt? The fact that he'd never been able to
convince Paul he'd done the right thing still bothered him.

Quinn wasn't the only one bothered by something. From
the parking lot, he suddenly heard raised voices from inside, so
he hurried back, only to find Angus Stanwood confronting his
daughter-in-law. "And you have the nerve to stand there like
you had nothin' to do with this!" Angus thundered. "The truth
about you is gonna come out."

Lizz stared at him without a trace of emotion, her calm all
the more obvious in the suddenly silent room.

That made Angus even angrier. "I always thought you
were a cold little bitch."

Quinn was trying to get to them so he could shut the old
fool up, but before he had a chance to slide past the people
blocking the door, he noticed his aunt had quietly stepped
between Angus and Lizz.

"It's true," Angus insisted, the whole time standing on his
toes and looking over Blythe so he could shout more directly
at Lizz.

Without agreeing or arguing, Blythe took Angus by the
elbow and led him in the opposite direction from Lizz, who
was quickly surrounded by mourners. *Thank God for Blythe*,
Quinn thought. Angus was the last person he wanted to deal
with at that moment. He had someone else he needed to con-
front—in person, especially since his attempts by phone hadn't
worked in the past twenty-four hours.

Quinn took Maria and Jack home, then drove to Becky's
Seafood Shack, a faded clapboard restaurant that sat precari-

ously next to the town dock and was plastered with brightly colored buoys, fishing nets and wooden lobster pots. Becky's husband, Ernie, was out front on a stepladder, painting a sign that was at least fifteen feet high and twenty feet wide, with each day's special slopped in dark red lettering. The ladder barely fit on a narrow strip of grass between the restaurant and town parking lot.

"That's a helluva menu," Quinn shouted up.

"It's a helluva restaurant," Ernie answered, without taking his eyes off the project.

"That's not what the health inspector told me."

Ernie's head snapped around so quickly that Quinn stepped back, afraid he'd be covered with paint, or worse, clobbered with the entire aluminum can. But as soon as Ernie saw who it was, he laughed heartily. "My wife hears that, she'll brain ya!"

"Just so she washes up before she goes back to the kitchen."

By then Ernie was off the ladder and extending a hand to his friend. But the smile didn't last. "It's just horrible about Paul." He slowly shook his head. "He was always on our side," Ernie said, and by that he meant the average resident.

Quinn agreed.

"Take this damn sign." Ernie nodded over his shoulder. "The rest of the numb-ass selectmen tell me my *own* sign in front of my *own* restaurant is *too big.*"

"You can't help but notice it," Quinn said in admiration.

"What it amounts to is a bunch of people from away telling the natives how to keep Stone Hahbah lookin' like an authentic coastal town," Ernie said, his voice trembling. "Look at me—ain't I authentic enough?"

Standing there in his paint-covered jeans and T-shirt, with a worn Red Sox cap and sunburned face, Ernie was the real deal. He'd come from a line of Stone Harbor swordfishermen, though the swordfish were long gone. His brothers had moved to Alaska to keep up the family trade, while Ernie stayed behind and ran a few lobster pots, drove a school bus, and during the summer months hauled tourists around the harbor in a battered forty-foot tub.

"Paul wouldn't let 'em get away with this," Ernie continued. "He'd a put the kibosh right on the notion before they had a chance to do anythin'."

"Hang on," Quinn said quickly, holding up one hand. "I'll be right back."

Ernie didn't go anywhere and kept right on talking, even though Quinn could no longer hear. He was particularly riled up about all the piss-headed ideas headed their way now that Paul wasn't around to keep the muckety-mucks in local "gov'ment" in check—especially that damn Bryan Bowen-Smythe, who'd already gotten himself named acting chairman of the town board.

When Quinn returned, camera in hand, he had Ernie pose next to the sign.

"It'll be worth a thousand words!" Ernie said while popping a gap-toothed smile.

Quinn motioned him closer and Ernie glanced back at the bright, bold lettering. "Steamers three bucks a dozen," he said, pointing to that menu item. "Make sure you get that in."

Quinn did.

"You tell 'em, Johnny!" Ernie said as Quinn headed toward the restaurant. "Just like you told 'em about the way old Silas Toomey was about to lose the last farm in town because they changed the zonin' to drive up his taxes."

Waving over his shoulder, Quinn said he would.

Inside, the Shack was crowded with tourists. They were a rowdy bunch, filling the benches and long wooden tables in the center of the dining room, ecstatic about the piles of clams and potatoes and boiled lobster before them.

Quinn found Police Chief Al Sears tucked in a corner booth, trying to enjoy his meal over the din and rattle. "So how's the investigation going?" Quinn asked as Sears crushed his package of saltines over a steaming bowl of fish chowder.

Sears just stared as Quinn sat down, uninvited.

"Well?" Quinn pressed.

Before Sears could answer, a stout woman showed up with her order pad. "Johnny, what can I get you?" Becky Gould asked.

"Whatever the chief's having," he said. "It's so good he can't talk."

Becky glanced down at Sears. "By the look on his puss, it's prob'ly a good thing he ain't sayin' nothin'. I just hope that ain't a commentary on his dinnah."

After she left, Sears finally leaned toward Quinn and spoke. "Why do you insist on plaguin' a man when he's tryin' to eat?"

"I don't know when else to get you, since you won't return my calls."

"That should tell you somethin'," the chief said before picking up his spoon, as though the matter were settled.

"What'd you find at the crime scene?"

Sears didn't answer.

"How about the autopsy?" Quinn pressed, this time in a louder voice that caused people at the nearest tables to stop talking.

Still nothing.

"Do you know where else Paul went that night? Did you get his cell phone records?"

"We don't comment on pendin' investigations," Sears said.

Unless it suited his purposes, Quinn thought. A month earlier the department had found a million dollars' worth of cocaine in a yacht, and before they had any idea who actually owned it, Sears came waltzing into the newsroom looking for reporters and photographers and anyone else who would tell the story. Now he was playing silent on something that involved one of their own and Quinn wasn't putting up with it. "Look—I'm more than a reporter this time."

"Yeah, you're a legend in your own mind."

"Can you even tell me why he was in the park?" Quinn asked.

Sears smirked, which had the intended effect.

Quinn's cheeks reddened. "Okay, if that's what you think, tell me this—what about all the gay bashing Danny Sloan said you never investigated?"

The chief tried to make it sound like he didn't care. "Why don't ya ask him yourself?"

"I will—in person—but right now I'm asking you."

"Like I said, we don't comment on pendin' investigations, no matter how many fruit loops get their panties in an uproar."

Now it was Quinn's turn to be angry, not that it did any good. "You don't even care what happened to those men!"

"My job is to protect and serve the decent people in town," Sears said evenly, "not to be browbeaten by you or your little pissant newspapah."

By then Becky had returned with Quinn's chowder. "Anything else?" she asked.

"Not for me." Sears put six dollars on the table and left.

Quinn and Becky both watched him stomp away, with his chin held high and his chest stuck out at the world. "What's eatin' him?" she asked Quinn.

"I think it's me."

"Wouldn't be the first time," she said with a wink.

That's for sure. The week Quinn got back in town he got a call from a clam digger who'd had three teeth knocked out by the chief after the man had too much to drink. Sears didn't deny it. The guy swung at him and he was only defending himself. But the man's lawyer insisted his client had been punched a half dozen times. Quinn learned it was the second lawsuit in three years alleging Sears had acted with excessive force, which became the basis of a weeklong *Pilot* series that infuriated the chief.

That was nothing, really, when Quinn considered what else Sears may have been hiding. Whatever it was, he couldn't wait to see the bastard's reaction once he found out.

4.

I wonder who paul blames now? Quinn asked himself as he moved out of the bright morning light into the gloom of the First Parish Church. Looking around, he didn't find an answer. He could barely see. The church was so dark that when he stopped, just inside the entrance, Marie and Jack bumped into him. As Quinn's eyes adjusted, he saw scattered mourners sitting stiffly in the hard, wooden pews. The sad thing was, more rows were empty than full.

Jack squeezed his father's hand. He'd never been in a church and was all eyes as they walked down the aisle beneath the spidery rafters and beams. First he stared at the ceiling, then the raised pulpit, and finally, the huge pipe organ that covered the back wall. He must have thought the church was as weird as the box up front stuffed with Uncle Paul.

Quinn regretted bringing him. He regretted a lot of things: his temper, the harsh, final words with Paul, and most of all, the distance that had developed between them during the last six months. As kids they'd been inseparable. Now that was just a memory.

A few rows in, the shaggy-haired acting chairman of the board of selectmen took a seat. No matter how many times he saw it, Quinn couldn't get past a grown man in a suit and Birkenstock sandals. The college brought all kinds to town, but at least Professor Bryan Bowen-Smythe showed up for the service. That was it from the political class, which was quite a contrast to a Stanwood funeral held three months earlier. When Paul's mother died, the governor, a U.S. senator and both Maine congressmen made the scene. Of course, breast cancer didn't carry the same stigma as being found beaten to death in a notorious gay pickup spot.

Quinn couldn't believe the hypocrisy, though he shouldn't have been surprised.

With each step came other faces and other stories, all pieces of a small-town puzzle he couldn't quite fit together anymore. It didn't help to see Al Sears in a boxed pew, dressed in a black suit, gray shirt and black tie.

Sears nodded.

So did Quinn, though he felt his right fist clench at his side when he looked at the other man. No use denying it. He would have enjoyed smashing the smug son of a bitch in the face.

Beyond Sears, his old friends Ernie and Becky Gould were there. Ernie looked stiff and uncomfortable in a white dress shirt and blue tie. It was the first time Quinn had ever seen him dressed so formally.

Just past them, the Quinns took seats in the third row, next to Aunt Blythe, who was with another nephew, Quinn's younger cousin Seth, the newspaper's blond and blue-eyed general manager. To Seth's right was Meredith Merrill, the bitchy heiress to a convenience store chain. She was pretty, short and stout and Seth doted on her. Though he was good-looking and presented himself well, Seth came up empty in the trust fund department. The poor guy had never been able to land the rich wife he sought, but wouldn't stop trying. That was also his philosophy in sales. "There's no harm in being told no," he liked to say. "The harm is in not asking." And Seth was always asking. Quinn liked to joke that he could sell cameras to the blind. The sad part was, he would have tried if the margin were there.

After ten minutes that felt like an hour, the family of the deceased came in. Angus Stanwood was first, beery-looking in a suit that fit thirty-five pounds earlier. He took a seat in the second row with his fifteen-year-old granddaughter and put an arm around her. Diane's black hair was cut short and streaked white. She was scowling and pissy and had every right to be. Angus understood. He tried to make up for the times he hadn't been around for his son by being there for his grandchildren, front row and center. You name it, he hit everything. Soccer games. Birthdays. School events. They could always count on Angus.

Quinn wondered if they could count on him to hold his tongue for a day; maybe Lizz and Pauly wondered, too, and that's why they continued on to the front row. Lizz looked tragic and beautiful in a small black dress and every eye in the room was on her—especially Quinn's. *Damn,* he thought, *I covet my neighbor's wife, even at his funeral.* He felt a pang of guilt and looked up at a stained-glass window's angry Moses and tried to imagine where the whole affair fit on the tablets the old boy was carrying down from the mountain.

Then there was Pauly, a little man in a blue blazer and khakis who had his father's dark hair and big grin, though it didn't show that day. He kept turning around, as if he expected someone behind him to explain what had happened. He saw Jack, smiled weakly and waved.

Jack waved back.

Quinn and Maria put their arms around their son. They wanted to do the same for Pauly, but he was on his own. Lizz was a mess, trying to compose herself and act dignified yet breaking down and sobbing loudly nonetheless.

Most of the pallbearers were ponytailed river guides who worked for Rock Coast Outdoors, an odd mix of college students, drifters, overachievers and screwups. The only thing they had in common was a love of nature and Paul. The longhairs, as Angus called them, had plenty of company, including dozens of young staffers, a canoe maker down from the Allagash and a couple of game wardens.

All told, it was quite a collection.

Quinn sat waiting for the crowd to sing its way through a monotonous hymn so he could get up and remind his neighbors there was a lot more to Paul Stanwood than the last few moments of his life. But he wondered how many of them would be able to get beyond its ending.

AFTER THE MINISTER INTRODUCED him, Quinn walked to the pulpit and faced them all. "I knew Paul Stanwood pretty much all my life," he began in a calm voice. "We were boys together. Teenagers. Young men. And there's something special about a friendship that helps shape the person you become."

He sighed at the memory. "One day you're on a baseball diamond, trying to turn a double play, and the next thing you know, you're the coach in the dugout, watching your own son." He shook his head, as though still surprised by that. Paul's great joy was his family. "Anyone who's ever seen a father smile at the sight of a sleeping child understands what I mean. He would have done anything for Diane and Pauly."

The little boy smiled, though his older sister's glare never softened.

"The cycle of life is also fragile," Quinn said. "We found that out a few days ago."

Quinn looked down at his notes, then back at the audience. "In case you hadn't heard, we could get mad at each other."

That got a few laughs.

"Oh, yes, it happened on more than one occasion," Quinn insisted, smiling and shaking his head. "Sometimes we wouldn't talk to each other for weeks on end. But if I ever needed him, Paul was there. I guess the story that sums up our friendship goes back to the cycle of life. Six years ago my son was born in a hospital in Key Largo during a hurricane. Now, if you've ever been in South Florida during one of those, you know things can get a little crazy. They board up stores. Everyone is trying to drive out of there and people are on edge. So that's the time my son chooses to come into the world."

Quinn shook his head and Jack covered his face with his hands.

"So my wife, a nurse and a doctor seem to be about the only people left in this hospital, which is sandbagged up for World War Three, and out of nowhere comes a guy wearing sandals, torn shorts, a soaking-wet T-shirt and one of those turned-up Australian bush hats.

"I asked Paul how he'd gotten down there and he shrugged and said from the looks of things, it was a lot easier than getting out.

"To this day I don't know how he did it. I'm not sure why he did it, either. I wanted to wring his neck for taking such a stupid chance, yet I was more touched by that gesture than anything else in my life."

Quinn paused for emphasis, then took in the whole room. "Now when I remember Paul I can look at him two ways. There's the dummy who was oblivious to personal danger, and there was the very decent guy who put the well-being of his friends above everything else."

That said, Quinn looked directly at Lizz Stanwood, who forced a small smile. "Now, I don't know about you, but I know which Paul I want to remember."

With that, he stepped down and left the rest to the padre. On the way back to his pew, he noticed Lizz stealing a look at her watch.

The Stanwood home was set behind a picket fence and a deep yard lined with elm trees and rosebushes. Simple and elegant, the two-and-a-half-story wood-framed house had been built in 1807 by a prominent architect from Salem, Massachusetts. Lizz was proud of that. She was also obsessed: in the past few years, she'd traveled up and down the East Coast looking at Federal architecture and made sure everything was exact in its reproduction, from the black shutters to the leaded glass windows and the fanlight over the paneled front door. After she put a fortune into the restoration, Paul dubbed it the White House.

At the moment, the place was overrun and John Fogerty's voice poured outside: *"I ain't no fortunate son."*

Cars filled the brick driveway from carriage house to street and small groups stood outside holding drinks. A few of the longhairs casually directed Quinn to a parking spot in the yard. The Stanwoods' two golden retrievers—and a handful of others that belonged to guests—were barking and bounding about in a wild game of chase.

"Is this a party?" Jack asked.

"Kind of," Maria said as they got out of the wagon. "But nobody is supposed to admit it."

"I won't say anything," Jack assured her. Then he went right at the goldens and was soon laughing hysterically in a sea of tan and red fur as they swarmed him, all wagging tails and licks and full-body rubs against his legs. He loved dogs, but Quinn was allergic and they couldn't have one at home.

Inside, they worked their way around the assorted guests who were spread all over the downstairs. Maria couldn't help noticing that saucers and glasses were piled everywhere, on the antique cherry desk, the bookcases, the stairs. She also couldn't help picking up a stack of china and silverware on the way to the dining room.

Aunt Blythe was listening intently to one of the canoe makers. She took everything in and would eventually find an outlet for the information in one of her columns. The woman had been compiling the town's happenings for fifty years and never missed a funeral, whether it was for the shipyard president or a retired ironworker. Seth and Meredith weren't doing as well, scrunched into a small couch with plates of food on their knees, obviously waiting for an appropriate amount of time to pass so they could leave.

Eventually, the Quinns found Lizz alone in the kitchen with her shoes off, holding a glass of pinot noir.

"Hey," she said when she saw them.

Jack hugged her.

"Thanks, slugger," she said. "That's just what I needed."

He blushed as Lizz and Maria exchanged girl hugs. After that, Lizz quickly squeezed Quinn's bicep before she turned back to Jack.

"So are you hungry?" she asked.

"A little," he admitted.

"Well, let me get you something. There's plenty to eat." The dining room table was covered with cakes and pies, roast beef, scalloped potatoes, salmon, shrimp and crab, fruit, vegetables, cheese and bread. Maria had added red beans and rice to the collection. "Careful, now." Lizz handed him a plate filled to his exact specifications—chocolate cake, chocolate pie, chocolate cookies and raw clams on the half shell.

He thanked her, then asked where Pauly was.

"In his room," Lizz said. "A bunch of kids are there. You should go on up. They'll be glad to see you."

Jack started walking that way—until Maria grabbed his arm and directed him to a flat-backed chair. "You can go up after you eat," she said.

He looked sadly at his full plate. "But I'm not really hungry."

"You can take that with you," Lizz said. When Maria started to object, Lizz grinned and shook her head. "Everyone else has."

"I'll be careful," Jack assured her.

"I know you will, honey." Lizz turned to Maria and Quinn. "Look, eat something," she said. "I don't know what we're going to do with it all. Somebody dies and the whole neighborhood starts cooking. Isn't it bad enough I'm in mourning? I have to be fat, too?"

Quinn smiled uncertainly at her attempt at humor.

Maria didn't seem to notice. "It's some sort of tradition," she told Lizz.

"We also have a bit to drink." Lizz pointed to a row of bottles on the counter. Tanqueray. Beefeater. Wild Turkey. Jack

Daniel's. Four flavors of Stolichnaya. Six types of wine. Even a bottle of tequila. "So, what's your pleasure?"

"I'll stick to tonic water," Quinn said.

Lizz paused, as though she were puzzled by that, then shrugged. "Suit yourself."

Maria refilled Lizz and poured herself a glass and raised it in a toast. "I'm with you," she said.

"Hey—aren't I supposed to be the hostess of this gathering?" Lizz asked.

"No," Maria said. "It's to help you."

"So in other words, it's a pity party."

Quinn and Maria exchanged quick glances. "I wouldn't put it that way," Maria said slowly.

"I know," Lizz said. "You're too polite."

Maria laughed. "I've never been called that before."

"I hear you," Lizz said as she turned to Quinn. "So what about you, John? Do you hear us?"

"A little too clearly," he said before he stood up. She'd already had too much to drink and he was more annoyed than he should have been, so he figured some distance might help. "If you'll excuse me, I'm going out for some air."

"You're excused," Lizz and Maria said in unison before saluting with their empty glasses.

He stepped onto the back porch, which wasn't original to the house but stayed because Paul wanted a place to watch the sun set. The view was worth it. Beyond a small fenced yard with a tire swing and cedar play set, the property opened into two wide acres bordered by loose stands of pine. Quinn saw Bowen-Smythe and a bunch of guides circled behind the carriage house beside a trailer loaded with an assortment of brightly colored kayaks and green and red canoes.

"What you said about Paul was quite nice," Bowen-Smythe said when Quinn approached.

"Thanks." What Quinn would have said about Bowen-Smythe wasn't nearly as nice, but he kept it to himself. He found it hard to believe that with Paul gone, the professor had become the highest-ranking elected official in town. That sneaky little shit now ran the board of selectmen.

If he knew what Quinn thought—or cared—Bowen-Smythe didn't let on. Instead, he was friendly and gracious. "Paul thought a lot of you and he was very happy when you decided to come home." After a pause, the professor added, "He said you'd add a broader perspective to the newspaper, given your background. He said you'd been all over Latin America. He said you even interviewed Castro."

"Six of us did." Quinn didn't want it to sound like more than it was. "We weren't exactly in an intimate setting," he said. "The U.S. had just invaded Panama and Fidel wanted to spout off to the press. After that, my mother-in-law didn't speak to me for years. She accused me of being a Communist."

"Were you?"

"No. For chrissake, I voted for Ronald Reagan."

"So how'd you square the Castro thing?"

"I didn't. Once our son was born, my wife told her if she ever wanted to see her grandson, she'd better get off her high horse, and that did the trick."

Bowen-Smythe forced a laugh and Quinn could tell the professor had other things on his mind. Maybe he was thinking of the coverage the *Pilot* had given the new sign ordinance. The day after the article and photo appeared in print, the paper received a half dozen angry letters complaining about the board of selectmen, which Quinn gleefully printed.

"So what's your sense of things?" Quinn asked.

Bowen-Smythe slowly folded his long, thin arms across his chest and rubbed his chin with his fingers, as if searching for an answer. "You mean the investigation?"

Quinn nodded.

"Chief Sears is pursuing some promising angles," Bowen-Smythe said. "They're looking at evidence from the crime scene. Waiting on the autopsy. Finding out where else Paul was that night. They're even checking his cell phone calls." Bowen-Smythe looked oddly at Quinn, who had started chuckling. "Please tell me why that's so funny?"

"It just sounds awfully familiar," Quinn explained, "but there is one other thing. Is Sears trying to find out why Paul was in the park that night?"

Bowen-Smythe blushed.

"What's the matter?" Quinn asked.

"He's assuming the obvious."

"Well, he's a fucking moron," Quinn snapped, his voice full of anger. "Everything he told you came from me. I asked him where he stood on all those things and if he doesn't have answers by now, I doubt he'll get them." Quinn noticed the professor was nervously tapping a sandal on the grass.

"He's doing the best he can," Bowen-Smythe said.

"And that isn't good enough. Do you know the last time this town had a homicide investigation?"

"No," Bowen-Smythe said, unsure of where this was going.

"In 1964 an old woman who lived alone on Front Street was strangled to death. Nobody could understand why. She wasn't robbed. As far as they could tell, she wasn't sexually assaulted. She was just dead and the case was never solved."

"They didn't have any suspects?"

"Her nephew had a financial motive, but the police never got anything on him," Quinn said, getting right in the professor's face. "They blew the case."

Bowen-Smythe was skeptical. "How do you know it was so simple?"

"He confessed on his deathbed to my father, twenty-five years later. The series of stories on the botched investigation was nominated for a Pulitzer."

Bowen-Smythe slowly shook his head. "And now I suppose you're hoping to use this latest case to achieve what your father couldn't."

"Hardly. But Danny Sloan has some interesting things to say about the police department and I need to talk to him."

"I already have," Bowen-Smythe said, grinning as though suddenly amused. "He also has some interesting things to say about your newspaper."

Quinn ignored that. "You know, there may have been a witness to Paul's death," he said before pausing for a reaction that didn't come. "Someone called the police shortly after he was killed. He may have even been alive at the time."

Bowen-Smythe's grin disappeared. "Why are you telling me this?"

"I thought you'd want to know," Quinn said. "I also thought maybe you heard something."

The professor averted his eyes. "This is all news to me."

"Really?"

"Yes, really," Bowen-Smythe said, now agitated himself. "Don't you think I'd come forward if I knew something?"

"You never liked Paul."

"We disagreed on many things," Bowen-Smythe admitted. "But it was never personal."

"That's not what I heard."

"Like you should talk, you arrogant asshole." As Bowen-Smythe spoke, the blue veins in his pale forehead throbbed like they were going to explode.

Quinn was shocked by the professor's sudden burst of anger and it must have shown.

Bowen-Smythe took a deep breath and tried to force himself to relax. "Look, I'm sorry," he said. "This whole thing just has me upset."

"I understand," Quinn said, though he really didn't. Still, he felt like he was getting warmer.

"So who else knows about the witness?" Bowen-Smythe asked quietly.

"The police, obviously."

"Can they tell who made the 911 call or was the caller ID blocked?"

"It was blocked."

Bowen-Smythe began to stare but he was no longer looking at Quinn. He was thinking of something else; whatever it was, he had no intention of sharing. "Look, I'll make some calls myself," he said. "If I learn anything, I'll let you know."

"Thanks."

"Don't mention it," the professor said, and he really hoped Quinn wouldn't.

By then they noticed the guides passing around a small pipe, something that made Quinn feel eighty years old as they walked his way. He laughed when one of them offered it to him. "No thanks."

"But I grew this myself," the kid said.

"Nothing personal. I stopped when my son was born."

"That's cool."

Quinn didn't know why, but he felt relieved to hear the kid's approval.

Bowen-Smythe was mortified.

"There are cops around," the professor whispered.

"Please!" Quinn said as the others started laughing. "A Stone Harbor cop couldn't find his ass with both hands."

"I'd still be careful," another voice joined in.

They turned and it was Sears.

The guide with the pipe grinned like an idiot sharing a secret and handed it to Sears, then hovered with the lighter. His eyes widened in disbelief as the chief walked to a nearby canoe rack and tapped out the contents. "Hey, man!" he shouted. "What are you doing?"

"Lookin' for my ass," Sears said. "What do you know." He pocketed the pipe. "I found it with just one hand."

When the guide continued to protest, Bowen-Smythe and the kid's friends herded him toward the house. Sears shook his head at the sight as they quickly disappeared inside, leaving him alone with Quinn.

"Alvah, what are you doing here?" Quinn asked in a pained voice.

"Observing."

"Everyone knows who you are."

"That clown didn't." Sears waited for a laugh that didn't follow, then looked Quinn up and down suspiciously. "I thought for a moment you were gonna join in."

"Fat chance."

"You never know." Sears crossed his arms and looked off toward the house.

Quinn thought the chief had no right to intrude, no matter how many times Sears had seen television cops do the same thing after a funeral. "So what are you finding out?" Quinn asked.

"That I'm not welcome here," Sears said.

"Does that surprise you?"

"Yeah. I thought Stanwood's friends would wanna help."

Quinn stepped from one foot to the other. "Maybe they don't think this is the time or place."

"I'm not sure we can be too choosy, given the circumstances," Sears said. "We're dealin' with a homicide. The last thing I care about is a few wounded feelings—especially among this crowd."

Quinn poked a finger into Sears's chest. "Just leave Lizz out of it. All right? At least for today."

Sears slapped the finger away. "I'll be the picture of discretion," he said, cocking his head to the side before looking around the empty yard, then back at Quinn. "You managed to get out of Sunday's problem pretty easy. But I guess that's life in a small town."

"I shouldn't have lost my head. I'm sorry." Quinn held out his hand.

Sears didn't shake it. Instead, he narrowed his eyes and said, "Don't fuck with me on this investigation."

"Just do your job and I'll do mine."

Sears smiled. "You got an answer for everything."

Quinn didn't respond. He figured that would get under the chief's skin, and it did. That's why Sears suddenly threw a hard uppercut to his solar plexus that dropped him to the ground.

Quinn didn't answer that time, either. He couldn't. His breath was knocked out of him and he was gasping for air. Sears started to follow with a kick but stopped himself halfway and just stood there, staring down at Quinn, who slowly got to his hands and knees despite the pain. His face was hot and flushed but at least he was able to take short, hard breaths.

Sears still hadn't moved as Quinn staggered to his feet.

Their eyes met. "Apology accepted," Sears finally said, before turning to walk away.

Quinn bent over, with his hands flat on his thighs, until things took a turn for the worse and he threw up. His throat burned and he felt humiliated and angry.

After he was done, Quinn went over to the garage and rinsed his mouth with the garden hose and washed his face. The cold water felt good and he didn't care how much dribbled down his disheveled shirt and tie. It was bad enough that Sears hit him. But why the sucker punch? What made him so sensitive to a little criticism? With that thought lingering, he wiped his face on his sleeve and headed back inside.

Lizz was still in the kitchen. "What happened to you?" she asked.

"Karma debt."

Her face tightened in concern. "That seems to be going around. For a minute I thought you'd been hit by a truck."

Quinn looked past her. "Where's Maria?"

"Checking on the kids." Lizz got up for more wine. "Another shot of tonic water?"

"No thanks, I'm driving. But I'll take a little Stoli."

She grinned as though she finally recognized her old friend, then gleefully poured the vodka over ice and handed it to him.

He took a gulp and realized it wasn't going to help.

Lizz understood. "This stuff only gets you so far," she said, before taking another sip of wine. "My God, you're soaked!" she said when she noticed his front.

"It's a long story."

"I know—it always is." She got a dish towel, put one hand on his shoulder, and used the other to wipe his face and chest. Smiling, she kissed him lightly on the cheek and let one hand fall to his thigh, where it lingered. Looking hard into his eyes, she tried to kiss him again, but he pulled back before she could.

He sat down, startled by the effect.

She moved beside him, mouthed a cigarette from her pack and lit up. He looked at her in disbelief and she shrugged. "Oh, don't act so surprised," she said. "We all need a vice or two." She leaned back and slowly, deliberately crossed her long legs in a way that was meant to hold his attention.

He couldn't help staring.

She couldn't help noticing. "Careful, cowboy," she said in a teasing voice. "I'm still in mourning."

Embarrassed by the entire situation, he turned away. "Sorry."

"Don't be." She straightened her dress, which fell perfectly on her lean body. She was athletic yet incredibly feminine. "Everyone likes to think they're attractive," she said. "Especially a woman whose husband was last seen in Sullivan Park."

"Don't say that."

"Why not? That's what everyone thinks."

So that's what it was about, along with a fair share of alcohol. Quinn suddenly felt more sorry for her than ever. "Who cares what people think?" he asked.

"Everyone cares what people think," Lizz said quickly, "no matter what they say."

Quinn understood, more than he cared to admit.

"Try this on for size," she continued. "My fifteen-year-old hasn't spoken to me since Paul died. Somehow she blames me for what happened."

That's what Quinn's wife had already told him, though he tried to act surprised. "She's not being fair," he said.

"Life isn't fair." Her mouth clenched as she spoke. "That's the one thing I've learned from this."

"Do you want me to talk to her?"

"It's something we have to work out on our own. Besides, she's at her grandfather's."

"Angus isn't here?" Quinn thought back to the scene at the wake and couldn't help feeling relieved.

"I guess you haven't heard," she said wearily. "The old bastard is contesting the will. Our lawyers say personal contact isn't a good idea."

"But he's already loaded."

"Yes, he is—in more ways than one." She stood up, walked to the window and blew smoke outside. "He also wants to take away my children, or as he puts it, his heirs, on the grounds that I'm an unfit mother."

"Because you let kids eat in the bedroom?"

"It's more than that." She gave Quinn a bitter smile. "The real reason has nothing to do with me. It's about Paul. You see, he was more than an idealist. The boy knew how to make a buck and left an estate worth millions."

Quinn was very surprised. "He couldn't have made that selling yurts."

"John, you've been gone a long time," she said, as though she'd finally run out of patience. "There's a lot about my husband you don't know."

"Like what?"

She ground her cigarette out on a porcelain saucer, then looked at him like she was about to say something important. He didn't know where this was going and found himself getting angry when she didn't answer.

"Well, don't worry," Quinn said. "What I don't know, I'll find out. And I'm sure as hell not gonna wait on Alvah Sears."

She looked at him uncertainly.

That's when Maria and Jack showed up. Jack looked upset and ran to his father. "Why'd he hit you?" he asked excitedly. "I saw it, right out the window."

Quinn imagined the scene his son must have witnessed, with Sears standing over him as he rolled helplessly in the ground. "Oh, it was an accident," he said, trying to make the remark seem casual.

"I saw out the window," Jack insisted. "He knocked you down."

When the women eyed Quinn with puzzled expressions, he tried to shrug it off.

Jack wouldn't let him. "Are you okay?" he wanted to know.

"Sure," Quinn said uncomfortably. "It was nothing."

"Why'd he do that?"

Then it was Quinn's turn to be stumped for an answer. How do you explain what happened to a six-year-old? Hell, how do you explain it to anyone? Paul had warned him about Sears a month earlier and Quinn had laughed.

"The guy is out of control," Paul insisted.

"Oh, he's just a bully."

Paul shook his head. "Just keep in mind that bullies like to pick on the weak."

The words continued to echo in his mind. Sears had certainly picked on him, but before he'd been lying in the Stan-woods' backyard dirt, he'd never considered himself weak. Then again, he'd asked for it. You don't threaten a cop like Sears and get away scot-free. So far Quinn had been charged with disturbing the peace. He'd been humiliated in front of his son. And he was left with a lot of unanswered questions.

Maybe Paul had been onto something.

"But why'd you let him do that?" The little boy's pleading brought Quinn back to the present.

He looked down at his son. "Jack, it was nothing," Quinn said again, to the same effect. "Come on. Let's go outside and play catch. Our gloves are in the car."

Jack hesitated a moment before bolting out the door to get them. He didn't notice that Quinn was holding his mid-section and grimacing as he slowly headed outside.

Lizz and Maria did, and didn't know what to make of it.

As Quinn stood in the front yard, waiting for Jack, he took stock of what had happened. As one of the most popular figures in Stone Harbor, Sears was used to getting his own way. Apart from Paul, the board of selectmen loved him and usually did everything they could to kiss his ass. Women thought he was attractive. Men thought he was a regular guy. Kids looked up to him for his work in school, his reputation as a jock, and mostly, Quinn thought, because they didn't know any better.

Paul Stanwood didn't give a shit. No matter how contro-versial the issue became, he stood up to Sears and made it clear the cops weren't supposed to be in the park. They weren't supposed to be anywhere near the place. That was one thing Paul had gotten Bowen-Smythe and the others to agree on, no matter how mad it made Sears.

And it really made Sears mad.

Anyone else would have cut his losses and accepted a lesson learned, but Sears was another story. He'd always held a grudge, even when they were in high school. Once when they were in tenth grade, Paul made an offhand crack in the locker room about the intelligence of the wrestling squad.

Sears, the senior heavyweight, heard about it second-hand.

The next day in the cafeteria he walked up to Paul, who was eating lunch with a group of classmates, and poured a pint of chocolate milk over his head. When Paul wouldn't fight back, Sears went berserk and it took Quinn and three teachers to pull him away. None of them had ever seen anything like it. Twenty years later, the memory made Quinn wonder: could Sears have killed Paul?

5.

"YOU'RE WRONG ABOUT THE chief."

Quinn looked up from the *Boston Globe* he'd been reading in line at Bliley's Newsstand. It was the proprietor, Bub Bliley.

"Both you and Paul always tried to make him out to be the bad guy," Bub said, his deep voice drawing stares from the half dozen shipbuilders in faded jeans and hooded sweatshirts. "Just because you nevah liked Al Sears don't mean he's doin' a bad job."

Quinn stared at him a moment. "Just because you've always liked him doesn't mean he's doing a good one, either."

"True enough," Bub admitted with a nod. "The same could be said about poor Paul. He shoulda been more concerned with his own family than the fairies."

"He always did what he thought was right," Quinn shot back.

Bub held his palms up, as if to calm the other man. "I didn't mean anything by that," he said when he handed Quinn his change. "He was my friend, too."

True enough. Paul had been everybody's friend, at least while he was alive. The distance and criticism came after he was gone.

For an awkward moment they watched the other men leave and slowly walk toward the giant cranes that towered over the west end. Some shipbuilders traveled as far as seventy-five miles to work each morning, piled in full-size vans. The wages were worth the time and trouble, and their arrival and departure were part of the pulse of the city, just like the pounding machinery from the ironworks, as steady and regular as the tide.

"You know, I grew up in a yellow wooden house that was close enough to the yard that the sound of poundin' steel and intercom carried into the kitchen each mornin'," Bub said. That's where his father, in a sleeveless T-shirt, would sip coffee and complain the sons a bitches could page him in his sleep. After breakfast the old man would put on a thermal undershirt and flannel top and head out, whether it was sixty degrees or zero, cursing and greeting the other shipbuilders as they came out of identical homes.

It was the kind of place where flags flew on porches and children played in the street, and if a man wrecked his back or smashed a hand at work, his neighbors would pass the hat and see his family through. "But things change," Bub said.

Quinn quickly agreed, thanked him for the papers, then left.

His next stop was Becky's Seafood Shack for takeout lox and a bagel. She had the order waiting at the counter. As he reached into his wallet to pay, she held his hand to stop him. "Not this mornin'," she said. "This one's on me."

"What's the occasion?"

"Business has been bettah than evah." She waved at several full tables that were usually empty. "People who haven't been in this place for years stopped by aftah that picture and story. They can't believe the nerve a those fools on the town board."

Quinn laughed. "Glad I could help."

"Well, it was a start. But Bowen-Smythe ain't gonna stop with the sign." She pointed at the public lot. "Now he wants to restrict on-street parking to fifteen minutes, which is fine for businesses with their own spaces."

"Since when?"

She slid a piece of paper across the counter. "Since this survey came out. It asks a lotta questions, but the only answer I have is they don't want our customers hoggin' spots that could be used for the yuppies shoppin' for wine and brie."

Quinn pocketed the survey.

"I already got three tickets for parkin' overnight," she added. That's because she and Ernie were living in the small apartment over the restaurant, since they could no longer afford the taxes on their cottage on the water and had sold it a month before.

They weren't the only ones. The gaping foundations of demolished homes allowed Quinn unobstructed views of the river on his way into the office. A quiet, working-class neighborhood had been bought and sold. The simple frame houses could no longer compete with the waterfront condos popping up in their place. The empty lots seemed naked, like someplace Quinn had never been. Thinking of the crews that would be ripping and prying the next house in line, he tried to picture what the street would be like tomorrow, or the day after that.

He didn't like the image.

IN THE NEWSROOM, HE was greeted by a dozen empty desks and the glow of a stray computer screen that had been left on overnight. He was always the first one in. That's because he liked the early morning quiet, the smell of strong coffee and the time alone to plan, read and think.

His routine was simple:

The lox and bagel.

The rest of the *Globe*.

The *New York Times*.

The Maine papers.

Then he hit the wires and by eight o'clock had a sense of what was going on in the world: oil prices were soaring, China was still stealing U.S. intellectual property, four Americans were being held by Islamic extremists in Sudan and Congress was debating the merits of amending the Constitution to protect the institution of marriage.

Great.

Once he got briefed on the local stories, he'd be able to pick and choose how to present it all in the twenty-four pages of the *Stone Harbor Pilot*.

Usually he had that first hour to himself, but when he was barely through the *Globe*'s regional section, Sarah Sewell came clattering into the newsroom in a flurry of shifting cloth, perfume and a bagful of notes and files. Quinn nodded and went back to reading about a man who'd quit his job as a bank executive to become the rigger on the USS *Constitution,* which was still a working ship out of Boston Harbor. "It's a cut in pay, but life's too short to spend at something you don't absolutely love," the guy was quoted as saying.

By the time Quinn finished reading, the rest of the staff had arrived and filed their story plans. Other than the Stanwood follow, they didn't have much of a local report. The city's only remaining cannery had laid off fifteen more people. A tourist from New York City had driven a rented Ford Explorer into a mudflat and had to be rescued by the volunteer fire department. Another clothing outlet had opened on Route 1, bringing the total to thirty-seven.

It was a pretty typical Monday.

After a while he felt like things were almost back to normal.

Then Sarah walked back into his office. "My story's done," she said. "If you need me, I'll be at the police station, checking the 911 tapes."

"Don't get arrested."

"Believe me, you'd be the last person I'd call if I did," she said.

"Let's hope your mother feels the same way."

Sarah ignored that.

Quinn was too busy reading to care.

SAVAGE BEATING CONTINUED
AFTER DEATH
BY SARAH SEWELL
Pilot Staff

Whoever killed Paul Stanwood continued to beat his lifeless body long after the fatal blow was delivered.

That's the conclusion of Maine State Medical Examiner Denise Deasy, who released her autopsy findings this morning. "He also suffered 23 broken bones," Deasy said.

She put the time of death at approximately 4 a.m. Sunday. His body was found an hour later in Sullivan Park.

A Wellsen psychology professor said it was probably an act of rage rather than a planned murder, though police said it's too soon to rule anything out.

"Whoever did this has a lot of anger toward homosexuals, for whatever reason," said Margaret Craig. "Finding out what caused the rage will be the key to solving this murder."

Police Chief Alvah Sears dismissed the theory: "I may not have any fancy degrees, but I know we have a homicide. I know we have evidence that I'm not at liberty to disclose in the middle of an investigation. And I know we're going to solve the crime."

Stanwood, the married father of two and a town selectman, had been critical of local police for arresting gay men who frequented Sullivan Park. Friends and colleagues speculated he was in the park to get the views of those men. Funeral services for Stanwood were held Wednesday afternoon at First Parish Church.

But Paul was a long way from being buried—something Quinn did keep out of the paper. In fact, his ashes were still in an urn on a Bangor lawyer's desk. Stanwood's wife wanted to scatter them over the Penobscot River. That's where he'd been happiest, and she couldn't think of a better resting place for a man who loved big water.

His father thought the remains belonged in the Stanwood plot with the rest of the clan. That was family tradition and had been for generations. Angus didn't want to break with it, especially over some half-wit idea that probably came out of a damn women's magazine.

He was impossible.

"This is what Paul would have wanted," Lizz had said.

"Well, that's not what our family does."

"Things change," she insisted.

"More than you care to admit," Angus countered. And that's when he served her with another injunction.

The rest was up to the lawyers.

That was the way things seemed to go. Everyone's first call was to an attorney. Even Danny Sloan—who Quinn vaguely knew—was threatening to get lawyers involved over his claims against the police department.

Why didn't Sloan just pick up the phone? Quinn would have gladly written about any cover-up by the cops. Instead, the little shit was trying to make the *Pilot* out to be an accomplice. Hell, Quinn hadn't even kept his own name out of the paper when he'd been brought up on bogus charges that the district attorney immediately dropped.

After the paper came out, he decided to pay the artist a visit.

SLOAN'S STUDIO WAS IN a low wooden warehouse along a pier that held a rickety collection of other buildings, the contents of which ranged from wrought-iron sculptures to used books and pottery. Sloan's place was filled with old fishing gear, watercolor landscapes and seascapes in various frames, along with piles of driftwood collected over the years.

"Well, well, well," Sloan said from one of the two stools he kept in front of a big bay window overlooking the harbor. "What can I do for you?"

"I'd like to talk about Paul Stanwood."

"Of course." Sloan offered Quinn the other stool and sat back down on his own. He was a small man with bright eyes and a thick body that could have belonged to a bricklayer.

"Did you know him well?" Quinn asked.

"In some ways, very well," Sloan said. "In other ways, not at all."

"What's that supposed to mean?"

Sloan shrugged, like he wasn't sure himself. "Paul was a

complicated man. I've done a lot of painting of the Maine woods. He knew and loved the territory. We became friends because we were both concerned about its future."

"So what was he doing in the woods of Sullivan Park?" Quinn asked.

"Your guess is as good as mine, though I do know the police aren't taking his death very seriously. They haven't taken any violence against gays seriously."

"Paul wasn't gay," Quinn said without emotion, as though he was tired of saying it and having people ignore him.

Sloan looked at him carefully. "Would his death have meant less if he was?"

"Not at all."

"Are you sure about that?" Sloan asked.

"I'm pretty sure he'd be just as dead." Quinn thought the guy had a lot of nerve, pressing him like that. He was used to asking the questions and didn't like answering them.

Sloan could tell. "Then what do you have against gays?"

"Nothing."

Though Quinn was annoyed and curt, Sloan remained calm and relaxed. "The subject seems to make you uncomfortable," he said gently.

Quinn rolled his eyes. "Please. Are you an artist or a psychiatrist?"

"I'm just a man who's concerned about the attacks."

"You're also the man who told Sarah we were keeping stories out of the *Pilot*," Quinn said. "Believe me, if those things happened, the police never told us."

Sloan crossed his arms. "That's not what Chief Sears said."

"And you believe that asshole?" Quinn asked.

Sloan raised his right hand as though taking an oath. "Now, I didn't say that."

"Well, you shouldn't." Quinn was off the stool and pacing. "I'm beginning to think he's the biggest problem in all this."

"I can see why. Some of us have had discussions about the department."

Unconsciously, Quinn fingered his midsection. "Have you talked to anyone on the council?" he asked.

"Paul. And I'm having dinner with Bryan Bowen-Smythe tonight."

Quinn gave a tight little smile. "Think you'll get anywhere?"

"Sure—after I raise the possibility of a lawsuit against the town."

"Is that just a threat or are you serious?"

"Hell if I know," Sloan admitted.

"So why is Paul dead?"

"I don't know that, either, but I'll keep making noise till somebody finds out."

"I'll do the same," Quinn said. "It would help if you gave me the names of the men who were attacked, along with anything else you might have."

"I was hoping you'd ask." Sloan walked over to a desk, reached in a drawer, and pulled out a manila envelope. "I've already made copies." Then he wrote his phone number on a piece of paper and gave it to Quinn. "Let me know if you need anything else."

"You, too." On his way out, Quinn hesitated in the doorway. "So what would you do if you were me?"

"Be careful."

●　●　●

He planned on it—especially since he was driving his wife's silver BMW convertible. She and Jack were picking up some landscaping supplies and she didn't want to get her car dirty, so she had the Volvo. Quinn made a point of parking the Beamer as far away from the other traffic as possible in the crammed lot. From the looks of things, both the sports car and his marriage had emerged unscathed.

As he drove down High Street, away from the waterfront, Quinn passed the old Lowell Mill, which was being converted into a giant antique boutique. Workers were hammering and sawing and carrying in finished cabinets and countertops. The new owners planned to put in a wine bar and an espresso shop, along with the town's second microbrewery. It was amazing. In his lifetime, Stone Harbor had gone from a tough town of fishermen and shipbuilders to a soft place that drew yuppies, trust fund brats and all their mush-headed sensibilities. In the past ten years, its population had nearly doubled and many locals felt like their own backyard had been taken out from under them.

The signs were everywhere:

"For Sale."

"Sold."

"Coming Soon."

The place had changed more than he realized, and the contradictions between then and now were laughable. The newcomers thought hunting was cruel, then cut up the woods for sterile subdivisions. They raved about rural Maine's charm but priced the natives out of their family homes. They wanted to get away from it all, then drove gas-guzzling SUVs to the strip malls that sprang up in their wake.

Tommy Hilfiger.

Victoria's Secret.

Saks Fifth Avenue.

At times like those he just wanted to hit the gas and go—especially when he looked in the rearview mirror and saw a black Lexus with tinted windows a little too close for comfort. The driver wore large aviator sunglasses and a navy baseball cap and stayed on his bumper. The car had Maine plates, but he figured with those roadside manners, the driver must be a Massachusetts transplant.

When Quinn sped up, the Lexus sped up.

When he slowed to a crawl, the Lexus did, too.

"Just pass me, Masshole!" Quinn shouted into his rear-view mirror.

It didn't do any good.

The hell with this, he thought. As Quinn downshifted and put the BMW's gas pedal to the floor, the engine roared, the lines on the curving highway blurred and suddenly he found himself on top of a stream of traffic with the Lexus in the same position, right on his bumper. Since he didn't have the patience to wait behind a Cadillac Escalade with three mountain bikes on the roof, a tour bus from Pennsylvania, two Subaru Outbacks, a Jeep Cherokee with a canoe lashed on top, and a giant RV from Kansas that was big enough to hold a touring rock group, he wheeled into the oncoming lane and just kept flying.

Seventy. Eighty. Ninety miles per hour. The Beamer handled much better than his boxy Volvo. He quickly lost sight of the Lexus and before he knew it, Quinn was going 100, 110, then 120.

Past the Cadillac.

The tour bus.

The Subarus.

The Cherokee.

The giant RV.

He wanted to leave them all behind.

He almost did when a banged-up truck was suddenly coming straight at him and a big Mainer in a black T-shirt leaned into the horn. With the sound still *blarrrrinnnnnnggg* and his tires squealing, Quinn jerked back to his own lane and cut off the RV. Quinn swerved onto the berm and kicked up sand and dust and a little uncertainty as his rear wheels went into a slide.

He eased off the gas until the speedometer dropped to the eighties and the car drifted past one more subdivision, over the Stone Crib Bridge and into what felt like the last open stretch of coastal highway. The Beamer ate it up and Quinn was starting to get the hang of driving a sports car as granite ledges and clumps of pine replaced the signs, facades and parking lots and the smell of salt water came off cold, clear Penobscot Bay. In the distance, wooded islands sat a mile offshore. He slowed all the way down to the speed limit and began to relax.

The Maine of his childhood began to emerge in the form of a roadside motor court and a general store that still sold gasoline from an ancient Gulf pump and discouraged unnecessary familiarity with a sign that said, "No public restrooms." The houses became sparser, older and more rustic as he passed Tripp's gravel pit, Niven's Nursery, the Morse bog. He traveled decades in a few miles until a stone fence paralleled the highway and there it was: Sullivan Park.

That stretch had changed very little in the past thirty years. When he was a boy, it was still in the Sullivan family, though by the early seventies the clan had been reduced to a pair of eccentric brothers with a small dairy herd, a lobster boat and firm notions on life, death and everything in between. Even then, the Sullivan boys didn't like much of what was happening to Stone Harbor. Their family had been in the area two hundred years, and Geoff and George were the end of the line. As a concession to that fact they eventually deeded their farm to the town and headed to Newfoundland, which they said was the last place on the Atlantic seaboard that hadn't turned into greater New Jersey.

Now most of their place—with the exception of a loose system of trails—had reverted to nature. The house, barn and outbuildings were gone, torn down to the foundations that were in turn reclaimed by fern and moss. But as Quinn pulled off the highway, he came to an unexpected stop: mounds of dirt were piled across the access road with no going around them.

He got out, slammed the door and walked to a chained gate posted with No Trespassing signs issued "under the authority of the board of selectmen."

That wasn't all. Downed trees had been dragged across four other spots along the road. So much for saving nature. Confused, Quinn walked back to the car for his camera.

He shot the brand-new signs.

He shot the torn-up road.

He tried to get the whole thing together in one frame to provide a little perspective, but couldn't quite pull it off. So he took the road by foot and looked around with a vacant curiosity, expecting, at any moment, to see whoever was responsible.

"Hey," he called out. "Anybody there?"

His voice echoed off the treetops. The park was isolated, yet he couldn't shake the notion that someone was watching. He called again: still no answer.

He was stunned by what was ahead.

The parking lot was empty, the picnic tables and pay phones nowhere in sight. Even the bathhouse had been razed. Nothing was left except a cracked concrete slab and bulldozer tracks.

He stood a moment longer and shot a few more images, then stared before turning to leave. It didn't make sense in the middle of a homicide investigation. The police shouldn't have allowed it. The same with the board of selectmen. But somebody wanted to make it seem like nothing had ever happened there.

Quinn was even more convinced when he got back to his wife's car. All four tires had been slashed, the windshield was shattered, the driver's-side door had been keyed and the folder from Danny Sloan was gone.

6.

"So where were you when this happened?" the young cop asked again, as if he really wanted a different answer than the one Quinn had given.

"I was in the park."

"Mr. Quinn, the park is closed."

Quinn stabbed a finger in the air, toward the sign. "I know it. *Now.* The problem is, nobody else does. This posting came out of nowhere."

"It was posted, just the same."

"But I'm working on a story," Quinn said. "You know that." Jesus. Earl Stufflebeam had spent five years as a carrier for the *Pilot* when he was a kid and knew better. He used to hang around the newsroom before the press run, soaking in the reporters' chatter and the gruff humor of Big Jake, Quinn's father, who roamed the place like a surly bear. Trying to take advantage of those days, Quinn leaned forward and spoke in a lower voice, as though confiding in him. "It's not like I was hurting anything."

"That's not the point," Earl insisted.

"Then what's the point? It's broad daylight, not four in the morning!"

"I still have to ticket you," Earl said somewhat reluctantly.

"For what?" Quinn couldn't believe what a tool Earl had become.

"You were trespassing on town land."

"On town land? I'm a taxpayer!"

"I give plenty of tickets to taxpayers," Earl said, "though I'd rather let you off with a warnin'." By then he was almost pleading. "But I want you to promise you'll stay away from places you don't belong."

Quinn knew Earl was acting on someone else's orders and wasn't really comfortable giving him a hard time. "So who decides where I belong and where I don't?" he asked.

That definitely troubled Earl. His slightly pimpled face stretched into a frown and he couldn't bring himself to answer. He'd been the most reliable carrier the paper had ever known and in some ways was too much of a straight shooter for his own good.

"Look, Earl, I won't go back again," Quinn assured the young cop. There was no use dragging him into his beef with Sears. He was just doing his job.

Relieved, Earl flashed a broad, toothy smile. "Okay, Mr. Quinn. That's more like it."

"Thanks for the break." Quinn waited a moment for his feigned gratitude to sink in, then asked, "So who do you think slashed my tires?"

"I have no idea," Earl blurted out so quickly Quinn figured he was hiding something.

"That's not very reassuring."

"Look, Mr. Quinn, there are lots of things going on I don't understand. That's why we don't want anyone out here. It's for your own good. I'll give you a ride into the station so we can fill out a report." Earl looked over his shoulder at the tow-truck driver, who'd been absorbing the scene from his perch in the cab. "Artie can take care of things from here."

The driver gave a salute from behind the wheel to acknowledge the fact.

They got in the cruiser and drove a mile or so in silence, with Quinn wondering who had vandalized his wife's car. Was it a coincidence or had someone tried to scare him off?

If that were the case, it had the opposite effect. He was enraged, not afraid, though he was doing everything he could to keep his cool. He needed to think and figure this out, not go off half-cocked.

Who knew where he'd been?

Had someone followed him? Could it have been the driver of the black Lexus? He'd never seen the car before, or at least never noticed it.

Or was it just another redneck who didn't like gays?

The hell if he knew. After turning things over in his head a few more times, Quinn decided to ask Earl about the homicide investigation. "Any progress in the Stanwood murder?"

"Yes."

Quinn waited for Earl to elaborate, but he didn't. "Well?"

"You have to talk to the chief," Earl said.

"I'd rather slice off my tongue."

Earl had a resigned look on his face as he glanced over at Quinn. "That's what I figured."

After that, silence, subdivisions, strip malls and increased traffic marked their progress. They moved slowly. Almost painfully. Thank God they finally got to the station, though Quinn didn't go inside. "Look, Earl, thanks for the ride. The more I think of it, I don't want to file a complaint."

"Don't you want to find out who slashed your tires?"

"Sure. I just don't see a connection between that and a bunch of paperwork." Quinn got out of the cruiser and walked down the street to the *Pilot*.

LATER HE FOUND OUT the new tires alone cost a thousand dollars.

"That's right, a thousand dollars," Seth Quinn said. He was staring out from behind the steering wheel of his own car, which had four fully inflated tires, an Italian leather interior, and a Jaguar V8 engine. Seth had a keen sense of what things cost—a stark contrast to Quinn, who rarely noticed the price of a gallon of gas, even though it had been rising all summer. His indifference to money drove Seth crazy. "And don't forget another four thousand for the smashed windshield and the damage to the door," he added.

"So it's five thousand," Quinn said from the passenger's side.

"No, it'll be more like six thousand when you count the labor," Seth corrected.

"We have insurance. For chrissake, we pay enough each month for the company fleet."

"It's a thousand-dollar deductible."

"Then deduct it."

"Deduct it," Seth said, like he couldn't believe what he was hearing. That struck Quinn as funny, since Seth had been the one who talked Maria into buying the car when she'd been happy with an eight-year-old Geo Prism. That had been the first week Quinn was back and Seth was eager to show off as the newly named general manager. He wanted to send the message that the Quinns were more successful than they'd ever let on. Come to think of it, Seth was the one who said it was no big deal to register the car to Stone Harbor Publishing.

How things changed.

"I can't believe you let this happen," Seth said. "What were you thinking?"

Quinn had to remind himself he was Seth's boss. "It's the middle of the afternoon in Stone Harbor," he explained. "I wasn't thinking anything."

"That much is obvious, but it won't do much for our insurance claim or the expense."

"It sounds like you don't want to deduct it," Quinn said in a way that made it clear the issue was closed—or so he thought.

"Of course I don't want to deduct it," Seth snapped.

"Then shove it up your ass."

"Why not?" Seth asked. "That's what I've been doing since you came back—taking it up the ass. I'm starting to feel like your buddy Danny Sloan. Only I don't have any secrets to share."

"Please."

"It's true," Seth said. "You go out and cause one mess after another, and I have to pick up afterward."

"My wife's car was vandalized."

"Your whole life's been vandalized!"

"What kind of thing is that to say?" Quinn asked as Seth steamed beside him in his cufflinks and tailored suit. "Look, I'm having a helluva day. I call the one person I can count on, and you just give me crap."

"My day hasn't exactly been a picnic," Seth said.

"What happened?"

Seth's cell phone rang before he could tell him. "I know . . . It's typical . . . I can't help it . . ." The call was from Meredith. The frantic look on his face gave it away. "Honey, I'll call you back as soon as I can . . . good-bye. Of course I love you." Seth was on the verge of proposing and was more attentive than ever to her moods.

Quinn couldn't help laughing, but in a good-natured way. "Do you have any idea what you could be getting into with that woman?" he asked.

Seth's face reddened against his blond hair. "Compared to you, she actually is a picnic."

"Does she ever let you turn that cell phone off?"

"I use it for work."

"There's more to life than work," Quinn said.

"How would you know? You've spent your whole life dicking around on Uncle Jake's dime. Now it's time to pony up with a little responsibility and you think it's a great big joke."

"So I've been told."

"In case you don't know it—and I'm sure you don't, since you never look at the financials I send you—we're having an awful month."

"What's a thousand bucks?" Quinn asked. "We're budgeted to make two hundred grand."

"We'll make half that."

"So we'll make half." Quinn shrugged as he said this. "There's always next month."

"The payment on the bank note is a hundred and twenty thousand."

"I can cover it."

"You shouldn't have to cover it," Seth said, turning sideways to look directly at him. "That's no way to run a business."

"It's only one month."

"It's been four," Seth said, holding up that many fingers. "And I don't think we can keep ignoring the problem."

"There's a difference between ignoring a problem and being consumed by it. Besides, the government told me this business was worth twenty-six million when my father died. Twenty thousand bucks shouldn't be a big deal."

"It's worth twenty-six million if somebody's willing to pay twenty-six million," Seth said. "In my book, that's an awfully big 'if.'"

By then, Quinn was seething, though not necessarily at Seth. "There was no 'if' when I had to borrow thirteen million to pay the inheritance taxes."

"That's why you have to start thinking about the bottom line."

Quinn glared at his cousin. "It's *your* job to think about the bottom line."

"Then let me do it," Seth pleaded.

"All right," Quinn said, giving in. "What do you recommend?"

"We need to cut some positions. Stoney's been in the pressroom forty-five years. He's old enough to retire. Aunt Blythe has been old enough to retire for the past ten years."

"Losing her job would kill her," Quinn said. He remembered her hand on his shoulder in the newsroom the day they learned about Paul. He also pictured her calming Angus down at the wake and chatting away at the Stanwoods' after the funeral. She was the most visible face of the newspaper and since her husband was long gone and they never had children, the newspaper was her life. "Why can't we just sell more ads?"

"I'd love to—only half our advertisers think your only mission in life is to stir things up. We're also in a recession. Nobody's spending money and if that's not bad enough, more and more people are reading the paper online, for free."

"Things will pick up."

Seth practically spat. "I'm glad you're so optimistic."

"Jesus—I thought we were supposed to be rich."

"You're rich," Seth corrected. "I'm just a poor relative who works for you."

"A poor relative who drives a Jag."

Seth smiled at that, since he loved his car. "I guess it's a matter of perspective," he admitted, and they both had to laugh. Seth had been successfully selling advertising since he'd been in high school. "But you're still the rich one," he insisted.

"Then why don't I feel rich?" Quinn asked. He pictured himself in a limousine with a chauffeur. Actually, for a moment he imagined Seth as his driver, complete with the cap and black uniform. Tailor-made, of course.

The idea was closer to the truth than he realized. "You don't feel rich because you don't act rich," Seth said.

"Well, how are rich people supposed to act?"

"Rich people would cut some positions," Seth said. "Besides, you're heavy in the newsroom."

"It's the same number we've always had."

"Yes, and Stone Harbor Shipping used to employ eight thousand," Seth said. "Now they employ fifteen hundred. Things change. We have to tighten up."

"We have seventeen newsroom staffers for a seventeen-thousand-circulation paper. That's the industry standard for a paper our size."

Seth couldn't believe what he'd just heard. "We haven't been at seventeen thousand in a while," he said. "It's more like fourteen thousand, which means we have to start making some tough decisions—something you like to avoid."

That sounded familiar. Paul always said he couldn't make a tough decision, though he'd once made a much tougher decision than Paul would ever know. It had affected them both, but Quinn was never able to tell him, and that was probably for the best.

"Hey!" Seth shouted, jarring Quinn back to the present conversation. "Have you been listening to a word I said?"

"Yeah," Quinn answered numbly. "So how long have we been at fourteen thousand?"

"Months."

Quinn couldn't argue. There was no point with Seth, the numbers man. "You're right," he finally admitted. "I'm just not in the mood today."

"When, then?"

"I'll let you know tomorrow."

"You're starting to sound like Scarlett O'Hara."

"Then why do you give a damn?" Quinn asked.

Seth exhaled sharply. "What makes you so sure I do?"

That was a pretty good point, Quinn realized. As his cousin pulled into the Stanwood Auto World parking lot to let him out, he wondered if he'd been taking Seth for granted. Seth had plenty of opportunities to move on to bigger things, but he loved Stone Harbor, his family and the *Pilot*. They might bicker and argue, but when you got right down to it, Seth had always been there for Quinn.

• • •

"WELL, THIS IS WHERE you get off," Seth said. They were at the entrance to what seemed like never-ending rows of shiny new and used cars: a thousand of them on five acres—Fords, Lincolns, Volvos, Lexuses, Range Rovers, BMWs—Angus had them all.

"You don't want to come in?" Quinn asked, as though he didn't already know the answer.

"Not this afternoon." Seth's trouble with Angus stemmed from an embarrassing mistake in a two-page advertising spread. Though it wasn't Seth's fault, Angus blamed him for the forty-eight-point typo.

"Don't worry," Quinn said as he got out. "I'll tell *Anus* you said hello."

Seth wasn't amused.

Quinn was. Laughing, he looked around the giant lot and thought of the owner. "You can always find a deal here," Angus liked to say in newspaper ads, on the radio and in tacky TV spots. Sometimes you could catch him after the local newscast, bellowing about another shipment of new cars that just *had* to *move*. Other times you might see him in the middle of the night, right after the lingerie babes pushing 1–900 phone lines. Whatever the hour, he was always making a pitch. He may have been the most recognized man in Georges County, if not the entire coast of Maine.

"Johnny boy!" Angus hollered when Quinn walked inside the main building. "Get your ink-stained ass on over here."

They shook hands and Quinn asked how he was doing.

"I feel like bloody hell."

"Well, you look it, too," Quinn said.

"At least I got my wits about me, which is more than I can

say about you," Angus insisted. "What kinda fool lets someone slash his wife's tires and scratch up her car?"

"You're looking at him."

Angus put his arm around Quinn's shoulder and led him into his office, which overlooked the showroom floor and was walled with one-way glass. He handed over a blue Stanwood Auto World coffee cup that had his own face superimposed on a cartoon globe. "What do you take in it?"

"Plain decaf."

"Decaf!" Angus exclaimed with great animation. "What's the friggin' point?"

"It's my doctor's idea."

"Oh, doctors around here have their heads up their asses," Angus said with the confidence of a man who'd been born and raised in Maine, and not counting seven trips to Disney World, had never left the state. "I haven't been to a doctor in thirty years," he said for emphasis as he poured out the unleaded, which he regarded suspiciously. "Has this made you feel any better?"

"I've had a headache for a week and I'm a little irritable."

"Well, you were always ornery, even as a boy." Angus roared at the thought.

Quinn didn't think it was *that* funny.

"You and Paul were quite a pair. That's probably why you got along so well." Angus paused a moment. "At least you had the sense to go into the family business."

Growing up, Paul had never wanted anything to do with Stanwood Used Cars, even when it became Stanwood Ford, and eventually Stanwood Auto World. This angered Angus enough so that long after Paul became prosperous himself, he gouged his son and daughter-in-law on the cars they bought.

Once Lizz threatened to price a competitor in Camden, but Paul drew the line at complaining. "I know he can be an ass," Paul said. "But he is my father."

"He sure as hell better hope I am," Angus said when he heard the story. From that moment on, any time Paul did something he disagreed with, Angus threatened to have blood tests taken. Paul always offered to pay for them.

"Oh, that Sharkey," Angus said softly as he shook his head at the memory. "Where'd you come up with his stupid nickname, anyway?"

"He brought that on himself," Quinn said. "On a ninth-grade ski trip. We were on a bus to Sugarloaf and, on a dare, he bit a girl on the ass."

"Right on the ass?"

"Yep," Quinn insisted with a touch of glee. "Right square on the ass."

"I'll be damned." At that moment Angus wore a look of pure admiration. "Then what happened?"

"She broke his nose with her elbow. It was the time he told you he ran into a pine tree."

"I don't blame the little pisser." Angus howled with delight. "I wouldn't admit to gettin' my nose smashed apart by a girl, even if she was a big strappin' bull dyke in a flannel shirt and knee-high lumberjack boots. But it served him right. He deserved a shot like that." Angus held his breath to keep from laughing any more. "So whatever happened to the girl?"

"He married her."

That did it. Angus's face turned a deeper red than normal. "I guess she really did pay him back," he said slowly.

Quinn thought that was unfair. "It depends how you look at it."

"It's how I see it," Angus said. "And if you knew her as well as I did, you'd see it the same way. I just don't trust her. Never have. She married Paul because I had money."

"There was more to it than that," Quinn said.

"There wasn't much more," Angus insisted. "She come from trash and figured he was her ticket out."

Lizz and her sisters were raised by a single mother. After their father left for parts unknown, Lee Anne Pert spent twenty-five years at Stinson Cannery. All three Pert girls used to deliver the *Pilot* after school and stuff inserts in the mail room to get by.

"She told me you were contesting the will."

"I'm contesting her version of it," Angus said. "That's for damn sure. I put a lotta money in that company. There were plenty of times they wouldn't a had a pot to piss in, out singin' in nature, for chrissake. Buildin' campfires. Chargin' Massholes so they could feel like a friggin' pack of Passamaquoddy Injuns. It was all fun and games—a great big lark, underwritten by me. Now Paul's dead and all I got is my grandkids. I'm not gonna lose them, too. I got my rights."

"Why would you lose them?"

"Queen Elizabeth doesn't want me near 'em 'cause I know she's nothin' but a money-grubber. You don't understand because your mind never worked like hers. That's 'cause you and Paul never learned the value of a dollah. You always had fathers who worked their butts off so you didn't have to."

Quinn didn't argue.

"Then little 'Lizabeth came waltzin' into the picture," Angus added.

Quinn didn't think that was fair. "She's always worked hard from the time she was a girl," he said.

"At some things," Angus admitted. "Other things just fell her way."

Quinn couldn't believe what he was hearing and it showed in the way his eyes sharpened on Angus.

"She had a financial motive," Angus explained, indignant that Quinn doubted him. "And what better way to cover her tracks than to make it look like he was a fairy, found dead in Sullivan Park?"

"You need to calm down and think about what you're saying." Quinn meant it as a final warning.

Angus waved him off. "Oh, that's a helluva bit of advice coming from a hothead like you."

"I'm not a hothead."

"Bullshit! That's why you flipped out on the chief." Angus roared at the thought, as only he could. Quinn found himself joining in, which broke the growing tension. "A normal person wouldn't a done that."

"I didn't flip out," Quinn said quietly, despite his smile, as if a softer tone could prove his point.

"Tell me about it," Angus said, his wide grin back again. "Why don't you just begin at the beginnin' and tell me all about it."

Quinn did. He told him about Professor Sloan's theory on the gay bashing.

He told him of his concerns about Sears.

He also told him about the bulldozed road and the razed buildings, which shut Angus up for a moment. Even after it sank in he was still pretty quiet.

"So you're saying the bathhouse is leveled?" Angus finally asked, without a trace of humor left in his voice.

"Flat as a pancake."

Then the older man exploded. He let loose with a whoop and hurled his coffee cup across the room, where it spun and sprayed and collided with the one-way glass that shattered and crashed into a thousand jangly pieces on the burgundy showroom carpet.

Nobody said a word.

Not Quinn.

Not Angus.

Not the young salesman, or the family that had been checking out the Volvo Cross Country with their Labrador retriever. They all looked over—rather sheepishly—except the dog, who wagged his tail and did a play bow, as if he wanted Angus to throw something else.

Angus tilted his head toward Quinn and shrugged, as though that were enough explanation for his customers till the salesman's quick reference to the full-time all-wheel drive drew their attention back to the Volvo.

Quinn was amazed. "I'm the hothead?" he asked, pointing at the glass. "What do you call that outburst?"

"That, my friend, was nothin'," Angus said. "You only seen the beginnin'. I'm gonna get some answers," he said to Quinn. "I'm gonna prove who did this, John. I really am, then I'm gonna kill her with my own two hands, so help me God."

"What if it's not her? Danny Sloan is complaining to Bryan Bowen-Smythe about the police department."

Angus scoffed at the notion. "Maybe he should discuss Bowen-Smythe with the police department. He's one little weasel you need to watch out for. Paul didn't trust him." The older man's eyes looked like they were far away, focusing on something he couldn't quite see. "Bowen-Smythe got all bent when Paul started thinking about a code of ethics for elected officials, which woulda been the end of the learned professor's little consultin' business—among other things."

"What are you saying?"

"Don't worry," Angus said. "I'll be sayin' a lot more and I'll be sayin' it publicly."

"Why won't you tell me now?"

"What's the friggin' point? I try to tell you about darlin' 'Lizabeth and you don't believe me. Why should I waste my breath on anything else? You just get your goddamn notebook ready when the time comes."

"All right," Quinn said in a way that sounded like it wasn't the least bit all right.

It had no effect, but as Quinn turned to leave, Angus stopped him. "One other thing." He held out a small pipe that looked oddly familiar, along with a bag of pot. "You don't want to be leavin' this in your ashtray. You're lucky the cops missed it when they went to the park to investigate your call."

It was the pipe Sears had taken from the guide after the funeral.

"That's not mine," Quinn said. "That son of a bitch must have planted it."

Angus nodded like that made perfect sense. "Now that's somethin' I wouldn't put past him. Either way, you bettah be more careful." Angus pushed the pipe toward Quinn. "So do you want this?"

"Not me."

"All right, then." Angus grinned. "I'm sure I can make some use of it."

Quinn had no idea what Angus had planned and wondered if the old boy even knew himself. As he got in his wife's repaired car and roared off, he tried to imagine why Angus blamed Lizz for Paul's death. Sure, he'd never liked her, but if the couple had the issues Angus claimed, divorce would have been the logical next step, not murder.

Then again, Lizz had an odd way of showing grief. She was also strong enough to beat a man to death. But Quinn knew she wasn't capable of murder. He knew her much better than Angus. There'd even been a time when he'd known her better than anyone, though that was something he didn't dwell on. But she'd certainly made him uncomfortable in the past few days. Despite everything that had happened, he couldn't get over the way her hand had lingered on his thigh after the funeral, or the look in her eye when they'd been alone.

7.

WELLSEN COLLEGE SAT ON a hill west of town, overlooking the harbor. Though Revolutionary War general Thaddeus Wellsen donated his personal library and the land for the school, he never traveled north of Boston, let alone as far as Penobscot Bay. That didn't keep future generations from erecting a statue of the founder lugging an ax and Bible through the northern wilderness.

His successors felt they carried the same burden.

Since Quinn didn't like the Wellsen crowd's attitude, he kept his distance. Dr. Bryan Bowen-Smythe reminded him of that when he stopped into the professor's small, cramped office. One wall was filled from floor to ceiling with books and papers. Another had posters of aging sixties musicians.

"John, I've never seen you on campus before," Bowen-Smythe said when he noticed Quinn. "I'm surprised you could find me."

"It wasn't hard," Quinn said. "Cole Hall was named after my great-grandfather."

"Really?" Bowen-Smythe asked as he cleared a pile of papers from a chair so Quinn could sit. "Are you a graduate?"

"Of the University of Miami." When Quinn saw the professor's mild surprise, he explained that he wanted to get away from home.

"But now you're back," Bowen-Smythe mused as he sat down himself. "So what can I do for you?" He leaned forward from behind his desk and put his chin in his folded hands, as though he couldn't wait to hear what Quinn had to say. He expected a question about the sign ordinance but that was the last thing on Quinn's mind.

"I was out at Sullivan Park this morning and was surprised to find the buildings razed." Quinn eyed the other man for a reaction that didn't come. "Did you know about that?"

"Yes. It was a public safety issue."

"Just whose safety did you have in mind?"

Bowen-Smythe shrugged. "Chief Sears didn't have a problem with it."

"The district attorney might."

Bowen-Smythe let his hands fall flatly on the top of his desk before he picked up a pen and began fidgeting. "So what are you accusing me of?"

"Nothing. I'm just trying to learn what's going on."

"So what great conspiracies are you uncovering?" Bowen-Smythe asked as he twirled the pen.

"Angus Stanwood said Paul was going to propose a code of ethics that would have cost you a consulting business."

"And he was trying to get you to consider a different set of ethics when it came to the way you reported certain items in your newspaper."

"But I haven't done anything that would impede the investigation into his murder."

"Neither have I." The professor slammed the pen on the table and stretched a forced smile across his face. "Thanks for stopping by," he said abruptly. "But I have a class in a few minutes and can't really talk any further." Bowen-Smythe stood up to leave, and to dismiss Quinn.

On his way out, Quinn tried to imagine what the professor really knew about his friend's murder.

PARK BECOMES THE LATEST MYSTERY
By John Quinn
Pilot Staff

Sullivan Park has been closed, its roadway torn up and its lone building razed.

While legal experts were shocked that the scene of a homicide would be so recklessly disrupted, Board of Selectman Chairman Bryan Bowen-Smythe said the measures were taken to ensure public safety. "Given the problems we've experienced this summer, this seemed to be the most sensible course of action," Bowen-Smythe said.

He insisted the removal of public conveniences and addition of barriers would end after-hours use of the park, which in the past month led to dozens of gay men being charged with public lewdness.

Chairman of the Board of Selectmen Paul Stanwood, a critic of the police crackdown, was found brutally beaten to death in the park June 7. Police Chief Alvah Sears said the physical changes at the crime scene wouldn't affect the investigation.

District Attorney Jeff McKenna disagreed. "I'm glad the chief is so confident," McKenna said. "But I wish someone had asked me about their little landscaping project."

He refused further comment.

University of Southern Maine law professor Thomas

Duvall had plenty to say. "In addition to being downright stupid, what the town did was illegal. Assuming the police are able to make an arrest—and that may be a pretty big assumption—this could make it very difficult to get a conviction."

Bowen-Smythe refused to respond to the criticism, but Sears answered it directly. "It's pretty easy for the professor to preach from his ivory tower, especially when he hasn't practiced a lick of law in the past 10 years, but I remain confident justice will be done," he said.

In a related matter, local artist Danny Sloan said Stone Harbor police failed to investigate six attacks against gay men this summer. This newspaper has filed a freedom of information request seeking all reports and paperwork related to the cases—a log of which should already have been made available to the media.

Sears wouldn't comment on that accusation, or the status of the investigation into Stanwood's killing.

"They still don't have any idea who did it," Maria said that night. "Do they?"

Quinn was at the kitchen table, trying to write a column on his laptop, but the going had been frustrating and slow, even before the interruption.

She leaned against him, put her hand on his shoulder and tried to peek at what he was writing. The truth was, she would rather have thrown the laptop out the window, but saved that argument for another day. At least he was home. For now. "So what do you think?" she asked.

"If the cops are onto something, they aren't telling us." He slowly closed the lid on his PowerBook. "The fact that we're in the dark may not be a bad thing."

"You make it sound like a bad thing in the paper," she said as her hands moved down his chest.

Quinn laughed. "Well, we don't want them to think they can walk all over everybody."

"Maybe they can." She slowly caressed his sore midsection.

He winced. "I don't think so."

"Really?"

"Yes, really." Quinn stood up and went to the fridge for a Geary's, hoping it would help him relax. No such luck. "Are we out of beer?"

She told him to check in the back.

"Ah," he said, beaming at the joy of finding the last bottle.

Maria couldn't help but laugh. He husband was passionate about what he liked and what he didn't. For example, he had an incredible capacity for work—as long as he was interested in something. At a paper in Belize he put in sixty straight days on a series on child labor that got picked up by the *Los Angeles Times* and changed the buying policy of a major American retailer. It also got the Quinns expelled from the country (an extra bonus, in her mind).

When he wasn't interested in something?

Nothing would change his mind. He didn't see the point in mowing the lawn, or washing their cars, or painting the shingle-style Victorian home that was built in 1897 by his great-grandfather. *That's why we have a checkbook,* he always told her.

When she suggested the house was too big for the three of them, he looked sadder than words could describe. "We can't give up this house," he said. "It meant too much to my mother. It would be like we were giving up part of her."

How could Maria argue with that?

Yes, her husband had his moments—like the time he showed up in her inner-city kindergarten class in Miami and bought the children Christmas gifts, a wonderful thing, considering most had nothing to look forward to anywhere else. Yes, when John wanted to, he had a way with people.

At other times he could really get under their skin—especially with his column. With that in mind she perched on the edge of his chair and opened his computer: he hadn't written a word. "I see the police aren't the only ones at a dead end," she said.

He walked back to her and put his hands in his pockets. "I know."

"Maybe you just need a break." She slowly rubbed his inner thigh, from just above his knee to his crotch.

He couldn't argue with that. "You're probably right."

"Oh, I'm pretty sure of it," she said as she stood up, put her hands on his chest and pushed him back into the chair.

"This seems like a good start."

She smiled and kissed his cheek, then his neck and chest. After loosening enough clothing on them both, she climbed onto his lap.

"Don't break the chair!" he said, laughing as much from her spontaneity as the feel of her soft breasts and hard nipples against his bare skin.

"Hey—I haven't gained that much weight."

"I wasn't talking about your weight."

"Just stop talking," she said. "Okay?"

He didn't say anything else. Instead, he held on to the chair and kept them from going over, which wasn't easy but was definitely worth the effort. The problem was, when the phone rang he grabbed it without thinking.

It was Danny Sloan.

"This really isn't a good time," Quinn said.

"You need to get over here as soon as you can."

Quinn looked up at his wife, who decided to quickly get things back on track by loosening the lower buttons of his shirt and working her warm tongue along the tightening muscles of his abdomen and beyond.

He let out a low moan and ran his fingers through her thick silky hair while she increased the pace. Moving his hands lower, he slowly, softly scratched her shoulder blades until she murmured something between a sigh and a giggle, then pulled up and climbed on top of him. Gripping his thighs with the soles of her feet, she churned forward, laughing, panting, kissing him.

And he wasn't going anywhere.

TWO HOURS LATER QUINN's hollow steps echoed loudly across Sloan's vine-covered porch. Wisteria, morning glory and clematis filled the white lattice work and blocked most of the bleached light from the single lamppost at the front of the cottage. Sloan's banged and dented work van and his blue Mercedes convertible were in the small drive, which was nothing more than two brick tracks through the high grass. Everything was still and quiet until Quinn turned the old-fashioned winding bell with its high, trilling ring.

Nothing.

He peeked through cupped hands into the house. It was too dark to see, so he tried the door, which to his surprise was unlocked. He cracked it open and called out, "Danny, it's John Quinn!"

Still nothing.

He stepped inside with his camera slung across his neck. "Danny?"

The silence was enormous, so he felt with his hands along the hall till he found the light switches. He clicked them up and down to no effect. By then his eyes had adjusted enough to make out the large shadows that were actually a leather couch, a recliner and an ottoman. He didn't see the cherry end table.

"Damn it!" He tripped and fell and burned his knees on the Oriental carpet.

That did it.

With his shin on fire and his elbow throbbing, he lifted the camera to get a better sense of where he was and hit the flash.

Whoosh!

In that black-and-white instant he could see the room was a mess. Another end table was overturned, a lamp was shattered and a throw rug was rumpled and uneven. The air was cool and he felt himself shiver as he wondered if anyone else was still there. Both he and the room were off balance so he shifted his angle, hit the flash and really concentrated.

Whoosh!

Georgia O'Keeffe's Southwestern landscapes flashed back at him from the walls.

Whoosh!

An Ansel Adams print from Zion National Park.

Whoosh!

He spotted the pale blue kitchen door and kept walking.

Whoosh!

He was halfway through without a second thought. He knew sometimes the most important thing in life was to look around the next corner, so that's what he did, step by cautious step.

Whoosh!

The flash shined off two bright eyes and Quinn fell back onto a bench against the kitchen wall. Danny Sloan didn't have much to say. His vacant eyes were still open, and above his thin goatee he wore the oddest smile. He looked dumbstruck, as if he were surprised by his predicament and trying very hard, in a faraway place, to figure out what had happened. Quinn wondered if that had been Paul Stanwood's final expression.

Quinn sat still a moment and tried to calm himself. His heart was pounding and he forced himself to take deep, reassuring breaths. Dim light was leaking through the narrow windows near the ceiling. As his eyes adjusted and the gray figure reappeared, he pulled up the Nikon and tried to focus, but it wasn't easy. Sloan seemed to be watching. His smile didn't change as Quinn snapped away.

Whoosh!

Taking in the whole kitchen at first, with its hanging pots and Shaker table and antique plumbing.

Whoosh!

Then just the body.

Whoosh!

The torso.

Whoosh!

The head and shoulders.

Whoosh!

And finally, the once ruddy face that had gone terribly white.

It didn't occur to Quinn that the *Pilot* never ran pictures of dead bodies. He just couldn't stop shooting: he was mesmerized by the encounter, haunted by the finality of the images, unable to let them go. That was probably his biggest mistake. He wasn't prepared for the sudden sound of human breathing.

Jesus. Sloan was still alive.

8.

WHEN QUINN FINALLY GOT home, Maria met him at the door with an anxious look. He'd called from the police station to let her know what happened and she'd been up ever since, waiting for him with every light in the house turned on.

"Is he going to make it?" she asked.

"They don't know," Quinn said as he stepped inside. "He was beaten pretty badly." Quinn kissed her and she buried her head in his chest. Her arms and shoulders were rigid and tense and he slowly stroked her shoulders until she relaxed a bit. "If I'd gotten there sooner this might not have happened."

Maria shook her head. "If you hadn't gone at all, he'd probably be dead."

"Maybe." He didn't tell her the police had found the back door ajar and thought someone else may have been inside when Quinn entered Sloan's cottage.

"John, I'm frightened."

He held her tightly. "There's no need to be."

Surprised and a little angry, she stepped away. "No need to be?" she asked, her voice rising. "Paul was brutally murdered. Now a man you've spoken to once was nearly beaten to death. You don't see a connection?"

"Sure, there's a connection," Quinn said. "That doesn't mean you have anything to worry about."

"I'm worried about you!"

"Nothing's going to happen to me."

"I'm sure that's what Paul thought," she said as the tears began to flow.

He gently wiped her cheeks with his fingers. "Well, I'm not Paul," he said.

"What's that supposed to mean?"

"It means he did things quietly, behind the scenes," Quinn said. "I'm loud and open, which is a lot safer."

"Wasn't that what Danny Sloan tried to be?"

She was right, but Quinn didn't admit it. He just pulled her even closer and promised himself, no matter what happened, he would always protect his wife and son.

GAY ACTIVIST STRUGGLES FOR LIFE AFTER SAVAGE BEATING
By John Quinn
Pilot Staff

STONE HARBOR—A 52-year-old artist and gay activist is in a coma after being found savagely beaten last night at his Elm Road home.

Dan Sloan, who has lived and worked here for the past 20 years, is in intensive care at Stone Harbor Memorial Medical Center. Reports said he suffered a fractured skull, two broken arms and a broken leg.

The attack comes after Paul Stanwood, a prominent local businessman and member of the town's Board of Selectmen, was found beaten to death in Sullivan Park. Like Stanwood, Sloan has been a vocal critic of the local police department's treatment of gay men who had been arrested while frequenting the park for sexual encounters.

His partner, local artist Jeff Morse, said he's expected to survive. "But in what condition, God only knows."

Police Chief Alvah Sears is confident his department will make an arrest. "I can't say anything more than that, since it's a pending investigation, but we have some pretty incriminating physical evidence that should help speed things along."

"Like what?" Quinn had asked the chief.

Sears didn't answer.

Quinn had barged past the front desk and into Sears's office despite the protests of the dispatcher, though the big cop hardly seemed surprised by the interruption. "Do you know he had dinner that night with Bowen-Smythe?" Quinn asked.

"Sure," Sears answered. "So do the thirty other people who were in the Wellsen House at the time."

"Were you there?"

"Nope." The chief shook his head. "Bryan told me about it."

"When?"

Sears smiled. "As soon as you might expect, since the bulk of the conversation was about me."

Quinn wasn't surprised. "And how'd you like that?"

Sears shrugged like it was no big deal. "Comes with the territory."

"Yeah, it's amazing, the things that come with the territory these days," Quinn said, thinking back to the pipe and pot that had been planted in his wife's car. He looked at Sears and wondered why he'd done it. "So was Danny Sloan beaten because he talked to me?"

Sears frowned like he was dealing with an idiot. "Why, you feelin' guilty?"

"No, just frustrated. I saw him the other day and he gave me a list of the incidents of violence against gay men your department didn't bother to investigate."

Sears raised an eyebrow, as though his interest had been piqued. "Let's see it."

Quinn gave him a hard look. "It's gone."

Sears laughed, leaned back and folded his hands over his lap. "That's awful convenient."

"Well, I don't think it's a coincidence."

"I don't think it's anything at all," Sears said as he sat back up. "Now, if you don't mind." He nodded toward the door.

Quinn hesitated, but realized he had nothing more to say. Sloan wasn't in a position to back up his story. Nobody was. When he walked outside, Quinn couldn't help noticing the car that was parked in the spot that was reserved for the police chief. It was a black Lexus. Sears had been the one following him on the way to the park.

He turned to go back inside and found himself stopping. How could he prove anything about the afternoon his wife's tires had been slashed? And who would he prove it to? This wasn't anything he could take on himself. He needed help and had a good idea where he could find it.

9.

EACH CREAK AND GROAN of the splintered wooden steps reminded Angus Stanwood how cheap the selectmen were, still meeting twice a month over the fire hall on High Street. Built during the First World War, the building could barely contain the big modern engines, despite the grandeur of its parapet and gables. The venue also added unexpected drama whenever an alarm went off, though that didn't seem to matter. As long as the schedule didn't conflict with the weekly bingo games held by the ladies auxiliary, nobody cared. Angus figured the town fathers played stingy-assed with the worn brick building so the public wouldn't notice when they were really getting screwed.

He stopped to catch his breath on the landing. Father God and Sonny Jesus, it was hot, but he wasn't about to be put off by a warm summer evening. He had too much to say, so he took another labored breath and trudged on. He felt as ancient as the pressed tin ceiling and his face and chest were soaked with sweat by the time he entered the council chambers and took a seat in the front row.

The selectmen—five men and two women—sat elevated behind paneled desks, with Bryan Bowen-Smythe proudly in the middle. A uniformed police officer stood by the door, solemnly chewing gum while a high school student worked the video camera for the cable access channel.

Quinn was in the back row, ready to make a quick exit if things dragged on longer than expected. When he noticed Angus, he gave him a solemn salute. Fitting, Angus thought, for such a ballbuster. No matter. Angus asked him to show up in person instead of sending some snot-nosed young reporter, and he was there.

Ernie and Becky Gould were there, too, already at the podium set up for public comment, though the meeting had yet to be called to order. They had a petition signed by 250 residents opposed to the sign ordinance and were ready to raise some hell, which was just fine. Angus liked the idea of unloading on politicians with both barrels.

Despite the tension already filling the room, Bowen-Smythe seemed unconcerned. After what seemed like an eternity, he called the meeting to order and led the Pledge of Allegiance before the town clerk took twenty minutes to read the correspondence. Then the jackasses had to pose and kick and carry on over the assorted old business, which included a proclamation declaring the weekend of August 23 the city's official clamfest, along with a short debate on whether to fine skateboarders caught downtown or sentence the little bastards to community service.

All the screwing around reminded Angus of a tree full of monkeys on the Nature Channel, howling and preening and putting on a show for one another till they got so turned on they began to pull their tiny monkey puds. By the time they reached the new business—naming someone to Paul's seat—Angus had worked up quite a lather. He could barely keep his mouth shut when the chairman started to speak.

"First I'd like to have a moment of silence for the late Paul Stanwood." Bowen-Smythe bowed his head and everyone but Angus did the same. He kept his eyes on the professor the entire time. "And let us pray for the recovery of Danny Sloan, who's in the intensive care unit, fighting for his life."

Angus showed what he thought of the piety with a loud grunt. He'd tried calling the acting chairman four times during the week, but each message had gone unanswered. Maybe Bowen-Smythe had been too busy praying, or just sitting in front of a roomful of stiff-necked dandies with a pained expression on his face, as he did then. Angus barely listened to a word he said, which didn't help any till Bowen-Smythe finally ended his prayer with "Bless his soul."

Then the professor looked up. "Now, I don't want to appear insensitive, but we have to move on. That's what Paul would have wanted. So, do we have any motions to fill his seat?" he asked, looking right through the Goulds as though they weren't standing in the middle of the room.

Becky Gould started to speak, but with the public microphone turned off, no one heard what she said.

Instead, they were treated to Selectman George Baribou standing up and practically shouting: "I motion that we name Seth Quinn to the remaining two years of the term."

The motion was seconded.

"Hold on there!" Angus thundered out of his seat, while farther away, Quinn practically choked on the news. "How can this be a done deal?" Angus demanded. "What about public input?"

"We still haven't voted," Baribou reminded the acting chairman, unmoved by the challenge.

Bowen-Smythe rapped his wooden gavel. "Let's have a little order."

"I'd prefer a little democracy," Angus said.

"You haven't been recognized by the chair," Baribou said.

"Then recognize me."

"Gentlemen, please," Bowen-Smythe pleaded. Despite a bachelor's degree in political science from Reed College in Oregon, a master's from Berkeley and a doctorate from Harvard's Kennedy School, he had a hard time accepting the fact that political theory often collided with small-town reality. Finally, when it was painfully obvious Angus wasn't going to yield to his authority, Bowen-Smythe shrugged his shoulders. "The chair recognizes Mr. Stanwood."

"I should hope so," Angus said. "I sold you that Lexus last year and gave you a damn good deal."

"I meant you could speak."

"Quite well, thank you." Angus straightened himself to his full height and took a deep breath. "Let me first just say no one is more suited to carry on Paul's term than his own father." He pointed an accusing finger at Bowen-Smythe, whose face reddened. "The fact that you want to put another little shitbird on the council amazes me."

It also amazed Quinn, who was sitting on the edge of his seat, bug-eyed at the news.

The other selectmen sat stiffly and stared straight ahead, as if by their reticence they could prove they never had, nor ever would, be amazed by anything.

Bowen-Smythe cleared his throat. "Angus, you've never shown an interest in town government before."

"That's 'cause I had no idea how bad you been muckin' things up," Angus said.

"And I don't remember you coming to any of our meetings," Bowen-Smythe said innocently enough, before adding, with just a hint of sarcasm: "You didn't even vote in the last election."

"How would you know?"

"I checked with the board of elections," Bowen-Smythe said patiently. "Anyone can do the same. It's a matter of public record."

"That don't make it any of your business."

"It does when you're asking to be named to a public office."

"I voted for my son every time he ran," Angus said.

"Do you think he would have voted for you?"

"Hell, yes." Angus waved a hand at Bowen-Smythe. "Especially if the choice was me and someone who give himself two last names."

The audience members laughed out loud and Bowen-Smythe's stare flattened on the older man. "Angus, I'm not sure mocking me is the way to make your case."

"If you find honesty insulting, perhaps you're the one not fit for public office," Angus countered.

Bowen-Smythe took a deep, calculated breath. "We know you're going through a difficult time. We're all shaken by what happened. That's still no reason to lash out at people who are trying to help."

"Help?" Angus said. "You'd rather pretend the whole thing never happened."

Bowen-Smythe looked indignantly at him. "That's not true!"

"You're damn straight it's true," Angus said. "That's why you closed the park."

"We removed a public safety hazard," Bowen-Smythe explained.

"You tampered with a crime scene!" Everyone in the room turned toward Quinn, who had finally stood up. "You think you can do anything. Just like you single-handedly pushed that idiotic zoning ordinance through." Quinn gestured toward the Goulds, who were too stunned to speak. Ernie had never been to a council meeting before but his big grin showed he found it terribly amusing.

The professor turned to Angus. "You, of all people, should understand what a safety hazard that park has become."

"I understand exactly what you're doing," Angus said as he pulled some folded papers from his jacket's inside pocket. "And I'll tell you why."

"No, you won't!" Bowen-Smythe quickly rapped his gavel. "The motion to name Seth Quinn to the seat has been made and seconded." This had the intended effect—at least on Quinn, who sat back down, fuming.

"Just who the hell do you think you are?" Angus shouted.

"The chairman," Bowen-Smythe said. "And you, sir, are out of line." He rapped his gavel again, this time so hard he broke it.

"I'm not finished." Angus pounded a meaty fist on the small oak railing that kept those standing at the public podium beyond choking distance of the selectmen. "You can't shut me off like that!"

But they could. No matter how loud Angus was or how long he went on, the town fathers weren't listening. Trying to regain his composure, Angus put his shaking hands on the podium. Veins bulged in his brow, a sign of deeper forces that were building inside. He started to speak but was too enraged.

His anger was a living thing that started somewhere deep in the pit of his stomach and was about to boil over. Preparing for the final eruption, Angus lowered his head, then hesitated, as if to catch a big enough breath to carry him through. Gasping, he grabbed his chest with one hand and fell sideways, pulling the podium with him with his other and taking out a row of fold-out chairs that snapped shut and slapped hard against the tile floor, where he flopped around in his bulging navy sports coat like a big fish.

While others stared, Quinn hurried to Angus, who was moaning with every tortured breath. Quinn looked over his shoulder at Officer Stufflebeam and said, "Better tell the crew downstairs." As he loosened the buttons to the older man's collar to help him get some air, Angus's eyes widened with fright, so Quinn took his hand and told him everything would be okay. "Just relax and keep breathing. I'm right here."

The selectmen looked on rather tentatively, not willing to get any closer as Angus wheezed and heaved. Sweat was pouring off him and his skin had turned pasty white. He leaned closer to Quinn, as if to tell him something.

"What is it?"

Angus threw up violently.

"That's all right," Quinn said, unshaken by the mess. He just kept holding his friend's hand. "Help is on the way."

THE PARAMEDICS WERE THERE in less than a minute. A solid-looking woman in her twenties knelt over Angus as her partner, a tall man about her age, lowered the gurney.

"It feels like an elephant's on my chest," Angus whispered hoarsely.

"Put this under your tongue." She popped a nitroglycerin tablet in his mouth. A moment later she had him chewing on a baby aspirin.

Quinn followed the stretcher downstairs to the ambulance, where he paused.

"You comin'?" the other paramedic asked.

Quinn jumped in, the heavy doors thudded shut and the siren began to wail.

Inside, the bright lights showed how pale Angus's skin was beneath the oxygen mask. At least he was still breathing, Quinn thought. Barely. "You're gonna be all right," he said, as much to himself as the patient, who was soaked in perspiration.

He didn't get a response.

The male paramedic ripped open Angus's shirt and the woman applied sticky pads for the chest monitor. Soon she was talking with the emergency control room on the radio. "He's got an elevation in ST." she said calmly, the whole time keeping her eye on Angus.

"How far away are you?" the voice on the radio squawked back.

Quinn leaned forward and braced himself as the ambulance sped toward the hospital, tires squealing with each bend in the road. The ride was taking forever and Quinn wondered if Angus would make it. He also wondered what else Angus had planned to say.

"Just be ready with your goddamn notebook," he'd warned Quinn that afternoon at the car dealership.

Whatever it was, the selectmen weren't concerned. Back above the fire hall, with no fanfare or further hesitation, they named Seth Quinn to the vacant seat.

10.

THE SOUND OF BASEBALLS pinging off aluminum bats carried over the bleachers at Baxter Park as Jack and his teammates endured infield practice. The *Pilot* Newshounds' play was uneven, complicated by the fact that most of them were scared to death of the ball.

Their coach, a bulging ironworker whose spindly legs stuck out of his moopy shorts like sticks, gently stroked grounders with a child-size bat and urged his players on. Not that it did much good. The second baseman cringed and turned his freckled head to the side when the ball came near. The lumpy first baseman managed to stiffly hold his glove in position as the erratic throws came his way, though he could never will his eyes to stay completely open. The tiny kid at third, faced with a hard chopper, simply ducked.

Jack was the exception at shortstop, charging the ball and scooping it cleanly. After every throw to first, he'd look to see if his father was watching. Quinn always was. He'd clap a few times and shout encouragement, whether the ball hit the nervous first baseman's mitt and promptly fell out, or sailed over his head. The important thing was to keep it fun. Jack was on his way to becoming a good player and the others would catch up. They just needed time, which would come soon enough.

Looking onto the familiar field, Quinn remembered when he and Paul were good enough as nine-year-olds to play alongside kids two and three years older. For the most part, they'd held their own. Late in the season, with a game tied and a man on first, a batter drilled a single to right, where Quinn took it on one hop, then bobbled the ball.

Embarrassed, he picked it up as the base runner headed for third, then rifled a throw to Paul, who was all of fifty pounds. With a kid who weighed twice that steaming down on him, Quinn figured he was dead. Spikes flew, dirt sprayed and Paul snagged the wide throw and applied a backhand tag without a second thought.

All those years later, Quinn was still in awe. Nothing ever fazed his friend.

A booming voice brought Quinn back to the present. "All right, men, that's enough," the winded coach told his charges, since he was hoping to sneak off for a smoke break. "Mr. Quinn has somethin' to reward your hard work."

The players, showing more enthusiasm than they had all day, swarmed as Quinn produced boxes of ice cream bars. He threw out the contents, which the smiling Newshounds snagged in midair like major leaguers.

"Here, coach," Quinn said, tossing one to the other man. "These guys are starting to come along."

"You betcha." The coach grinned like they were ready for the World Series.

DRIVING AWAY FROM PRACTICE, Quinn asked his son where Pauly Stanwood was.

"He doesn't come anymore," Jack answered, twisting his face as he spoke. "I wish he did."

"Give him some time and he'll be back."

"I hope."

So did Quinn, who tried to imagine what the poor little boy was going through. "Maybe you should invite him over sometime."

"Okay." Jack was a good kid and Quinn was proud of him.

"Right now we need to stop at the hospital and see Pauly's grandfather."

"Is he sick?" Jack's eyes grew even bigger than normal as he looked up at his father.

"He's getting better," Quinn assured him.

THEY FOUND ANGUS ALONE at Stone Harbor Memorial Medical Center, third floor, second room. He was propped up in a reclining bed, staring listlessly at nothing in particular on the ceiling. When Quinn rapped on the door and they entered, Angus slowly turned his head their way.

"How you feeling?" Quinn asked.

"Like hell." He looked it, too. His unshaven face was gray and the words came out slowly, but since it was Angus, the words still managed to come out.

Jack hung behind his father, curious but a bit frightened.

"You need anything?" Quinn asked Angus.

"Beer," the older man managed. "Cigarettes." He'd smoked two packs a day for fifty years and was having a hard time going cold turkey, despite the circumstances.

"How about a swift kick in the ass?" Quinn asked.

Angus slowly rolled his eyes toward Quinn, as though the movement took an effort. "Had it."

"I see that. But you're a tough old bird. If you listen to the doctors and do what they say, you'll bounce back from this."

"Yeah." Angus tried to mouth a crooked smile, which only made him seem weak and helpless.

"Look on the bright side," Quinn said. "You got some great press. The front-page coverage alone was worth five of your stupid infomercials."

"Not finished."

"Well, maybe you should give it a rest." Quinn shook his head, leaned forward and got in Angus's face. "You've done a lot of stupid things, but trying to get on the board of selectmen tops them all. What were you thinking?"

"Land."

"What land?"

"Long story."

"Well, let's hear it," Quinn said. "You're not going anywhere."

"Gone tomorrow."

"Think so?"

Angus moved his head in what seemed like a nod, then fell asleep.

Quinn had no idea what land he was talking about and hoped the notion wasn't as misguided as the accusations against Lizz. Quinn patted Angus on the shoulder. From the other side of the bed, with the help of a chair he was standing on, Jack did the same. The older man was fleshy and soft. At one time Angus could pick up Paul and Quinn, a boy in each arm. Back then Angus seemed like the strongest man in the world and was never at a loss for words. Now he was old and a little confused.

Time had a way of catching them all.

As Angus drifted off, Quinn thought of his own father and wondered how he would have handled the events of the past month. Quinn didn't know what Jake would have done, but there would have been no looking back once he'd done it.

Sitting in the stark hospital room, Quinn looked at his own son. Jack hadn't said a word the whole time they'd been there; he just sat quietly with his father and Angus. Before long, the older man was snoring. Every so often he'd moan or twitch and Quinn wondered if, in those troubled dreams, Angus saw his murdered son.

AFTER HE'D TAKEN JACK home, Quinn headed back to the newspaper. To his surprise, Seth was still there, sitting behind his desk in the same office Quinn's grandfather and great-grandfather once occupied. He was studying paperwork that told the *Pilot*'s financial tale. The annual audit was approaching and Seth wanted to make sure everything was in order for the bankers.

Quinn had other things on his mind and didn't hold back. "You can't serve as a selectman! It's a terrible conflict of interest. The newspaper has to cover city government."

"I'm not going to stop you," Seth said, unaffected by the outburst. Then he looked down at the report he'd been reading, as though the conversation had ended.

"It just doesn't look good," Quinn continued.

Seth stopped reading, sighed, and gave him a long-suffering frown. "Who cares what it looks like? Do you think the town would be better off with Angus making a fool of himself every meeting?"

"You're an employee of this newspaper!" Quinn answered, his voice rising.

"Everyone knows I don't have anything to do with what you write," Seth said. "Believe me, I make that perfectly clear. I said it to Paul after the first park arrests and I'll say it to Sears the next time you take a cheap shot at him in print."

Quinn gave him a hard look and slowly asked whose side he was on.

"I don't take sides and you should be grateful," Seth said. "That's why Bryan wanted me to serve out this term on the council. That's why Uncle Jake trusted me. That's why I'm the first person you called when you were arrested for threatening the police chief."

Seth was so full of himself, Quinn couldn't help but laugh. "Actually, you were the second," he explained when Seth looked at him like he was crazy. "Maria didn't answer when I called."

Seth didn't see what was so funny. "It's a good thing, too, because I don't think she would have had the same luck getting the district attorney to drop the charges against you and Sarah." He was beginning to lose his patience with the conversation, especially when he saw the changed expression on Quinn's face. "You have a problem with that?"

Quinn thought about what his cousin had said. "I have a problem with a lot of things around here."

"Well, you shouldn't have a problem with me. I just sell ads. I just make the money despite your best efforts to put this place under."

"Oh, please!"

"Have you ever sold anything?" Seth asked. "It's not as easy as it looks."

Now Quinn was visibly angry. "I worked in circulation all through high school."

"You took orders."

"I made sure every paper we printed got delivered."

"So you were a paper boy."

"It doesn't matter what I was," Quinn said, furious that Seth had turned the conversation away from his own conflict of interest and into a debate about Quinn's qualifications to run the paper. "Right now I'm the owner and that means I sign your check."

It was Seth's turn to laugh. "Well, I'm staying on the board of selectmen and you can fire me if you like. Otherwise, get off my back." He leaned across his desk and picked up a sheet of paper. "In case you're interested, Bryan asked me to give you this."

He handed the press release to Quinn.

"What is it?"

"An announcement," Seth said. "But before you get your hopes up, I don't have any comment."

"You know," Quinn said, "that kind of crap would have sent my father to the moon."

Seth knew better than to respond as Quinn bolted from his office and took the stairs to the newsroom. Like Jake, he had an Irish temper, though Quinn was the only one who failed to see the similarity, even when Aunt Blythe suggested it in a gentle way. Still, Quinn felt the weight of the old man's presence and after he closed the door to his office, he sat in the same hard, wooden chair Jake once used. No matter how uncomfortable it was, nobody could convince him to replace it. And as he did so often, Quinn thought of his father. No one would ever have questioned anything Jake had said.

Then he picked up the phone and started making calls.

IT'S ALL OVER FOR
SULLIVAN PARK MEN
By John Quinn
Pilot Staff

All charges have been dropped against the 23 men accused of public lewdness in Sullivan Park this summer.

Citing "a respect for community sensitivity," District Attorney Jeff McKenna and Acting Board of Selectmen Chairman Bryan Bowen-Smythe announced the decision in a joint press release and refused further comment.

Police Chief Alvah Sears, who made the crackdown on gay men who used the park a personal crusade, failed to return several phone calls.

Public reaction wasn't as muted.

"That shows what happens when you stick your nose where it don't belong," said shipbuilder Danny Miller over breakfast at the Magic Muffin Bakery. "And I mean that quite literally."

Another customer agreed.

"We've heard more than enough about the goings-on there," Rick Marsh said.

One of the men who'd been charged, Pat Bourque of 113 Court St., is considering legal action against the city. "A lot of innocent reputations have been smeared," he said. "And for what? To give a small-town police chief something to do?"

None of the remaining suspects would talk on the record, citing the recent beating of police critic Danny Sloan as reason to keep quiet.

That night, Quinn was still trying to piece it all together after he'd put Jack to bed and he and Maria were finally alone.

"Maybe Paul's death put things in perspective," Maria said as she pulled a hanger out of the closet. "Compared to that, who cares that some nasty men got a few thrills?"

Quinn paused as he undid his belt. "That depends what you mean."

Maria stepped out of her flats and let her thin blue skirt fall to the floor, revealing smooth olive thighs. "Well, what did Seth say about dropping the charges?"

"He was more interested in taunting me."

Maria pulled off her white tank top and tilted her head to one side and considered how frequent the flare-ups between the two men had become. "I know he can be difficult, but are you sure he's not just looking out for you?"

"I'm a big boy."

"No, you're a father and a husband," Maria corrected. She bent over to toss her skirt into the hamper, then stopped. "And you need to keep that in mind."

"I do." Quinn stepped out of his pants. "I'm also the editor and publisher of a newspaper and need to let people know what's going on."

"Are you sure they care?" Maria asked as she pulled off her bra.

"Yes, I'm sure. Why would you ask something like that?"

Maria shook her head. "I don't know." When she walked slowly toward him, his anger melted and the last thing he wanted to talk about was the newspaper.

"I know this hasn't been easy." He gently caressed her upper back. She had a long, beautiful neck and her breasts were soft and warm. The smell of perfume covered him even when she stepped back.

"You certainly have a way of changing the subject," she said.

"You make it hard not to." He kissed her softly on the mouth. "Did I ever tell you how beautiful you are?"

She rolled her eyes as if she'd heard it all before.

He moved his right hand lower, down the curve of her hip. "You're still as hot as you were when I first saw you in South Beach."

She kissed him quickly, then held a hand up to his mouth for him to stop. "Let me take off my makeup."

"Okay." He followed her into the bathroom, lowered the lid on the toilet and sat down as she mugged in the mirror and wiped off her mascara.

"I'm worried about you," she said.

"You shouldn't be."

"How can I not be?" she asked. "Paul is dead. Gay men are being brutalized. Danny Sloan is in the hospital."

"I'm more careful than them."

Her eyebrows arched in the mirror. "Then why were my tires slashed?"

She had him there. "You're right," he said. "I'll be more careful." He had better things in mind than arguing and hugged her from behind.

"I'm sorry," she said patiently as she dropped both arms to her side, "but I'm just not in the mood for sex."

"What makes you think I want sex?"

"You always want sex."

He shrugged. "What's wrong with that?"

"You're not paying attention to me."

"My God, I can't think of anything but you right now."

She stepped away from him and put on her robe. "That's not funny."

He followed her into the bedroom, where she plopped

down on the edge of the mattress. "I'm not trying to be funny," he said.

"You just don't get it."

"No, I don't," he admitted.

"Everything is starting to get to me." She pulled back the covers and slipped between them.

"I'm sorry." He kissed her on the cheek as modestly as possible to avoid further offense.

She smiled. Sometimes he could be quite sweet. "Are you coming to bed?" she asked hopefully. That way he would be beside her. That way she would know he was safe, at least for the night.

"I'm not really tired," he answered. For some reason, he was reminded of the time a girl in high school complained that he was the horniest boy on the planet. Laughing, she wanted to know why he couldn't be more like Paul.

"He's always the perfect gentleman," she had said. "Everyone thinks so."

For some reason, that had really bothered him. Remembering it, he went downstairs, ready to scream.

11.

THE NEXT MORNING AL Sears shuffled into the newsroom with his hands in his pockets, looking humbled. As soon
as they saw him, staffers stopped what they were doing and
stared, though Quinn wasn't the least bit bothered by the
chief's unexpected presence.

"Finally have something to say?" he asked.

"If you can spare a minute."

"That depends." Quinn was leaning over a reporter's computer screen, pointing out changes he'd made to a story on red
tide poisoning. "Is it business or personal?"

"It's important."

Quinn figured it must be, so he stood up and slowly
walked into his glass office as a handful of reporters began to
whisper.

Sears followed and shut the door.

"They can still see, even if they can't hear," Quinn said.

When Sears turned around, he was grinning. "Relax—I'm
here for a favor."

"No wonder you shut the door." Quinn got up from his
desk and pushed it open.

"Did you hear about Angus Stanwood?" Sears asked.

Quinn hesitated. He couldn't imagine where this was going. "I stopped in to see him yesterday afternoon," he said tentatively.

"The old fool walked out last night." Sears shook his head. "The doctors didn't even think he could get out of bed, but when the nurse made her midnight rounds he was gone—just like that—because they wouldn't let him smoke."

Quinn was alarmed yet a little amused. "He's stubborn, but he couldn't have driven."

"All I know is that when the shift changed, he was gone. I'm told he's restin' at home. His granddaughter is there, keepin' an eye on him."

That was a relief. "And they're not trying to get him back?"

Sears's mouth dropped open in surprise. "Would you?"

"Probably not."

"Well, you said it, not me."

"True enough," Quinn admitted, grateful that Sears had filled him in on the situation. "So what's the favor you're looking for?"

"I need Sarah's crime scene negatives." Sears said this casually, like it was no big deal. "Our pictures never came out."

Quinn was mildly amused. "I hope Wal-Mart gave you a refund."

"This isn't a joke." Sears looked Quinn steadily in the eye as he said this.

"Then what is it?" Quinn couldn't believe what he was hearing. "You have the town's first homicide in thirty years and can't even get pictures of the crime scene? No wonder you won't comment on the case. You're probably too embarrassed."

"I don't answer to you."

"Who do you answer to?" Quinn asked.

"My conscience."

"Your conscience," Quinn repeated, as though he liked the sound of it. "Well, let me ask you something: have you been sleeping at night?"

"I nevah need much sleep." Sears leaned over Quinn's desk and picked up a framed picture of Maria coming out of the water at a Puerto Rican beach—one of six shots of her that were on a shelf full of family photos and Jack's drawings. "You have a beautiful wife." With eyebrows raised, he admired the sleek, bikinied body. "I see her when she takes your son to the park. They go almost every day."

Quinn's face flushed with anger. "Is that a crime?"

"No." Sears smiled and lingered a bit longer over the photo. "I'd say it's a community asset. So how's she like it here?"

"This town's taken some getting used to." Quinn snatched the picture from Sears and, for a moment, was tempted to smash the glass frame across his leering face. "For one thing, she can't understand how nosy everyone is."

"It's my job to be nosy," Sears said. "Yours, too."

"What's the board of selectmen think of the job you've been doing? One homicide and a beating that may turn into another."

"I haven't had any complaints." Sears tried to sound matter-of-fact but the criticism stung.

Sensing this, Quinn didn't let up. "Oh, you've had some pretty big complaints. And from what I heard this morning, they're about to get even bigger."

Sears tried to dismiss that with a wave of his hand.

"Then there's the district attorney," Quinn continued. "I can't believe his office is dropping all charges against those pervs in the park."

"That was outta my hands," Sears objected, the hurt apparent in his voice. "As you well know, I don't always see eye to eye with the DA, or his good friend Professor Bowen-Smythe."

"You must be pissed," Quinn said. "A few of those nature lovers had to know something about Paul's death. You could have used the leverage."

Sears lowered his voice, as though confiding in or threatening Quinn. It wasn't really clear. "What makes you think I didn't?" he said quietly.

Quinn leaned forward, his own voice barely above a whisper, and said, "Because you're here, asking for those negatives."

"Well, you gonna hand 'em over?" Sears asked in a suddenly hopeful tone that was completely out of character.

"All our photography is digital," Quinn said. "We don't have negatives. We have disks and electronic archives."

That seemed to disappoint the chief.

"Do you want evidence or are you trying to get rid of it?" Quinn asked.

"I can get a subpoena," Sears pressed.

"Then get one."

Sears looked like he was considering it, which made Quinn wonder just what was on that disk. He couldn't bring himself to look, though he made a note to talk again with Sarah. Maybe she'd actually stumbled onto something more important than she'd realized? Maybe that's what Sears's interest was really all about?

As Quinn considered this, the chief's expression gave nothing away. Once he realized the conversation was going nowhere, Sears stood up to leave, then hesitated a moment. "I'm not sure this is evah gonna sink in, but I'm not the problem here."

At least not anymore, Quinn thought as the chief walked away. It seemed as though Bowen-Smythe had finally started to rein him in and the dumb shit had no idea how to respond.

A FEW HOURS LATER, Lizz Stanwood was waiting in a booth at the Wellsen House, staring vacantly through the paned glass at the brightly colored sailboats in the bay. She was wearing low-cut jeans and a small red top with thin straps. Her short hair accented high cheekbones, and from a distance, she looked like a college coed. Close up was another story: crow's-feet lined her eyes, and despite the noise and bustle of the midweek lunch crowd, she seemed withdrawn and very much alone.

Quinn startled her when he sat down. "Oh, John," she said. "I didn't see you come in."

"Sorry." He gently touched her forearm. "Have you been here long?"

She smiled a little crookedly and said it was her second glass of wine.

Quinn ordered an unsweetened iced tea and glanced at the menu. "So what do you recommend?" he asked.

She paused, as though she couldn't believe what she'd just heard. "I'd go with something a little stronger than iced tea."

"I'd love to, but I have to go back to work."

"That figures," she said wearily. "You're always going back to work."

She'd obviously been talking to Maria. "Well, I must have a prick for a boss," he said, trying to make light of it.

"That's the word around town."

That stung, and it showed in the way the smile dropped from his face. "You shouldn't believe everything you hear," he said.

"I don't," she said. "And believe me, I hear a lot."

Quinn wondered what she meant and was about to ask when the waitress appeared. Lizz ordered a pickled herring appetizer, a Caesar's salad and pasta primavera. For a slender woman, she had a big appetite. Inspired, Quinn went with the plowman's lunch and a pint of Newcastle. "I hope I'm not a bad influence," she said.

"Nah—I'm starving," he said. "So tell me, what else have you heard?"

"That your cousin resents you," she said, raising a hand and beginning to count. "That you spend a lot of time with Sarah Sewell. That the newspaper has money problems and that Seth flipped out when somebody took a stiletto blade to Maria's car tires."

"Now that last one surprises me," he said.

"But you're not denying it." She dropped his hand to the table and squeezed his playfully.

"No, I'm just trying to figure out how you knew."

"Like I said, I hear a lot of things. Mostly I hear how surprised people are that you came back to Stone Harbor."

He pulled his hand away. "This is my home."

"That never mattered before," she said with a sudden edge in her voice.

"You're right," he said softly. "Things change as you get older."

She let out an exaggerated groan. "Yeah, you put on a few pounds. Your ass droops. Your tits start to sag."

"That's not what I meant," Quinn quickly said once he realized he'd been eyeing the freckled tops of her breasts. As he brought his eyes level to hers, he saw that she found his reaction amusing. "I'm talking about how you start to see things a little differently," he insisted. "Your perspective changes."

She gave an exasperated sigh.

For a while, they both stared out at the bay. The sky was blue, the water was shimmering and lobster boats were beginning to come in and tie up. "It really is a beautiful day," Quinn said.

"Too beautiful to spend worrying about the paper." She lifted her glass and took another drink. "I'm surprised you haven't thought of selling it. The inheritance taxes must be killing you. The real estate alone has to be worth a good bit—you'd be shocked at what's being bought and sold around here."

He shook his head. "The *Pilot* meant too much to my father."

"You never cared what your father wanted while he was alive."

"I know." He took a long drink of Newcastle, then wiped his mouth. "And I can't tell you how much I regret it."

"Would you be here if he were still alive?"

He glanced over her shoulder at nothing in particular. "Probably not."

"That's a shame."

"A lot of things are," he admitted.

To Quinn's surprise, the memory of Jake brought tears to

her eyes, though he should have known better. When she was a skinny thirteen-year-old, Jake Quinn had given her an old Speed Graphic camera so she could learn how to take pictures. She still had it, along with photo credits in scores of publications, including *Condé Nast Traveler*, *Outside* and *National Geographic*.

"He was a good guy," she said.

Quinn thought back to the complicated relationship he'd had with his father. "The old man had his moments." When they were younger, Jake Quinn wanted him to marry Lizz. When that didn't happen, he figured Paul was the next best thing and was happy with that. "He had a lot of compassion for other people, yet no matter how painful, he wasn't afraid to tell the truth," Quinn said.

"Are you?"

"Not at all."

"All right, so tell me." She smiled slyly. "What's the real reason you came back to Stone Harbor?"

"You really want to know?" he asked.

"Yes." She twisted back in her chair as a red strap slipped lower on her shoulder.

"I thought I could make a difference."

She put a hand over her mouth and laughed bitterly. "My husband thought he could make a difference and look where it got him. Dead. That's where."

"So who do you think killed him?"

"Take your pick," she said flatly. "An angry queer. A cop. Maybe a local goon who didn't like the idea that grown men were doing all kinds of depraved things to one another out in the woods. The possibilities are as endless as the speculation—and that's saying a lot, the way this town talks."

"They're missing the larger point."

"You have to be careful when you make assumptions, because to tell the truth, you're wrong about my husband." She pulled her wineglass closer and Quinn felt his face turning crimson.

"So what do you want me to say?" he asked.

"I don't want you to say anything. I just want you to know it's like Al Sears said—we're lucky he didn't die with a dick up his ass."

Quinn felt his hands clenching. "How do you know Sears said that?"

"He told me."

"When?"

She looked him straight in the eye. "Right before he put his dick up my ass."

Quinn slammed a fist on the table, rattling their plates and drawing stares and hushed comments from the other customers. He didn't want to believe it. He told himself he couldn't, yet there she was, sitting across the table with an odd mix of defiance and shame all over her face. He wasn't sure what his own face showed, but Lizz didn't like it.

"Don't look at me that way," she said. "You of all people. Don't you dare look at me that way."

Instead, he looked down at his hands before he picked up his pint and drained what was left. The dregs left a bitter taste. "How could you?" he finally asked.

She narrowed her green eyes and tightened her lips. "Oh, it hurts like hell, but for some reason, I really get off on it."

He stood up to leave before the image made him scream.

"So I've been fucking Al Sears," she said. "At least he never pretended to be Paul's friend."

"I never pretended anything," Quinn said, his voice filling with rage. "I *was* his friend."

"Then why didn't you know what I had to deal with all these years?" She said it loudly, and throughout the restaurant, any remaining customers who weren't already quiet stopped talking, though she didn't seem embarrassed or even concerned.

Quinn felt his eyes welling with tears. He couldn't understand why she was doing this.

"Well, aren't you going to say anything else?" she asked.

He dropped his napkin on the table. "Thanks for lunch."

With the eyes of the entire room on him, he turned and walked out—but he couldn't walk away from her words. They stayed with him, just like the burning in his cheeks. He'd made a fool of himself and had been making a fool of himself for weeks, every time he'd written a story, argued with Sarah, or snapped at people who disagreed with him. John Quinn, the man who always accused the rest of the world of fearing the truth, had been living in the worst kind of denial.

So PAUL REALLY HAD been queer, he thought, lingering on the ugly word—a word he no longer would have said out loud, at least not in the presence of someone who actually was queer. Growing up, he and Lizz had used it hundreds of times, no, thousands, not that they had any idea how it must have hurt Paul. Looking back, Quinn tried to remember possible signs—a certain glance, an awkward moment, an inappropriate bump. Nothing came to mind. If it had, the taunts of their classmates would have been unbearable. As a kid, he hadn't known of an openly gay man in their hometown.

Sure, they had their suspicions: Mr. Michaud, the sixty-year-old bachelor who taught tenth-grade English; Jane Moss, the woman's golf champ at the Georges County Country Club for twelve straight years; even Billy Gallagher, a classmate who used to stare at everyone in the shower after gym.

Paul even went along with the cruel speculation. Once when Mr. Michaud left the class for a moment, he went to the front of the class, begging the suddenly rowdy students to settle down. "Do I have to spank you boys?" he asked his fellow jocks, who were roaring at his lisping imitation. "Because if I have to, I'll spank you *so* hard!"

What made it even funnier was the quiet way the subject had returned to witness the exaggerated routine. "Paul, take your seat," the effeminate teacher simply said, which caused Paul to react with horror. The pained silence that followed did more to shame him than any angry words could have.

When Quinn joked about it after class, Paul kept quiet, as though a switch had gone off inside him and he'd known—far more than the others—how cruel he'd really been. Speaking of cruelty, as Quinn drove back to the office, he wondered if Lizz had any idea how much she'd actually hurt him.

"WHY DIDN'T HE EVER tell me?" he asked Maria when they were in bed that night.

She didn't answer. He had come in late and had woken her up and now they were both a long way from getting any sleep.

"I was his best friend," Quinn said slowly. "I thought I knew him better than anyone."

"Maybe you did." She rolled on her side to face him. "But that was a long time ago. I'm sure there are other things you didn't know."

"Like what?"

"I'm not the one to ask," she said vaguely. "He wasn't my husband."

"But you knew him," Quinn said.

She shook her head. "Not very well. Mostly I've seen Lizz and Pauly since we moved here."

"We saw the whole family every summer for the past seven years," Quinn said.

"Yes, for a week on vacation. And when they came to visit, you spent most of the time entertaining the children."

"Paul and I talked."

"Sure, about old times."

"So what? This didn't happen overnight."

"No, he was probably always that way." She rubbed his shoulder with a hand.

"He never showed it."

"Maybe you never noticed," she said. "But if you had, would it have changed anything?"

"Of course not," he lied. He was ashamed to admit it would have. Growing up in Stone Harbor, he never could have handled the knowledge that his close friend had been gay. None of them could have and that was the problem.

"Does it change anything now?" she asked.

"I'm not sure." He sat upright and turned to her. "This is different. It's like he was never really honest with me."

"It was probably hard for him to be honest with himself," she said. "And how was he supposed to bring it up? 'Excuse me, John. Do you have a minute? I just stopped in to tell you I'm attracted to men. Have been all my life. It's really nothing I can control.'"

That only explained part of it. "He didn't have to be so self-righteous about the park," Quinn said.

"He thought he was doing the right thing."

"Oh, he was doing a lot of things," Quinn said bitterly, trying to imagine a few of them. "I'm just not sure I'd classify any of them as right. I'm not even sure they'd pass as R-rated. They sound more like some triple-X cock movie."

She sat upright herself and turned to face him. "You don't mean that!"

"He was a pervert!"

"He was gay," she said.

If only it had been that simple. "He was married. He had two children. He had a lot more to worry about than his own gratification."

"He's not the only one guilty of that."

Quinn stared at her. "What's that supposed to mean?"

Maria ignored the question, but it didn't matter. He knew exactly what she meant and really couldn't argue. Quinn could be self-absorbed and his wife deserved better. He'd been trying to change, before everything happened and he found himself caught up in it all.

"Just imagine what poor Lizz went through," Maria said. "I don't know what would be worse: the embarrassment or the rejection."

Quinn recalled how she'd been that afternoon. "Look, I love her like a sister, but she probably drove him to it," he said. "You haven't seen her other side. I'm telling you, she enjoyed seeing how hurt I was."

"How can you say that?" Maria asked. "She's gone through things nobody should have to endure."

"So she deals with it by screwing Alvah Sears?"

"She was lonely."

"But Sears? That makes my skin crawl."

"I don't know," she said in an offhand way. "He's an attractive man and he seems decent enough. He always stops to talk to me and Jack in the park."

"Oh, please." That really got to Quinn, even more than anything he'd heard that day. The fucker was putting the moves on his wife and she was actually charmed. "I can't believe you, of all people, can't see through that guy."

"He was probably there for her," Maria said. "God knows Paul wasn't."

Quinn looked at the ceiling as he spoke. "Oh, if you believe what she says. Maybe she's just covering up for her own behavior."

"That sounds like a stretch."

"What doesn't? Two weeks ago I wouldn't have believed any of this."

"Would you believe the cops were monitoring the park the night Paul was killed?" Maria asked.

He grabbed her elbow. "How do you know that?"

She shook her arm loose. "Lizz told me."

"And you believe her?"

"Why would she lie?"

It was a good question, one of many Quinn was having a hard time answering. In the next hour, they gnawed at him so much he couldn't begin to fall asleep. He just kept replaying things over and over. His conversation with Lizz. His arguments with Paul. His curiosity about who his friend had been involved with. The possibility that he'd been killed by an angry lover.

He couldn't turn things off—especially the memory of the last time they'd talked about Sears. Now he was suffering from a combination of guilt and betrayal and a sense that he could have done more to convince Paul to be careful.

And to think, the whole time Sears had been screwing Lizz.

It was obvious Quinn wasn't going to sleep that night, so finally, around two o'clock, he put his nervous energy to good use and went to the office.

12.

As the empty newspaper building creaked and settled, Quinn was immersed in computer searches of the men who'd been arrested at Sullivan Park. He'd found details that never made the black-and-white listings of the *Pilot*'s police reports: Pat McKenna was a Stone Harbor grade school teacher who'd been honored by the University of Maine for his work with developmentally disabled students; John Brennan of Camden had been in the Peace Corps; Paul Hale of Rockland was a Congregationalist minister. Many of the men were married. Only one had a criminal record. None had any apparent ties to Paul Stanwood, at least none that could be found in a back issue or on the Internet.

The biographical snippets, road race finishes, political contributions and other shreds of info formed an electronic maze Quinn scurried through as minutes blurred to hours. He'd started with all the names and addresses from the original stories. Before long he had most of their phone numbers, including a few he planned to call at a decent hour. He wondered how safe they felt, knowing two gay men had been savagely attacked, with one dead and the other close to dying. He also wondered about Danny Sloan.

Why had someone tried to kill him?

• • •

NOBODY ON THE HOSPITAL'S overnight crew even blinked when they saw Quinn walking through the empty halls. Either the staff knew who he was or they just didn't give a damn. When he finally found the right room, the smell of bandaged wounds and institutional disinfectant made him cover his nose and mouth as he approached the patient's bed. The only sound was the mechanical breathing of the ventilator that kept Danny Sloan alive. Stepping closer, he waved a hand in front of Sloan's vacant gaze.

Nothing registered.

"It's amazing he's even alive," came from the other side of the room.

Quinn jumped back. "Jesus," he said toward the voice. "You startled me."

"Sorry." A man walked from the window and sat down in a chair next to the bed. "I thought you saw me when you came in."

"No, I didn't."

Jeff Morse smiled. "I never knew you were so jumpy." He was the victim's partner.

"This isn't anything I'm used to." Quinn's heart was still racing from the surprise and he knew the words sounded lame.

"It's hard to see him like this." Morse slowly stroked Sloan's forehead. "But don't worry. Our guy's a fighter. Otherwise, he wouldn't have gotten this far." Then he moved another chair closer, almost apologetically. "Please, have a seat."

Quinn turned away from the bed.

"John, it's okay," Morse said gently. "This is an emotional time for all of us. Sit down. Please."

Quinn took a seat and looked at the floor, the ceiling, the

walls. The pictures Morse had hung were a shrine to a life to-gether. They included a shot of the couple on the pink granite shores of Schoodic Point. A celebration at a Portland restau-rant. Sloan leading the first (and last) annual gay pride march at Wellsen College. The display's centerpiece was a pair of pic-tures of the couple's Provincetown marriage. Both men wore dark, conservative tuxes on a bright, sunny day. In the first frame, they had their arms linked and were smiling like groomsmen at a friend's wedding. In the second, they were kissing.

"That was a great afternoon," Morse told him.

"Yeah," Quinn said, staring longer than he intended. "I'm sure it was."

Morse smiled at the memory. "Just when the world was lightening up, something like this slams us back to reality. That's what I told an art dealer on the West Coast. He said we should have left a long time ago, but we've always been drawn to this place." Like his partner, Morse was a well-known watercolorist, but his art was on hold that week. He'd barely left the room since Sloan had been admitted. The staff stretched the visiting hours because he was a sweet man and any mo-ment could have been the last they'd spend together. "It helps to know that a lot of people love him and will be with him every step of the way," Morse said.

They sat together a moment longer. No matter how much he tried, Quinn wasn't comfortable, so he finally just spit out what he had to say: "Do you mind if I ask you something a little awkward?"

"I thought we were through the awkward stage," Morse said.

"I wish it were that easy." Quinn tossed his head toward

the door and Morse followed him into the hallway, where his tone grew more serious. "How long had Paul Stanwood been openly gay?"

"He was never that open about it."

"But you knew."

"Yes." Morse looked Quinn straight in the eye before quietly adding, "From firsthand experience."

Quinn tried not to look surprised.

"Danny and I had a bad fight," Morse quickly explained. "Look, I love him but I'm not perfect. He knows that and accepts it."

"I'm not judging you."

Morse smiled and shook his head. "It doesn't really matter."

"So who else was he involved with?"

"John, really!" Morse frowned and cringed a little at the same time.

"Don't you think it could help shed some light on the situation?"

"He was involved with a few people," Morse said reluctantly, his eyes searching Quinn's. "None of them regularly."

"Would any of them have wanted to kill him?"

"I'm not sure they even knew his name."

"Oh, Christ!" Quinn brought his hands to his mouth as soon as the words came out, but it was too late.

"He was discreet," Morse assured him. "He had a family. You didn't know, even after all these years."

That's when Quinn decided to change the subject. "What time did Danny have dinner with Bowen-Smythe?"

"Early. I was with him and it was awful."

"Did they argue?"

Morse nodded. "Danny said he had evidence that could prove the police were brutalizing gay men. Bowen-Smythe told him not to jump to any conclusions."

Quinn could just imagine his condescending tone. "Do you know why Paul didn't like Bowen-Smythe?"

"I don't know—it seems like a natural reaction upon meeting the man." Morse shuddered in an exaggerated way to make his point.

"Could Bowen-Smythe have done this?" Quinn asked, looking toward Sloan's bed.

"I don't know how anyone could have done this. But that spindly man? Danny could have crushed him like a bug."

"Even if Bowen-Smythe had a weapon?"

Morse hesitated. "I don't know," he said tentatively.

"What about Sears?"

"I wouldn't put anything past that animal," Morse said without hesitation.

"How about Lizz Stanwood?"

Morse shook his head. "That poor woman?"

"She's been fucking Al Sears," Quinn said in an effort to dispel the "poor woman" notion. "And somewhere in all this, something else is at stake."

Morse tried to absorb what he'd been told. Then he touched Quinn's forearm. "Please excuse me. My biggest fear is Danny will get the sense he's alone and he has to know he isn't. He has to know he never will be."

"Hang in there, Jeff," Quinn said before he turned to leave, though he was left with the feeling that his words were terribly insufficient.

LATER THAT MORNING, QUINN found Sears at the dock, hosing down the teakwood deck of his thirty-foot sailboat,

The Alibi, which is where he spent most of his free time. The big cop was sculpted in a pair of cargo shorts and a sleeveless T-shirt and looked like he'd never eaten a donut in his life.

"Alvah," Quinn said when the chief looked up.

"Well, look what the tide brought in," Sears said cheerfully, as though Quinn were a long-lost friend. "Come aboard. Coffee's on and I could probably dig up some breakfast."

"Thanks, but I've already eaten."

"At this ungodly hour on a Sunday mornin'?" Sears asked. It was eight a.m., not exactly the middle of the day, but hardly the crack of dawn, either.

"I thought we might talk a bit," Quinn said.

"All right, then talk."

"Who was Paul linked with romantically?"

Sears didn't know.

"You haven't found that much out?"

"In case you haven't noticed," Sears said, laughing, "Sullivan Park didn't require dinnah and a movie."

"That's not what I'm talking about," Quinn said.

Sears eyed him a little more seriously. "You know somethin' I don't?"

"To start with, I heard something pretty interesting about the investigation—that you were there when it happened."

"I was there when a lot a things happened." The chief's tone had definitely lost the friendly pitch. "And quite a few of those things would turn your stomach."

"You were in Sullivan Park the night Paul was killed," Quinn said.

Sears didn't say anything. He seemed puzzled that Quinn had heard.

"You're not denying it?"

Sears turned off the hose and let it retract into its holder. "Right now I'm not doin' much of anythin'."

"That's been the problem all along."

"We have a number of problems." Sears said. "I'm tryin' to sort through them, one at a time." He looked at Quinn as though he was the worst of those problems. "We don't have any witnesses. The physical evidence is enough to make your head spin."

"And now none of the men who were arrested in the park will speak to anyone, on the advice of their lawyers."

Sears didn't seem to care. "Believe me, they don't know anything."

"Who wanted Paul dead?"

"That's a good question," Sears said. "But the answer might not mean anything. Plenty of people would just as soon see you dead, but my guess is you're not in any danger."

Quinn wondered if the chief was one of them. "Thanks," he said. "That's a real comfort—even with you in charge of the Keystone Cops."

"We have a fine department," Sears said as his tan face reddened.

"Then why haven't you made an arrest?" Quinn pressed. "Is it because you're too arrogant to ask the state police for help? Or do you have something to hide?"

Sears snorted. "I've got nothin' to be ashamed of."

"You couldn't even handle the crime scene photos!"

"Oh, that's been taken care of." Sears was almost gloating when he said it. "Sarah gave me the disk. I told her not to go outta her way, but she said it was no big deal."

"She shouldn't have given you a copy."

"I'm pretty sure it was the original," Sears said. "But hey—why don't you ask her?" He called into the cabin. *"Sarah!"*

Quinn couldn't believe she was there on a Sunday morning, especially with no sign of Ginny. When Sarah walked out barefoot in one of Sears's bright polo shirts, he figured she wasn't exactly working.

"Oh," she said when she saw him. "Hi, John!"

"Don't let your jaw hit the ground," Sears added, clearly enjoying Quinn's discomfort.

"Did you have to arrest her, or did she come willingly?" Quinn asked.

"There was no resistance," Sears said, "if that's what you're askin'."

Sarah started to giggle but caught herself.

"What are you doing here?" Quinn asked.

"That's a pretty personal question," Sears said.

Quinn slowly looked from Sarah to the chief. "And I'd like an answer—from her—if you don't mind."

"Well, we just started talking about the investigation," Sarah said self-consciously. "Then we stopped at the Laughing Gull for a beer."

"You don't even drink!"

Sears winked at her. "There's a first time for everything."

"So how'd you end up here?" Quinn asked, though he knew the answer.

"She was invited." Sears put his hands on his hips as he said this.

"Unlike me, I suppose."

Sears drew his right hand in imitation of a pistol and fired at him. "You catch on quick."

"Not always." Quinn suddenly felt drained. "Right now this is a little much for me to process."

"What's so complicated?" Sears asked.

"Christ, I don't know where to begin."

"John, I'm an adult," Sarah said. "I'm twenty-two years old."

"He's almost forty!"

"It's really none of your business," Sears said, moving between the two.

Quinn sidestepped Sears to speak directly to Sarah. "Well, there's a lot more to this than age."

"Neither of us is married," she said.

Quinn pointed to the other man. "He's *been* married—three times!"

"Really?" Sarah turned to Sears, more curious than concerned about the figure.

Sears shrugged. "I thought you already knew."

"I suppose he also never bothered to tell you when he was showing you his . . . boat . . . that he's also involved with Lizz Stanwood."

"Now, wait just a minute," Sears said, "you . . ."

". . . slimy prick!" Sarah finished.

"Yeah," Sears said as he shoved Quinn in the chest with the flat of his hand. "Get lost."

Sarah grabbed Sears by the arm. "I was talking to you."

"Me?" Sears asked as he stepped back from her. "Now hold on a minute—that was before we got together!"

"We're not together," Sarah said.

"Then what are we?"

"Just a mistake I made." She folded her arms across her chest, then burst off the deck and up the dock to Quinn's Volvo.

"Oh, come on," Sears said. "Where you goin'? We haven't even had breakfast."

"I can't think about eating when I'm sick to my stomach," Sarah said as she fought back tears.

"He's just tryin' to cause trouble," Sears said. "That's all."

She ignored him.

"Sarah, come on." By then it was clear he was getting nowhere, so Sears changed tactics. "I'll call you later, okay?"

She stood by Quinn's passenger-side door with her back to them both.

"You can't tell me you didn't have a good time!" Sears shouted after her.

She turned to face him. "Well, I'm not having one now."

"All right. I can take a hint." He hesitated, as though he couldn't decide what to do next. "Aren't you forgettin' somethin'?" he finally asked.

By then she'd turned away again.

"Her panties are still hangin' off the lamp," Sears told Quinn.

"Consider them a keepsake," Quinn said, happy that Sarah had come to her senses. "You're probably the type who would."

It took a second, but Sears finally came back again. "So now you're playin' the big hero who rescues her, you pathetic jerk."

"I might be pathetic, but I don't prey on children."

"Children don't come with bodies like that." Sears looked over at Sarah. "But she does have a few issues."

As if to prove his point, Sarah kept trying the car door— even though it wouldn't open. Then she slapped the window with her palm. When Quinn reached her, she asked why he'd locked the damn thing.

"You can never be too careful," Quinn said over his shoulder, loud enough so Sears could hear. "Strange things have a way of turning up in unlocked cars around here." He opened both doors with his remote and got inside. "You okay?" he asked.

"I'm fine," she muttered. "Just drive."

Slowly, calmly, he backed away from the dock and pulled through what he realized was a crowded public lot. More than a few people were gawking. "I can't believe you're fucking that jerk," he said to Sarah.

"It was only last night."

"So that makes it all right, since it was only once?"

She blew a breath upward, which caused her bangs to rise and fall. "Actually, it was three times, if you're counting."

"Jesus," he moaned as his hand slipped on the steering wheel and his body slouched forward. "I don't need to know that."

"Then you shouldn't have asked."

"I know." He was determined not to make that mistake again—at least not until he'd taken her safely home.

That's when they heard honking behind them. Quinn looked in his rearview mirror. Maria and Jack were in her silver BMW, so he pulled off to the side of the road and let them come alongside. Maria rolled down her window and Quinn did the same. "John, where've you been?" she asked. "Did you forget we were supposed to go to the beach?"

He had—completely. "I got up early and ran an errand," he said in a voice that felt as lame as it sounded.

"And you're still running it?" Maria's eyes sparked when she noticed he had company.

"Hi, Mrs. Quinn!"

"Sarah," Maria said flatly. She hated to be called Mrs. Quinn, which made her feel withered and old, especially when it came from someone who was so young and fresh. "Where's your mother?"

"Probably at home," Sarah said. "She didn't feel like going out last night."

"Last night?"

"It's not like it sounds," Quinn quickly added, in deference to his wife's jealous nature.

"So how does it sound?" Maria asked.

Quinn smiled uncomfortably. "I don't really know where to begin," he admitted.

"Try the beginning," Maria said. "What time did you leave the house?"

"Two o'clock this morning."

Sarah started to speak but Quinn cut her off. "I had to talk to Sears," he explained.

"Both of you?"

"I needed a ride," Sarah said.

"Is your mother's car broken down?"

Quinn winced. "It's really a much longer story than we need to get into right now," he said.

"It always is." Maria got out of her car and in his face. "Jack has barely seen you all week. Last night you said we could go to the beach. Then you got up in the middle of the night . . . You were still gone this morning and we've been waiting around for two hours."

"I stopped in the office," Quinn said. "I was doing some work online."

"We have a computer at home." There still was an edge to her voice.

"I had files at my desk," Quinn said. "I figured I'd be back before you woke up."

"Well, you figured wrong," Maria said. "It's Sunday morning and you don't even publish one of your shitty papers till tomorrow." She looked inside the car and couldn't help noticing Sarah had a cute pair of legs tucked under her chin. "Aren't you a bit underdressed?"

"Yes," Sarah admitted. "It's a little awkward."

"John, get out of the car," Maria said. "This looks terrible."

He did, then glanced over at Sarah, but kept his opinion on how the curve of her thighs looked to himself.

"What's going on?" Maria asked.

He told her.

She couldn't believe it. She was trying—Mother of Christ, she was trying—but that didn't mean it was easy or made much sense. "Why is it you're always tied to the Sewells?" she asked as they walked a distance from the car.

"Sarah works for me."

"You worry an awful lot about her," Maria said, her voice full of hurt. "Do you know that? And I think it goes even further."

"That's nonsense," Quinn said softly, trying to reassure her.

"Then why do you spend so much time talking about her?" Maria asked. "And when you're not talking about her, you're thinking about her. My God, I remember the day you promoted her from clerk to reporter."

"I was proud of her."

"You just wouldn't drop it."

"Why should I have?"

"Because it was my birthday," Maria said, striking his chest with the palm of her hand. "My thirtieth—if that wasn't bad enough."

Quinn reached for her shoulder. "I bought you roses and took you out to a great restaurant."

Maria pushed his hand away. "Where you went on and on about another woman."

Quinn threw his hands in the air. "She's not another woman—she's just a kid I work with!"

Maria let that hang in the air without responding.

"Honey, you're exaggerating," he said slowly for emphasis.

"Am I?"

He paused and thought things through. Maybe she wasn't.

By then, Maria's tears were flowing and it had grown into another awkward moment between them.

"Look, she's the only reporter I have who's worth a damn," Quinn said. "I need to take care of her."

"Why don't you take care of your son once in a while?" she asked. "Or your wife. We never even see you anymore. It's as though a stranger lives with us."

"I've been going through a rough time."

"And we haven't? You selfish man! We're going through everything you are, only we can't throw ourselves into our work. Instead we sit at home, waiting around for you, worrying about what's going to happen next. What do you think that's like for Jack? You never spend any time with him."

"I took him to visit Angus the other day," Quinn said.

"Yes, you did. And do you know what he picked up? Your language. When I told him to finish his breakfast this morning he said he didn't have to. When I disagreed, he said he was gonna kick my ass."

Quinn couldn't help laughing. He knew it was wrong, but he couldn't imagine anyone—especially anyone who was only thirty-two inches tall—saying that to Maria and living to tell about it.

Her face was redder than he'd ever seen it. "This isn't funny! After I slapped his mouth, he said that's what you told Angus in the hospital."

"I was joking around."

"Well, I'm not," Maria said. "Things have to change and I'm serious. I'm more serious than ever."

"Come on." Quinn looked past his wife and directly at Jack, who was clearly uncomfortable in the passenger seat. "As soon as I take Sarah home, I'll meet you at the beach."

"Don't bother," Maria said.

Quinn didn't know what to say. As they drove away, Quinn noticed his son had tears in his eyes as he waved good-bye.

He slowly waved back.

Still in Quinn's car, Sarah was just as upset. "John, I'm sorry. I made a fool of myself."

"Don't worry about it," Quinn said, the last words spoken during the drive. He was no longer going to get caught up in Sarah's personal drama. She was a big girl and he had his own problems to worry about.

After he dropped her off, Quinn drove down to Quahog Point, which took nearly half an hour—on a crowded, winding road down a peninsula that led to the only sand beach within fifty miles. When he parked in the unpaved lot and walked through the warm dunes to the water's edge, he could feel a cold, steady vein of air that seemed to come from the middle of the North Atlantic. A half dozen people were huddled in blankets and hooded sweatshirts. August or not, this beach in that breeze would never be mistaken for the tropics. Maria and Jack were nowhere to be found.

He couldn't really blame them.

They weren't at home, either. The place was empty, its three stories, turret and massive second-floor porch magnifying Quinn's growing sense of being alone. Maybe it was for the best. Maria would probably stay angry the rest of the day and quite frankly, he was too exhausted to argue with her. But he needed to talk to someone. Aunt Blythe wouldn't necessarily be sympathetic, yet she'd listen, though after the events of the past few days, he wasn't sure where to begin.

"Well, you're not always the most considerate person," Blythe said matter-of-factly, "but your intentions have always been good." They were sitting in her kitchen over tea and shortbread. "In some ways you have tunnel vision, just like your father."

"I'm not like my father."

"Oh, really?" she asked, a smile curling on her face as she raised a cup. "Since he was my younger brother and you're my nephew, I'd like to think I'm in a better position than you to make that judgment."

"Whatever."

Blythe sat up straight and set her cup back down. "Don't talk to me as though you're still seventeen years old, Jonathan," she said rather sternly. "I've seen that phase of your life once and really don't want a repeat performance."

"Neither do I," Quinn mumbled.

"Whether you like it or not, you are your father's son."

"That doesn't mean I'm him."

"Of course not." She patted his hand to reassure him of that fact. "But one of the reasons you still resent him was the amount of time he spent at the paper and now you're doing the same thing."

"I never resented him for not being around," Quinn said. "His behavior in person was the problem. And besides, circumstances at work have gotten a little beyond my control."

"They always do." She slowly shook her head. "That's part of the business, especially at a small paper during a tough financial stretch. I understand that. Your mother understood it. That doesn't mean Maria has any frame of reference."

"This is a lot more than business," he said, thinking of his friend's murder.

"Of course it is," she said, thinking of his family.

Quinn knew what she meant, but what kind of father and husband would he be if he sat this out? "Do you honestly think the police are going to find out who killed Paul?"

"No."

"And that doesn't bother you?"

"Not really." She gave him a long, searching look, as though reassessing him after years of disappointment. "That's because I'm counting on you."

13.

"That's it for today," Bryan Bowen-Smythe told a dozen students who were lounging in a circle on the Wellsen College lawn. "But don't forget term papers are due Monday."

Unlike the board of selectmen's meetings, where he was stiff and uncomfortable, Bowen-Smythe was relaxed and happy. He was wearing a faded denim shirt and cutoff jean shorts that showed off the long, spindly legs that led to his undergraduate nickname, Chicken. Blue veins showed through his marble skin, and the one constant to his wardrobe, his Birkenstock sandals, were off in the grass. He smiled when a young Republican with red hair and a look in her eye raised a hand.

"Does that mean you'll cut us some slack?" Red asked.

"Not when I've already extended the deadline a week," Bowen-Smythe said.

A collective groan rose from the grass.

Despite their disappointment, the students loved Bowen-Smythe, more for his affable nature and willingness to throw keggers than any academic ability. In fact, after his fall reelection to the town council, the police had been called to a particularly rowdy victory party at his home, a few blocks from campus. No formal charges were pressed and Bowen-Smythe held the news stories that followed against Quinn. Still, he acknowledged him with a grin.

Quinn nodded, though he wondered why the professor was so giddy.

Once class was dismissed, the students were in no hurry to leave. They milled about in small groups, waiting for a chance to speak to Bowen-Smythe in private. He was chatting up the redhead when Quinn made his way toward him.

"Professor."

"John."

"Bryan, who's this?" Red asked, surprised the professor had taken his eyes off her.

"Oh, excuse me," Bowen-Smythe said. "Julie, this is John Quinn. John, this is Julie Chapman, one of my brightest students."

Quinn held out his hand and she shook it.

"John owns the local newspaper," Bowen-Smythe said.

"Can't say I've ever read it," she confessed.

"You should give it a try sometime," Quinn said. "We write an awful lot of interesting things about Dr. Bowen-Smythe. In fact, he was in a story today."

"Really?" she asked. "Why's that?"

"We write about government's responsibility to its citizens, the same sort of thing the professor was lecturing about."

"Along with plenty of bake sales and bean suppers," Bowen-Smythe added, trying to lighten the mood. "They also print a mean church listing."

"I'll have to check out an issue," she said.

"Just ignore the editorials," the professor said. "He'll take any position to get a rise out of his readers—especially at the expense of the public servants on the town council."

She considered this with a smile, which caused the professor to shake his head and move her along with a subtle hand on her hip. "So I'll see you at eight?" she asked.

Bowen-Smythe winked. "Not if I see you first."

"Office hours?" Quinn asked.

"The Laughing Gull," she said. "A few of us are Tuesday night regulars. It's a summer session tradition. Stop in if you get a chance."

Quinn said he'd think about it.

"Well, it was nice meeting you." She waved over her shoulder as she walked away.

"Likewise."

Julie Chapman was tall and angular and had a hitch in her stride that made the professor breathe a little deeper as he watched her go. "Working on a little extra credit?" Quinn asked.

Bowen-Smythe ignored that. "So what can I do for you?" he asked as he began putting his notes in a knapsack.

"I'm troubled by the investigation into Paul Stanwood's death," Quinn said, "And now we have another critic of the police department in the hospital, near death."

"Have you talked to Al Sears?" Bowen-Smythe asked.

"No," Quinn said. "He's what's troubling me, and Danny Sloan would agree, if he were conscious."

That touched a nerve. Sloan was a popular adjunct professor at the college. "Is he going to live?" Bowen-Smythe asked.

Quinn thought back to his hospital visit. "Probably like a vegetable."

"Do you know that for sure?"

"That's what his partner told me," Quinn said. "Does that mean you haven't visited him yet?"

"No, I haven't." Bowen-Smythe looked at Quinn sadly. "I'm not proud of that."

Quinn considered him closely. He was acting nervous but there was no way he could have beaten two men so brutally. "Do you know him very well?"

"This is a small college with a close faculty," Bowen-Smythe said. "Danny is respected by both his students and peers. He cares about this place and knows the difference between right and wrong."

"He was also very critical of town government."

"I know," Bowen-Smythe said. "We had dinner the night he was beaten."

"Did you argue?"

The professor zipped his knapsack shut. "What makes you think that?" he asked.

"No reason."

"John, I'm not a confrontational person."

"Well, you certainly pissed off Angus Stanwood at the last council meeting."

Bowen-Smythe slung his pack over his shoulder. "You were there. You know I didn't start that."

Quinn shrugged. "He did manage to get under your skin."

"Some people have a way of doing that."

"Did Paul Stanwood?"

"Occasionally." Bowen-Smythe eyed Quinn evenly. "That's part of the give-and-take of government."

Quinn didn't blink. "Angus said you hated each other."

Bowen-Smythe slowly shook his head. "That doesn't make

it true, any more than his crazy accusations that Lizz Stanwood killed his son." Then he started walking.

Quinn hurried to keep up. "You know, I talked to him in the hospital."

"Oh?" Bowen-Smythe seemed surprised. "How's he doing?"

"He said this whole thing centered around some land."

"It does." The professor stopped walking and turned to directly face Quinn. "Can we go off the record?"

"Of course."

Bowen-Smythe told him what was going on. Quinn printed it anyway.

SULLIVAN PARK ON THE BLOCK
By John Quinn
Pilot Staff

Sullivan Park is for sale.

That's the word from Acting Board of Selectmen Chairman Bryan Bowen-Smythe, who said a potential buyer had already expressed interest.

"We haven't been able to use it as a park, so the expense of maintaining it can't be justified," Bowen-Smythe said. "The best thing we can do is get the land back on the tax rolls."

He said the town attorney had already drawn up a purchase agreement, though he refused to release any details.

"We'll announce things as soon as we can," he said. "But the emphasis will be on sooner rather than later. This is something we want to act on quickly, and if you don't mind, quietly."

That may not be possible.

The proposed sale has already drawn a negative reaction from environmentalists.

"That land was put in public trust to preserve a unique part of Maine's heritage," said Jeri Moneghan, a member of the Coastal Trust. "Selling it is a violation of the spirit of the donor's intent."

Others questioned the wisdom of doing that without putting it up for public bid.

"Just when you think this crowd can't do anything number, they go out and do this," Angus Stanwood said. "If they were looking out for the public, they'd try to get the most money they could."

The property was deeded to the town in 1973 by Geoff and George Sullivan. It had been in their family since 1683, according to the Georges County Historical Society.

Bowen-Smythe said the town had every right—legally and morally—to sell the land. He insisted any sale would include provisions to maintain the preserve's unique natural habitat.

"This place will remain protected," he said. "That's a guarantee I make to every resident."

He said the way to protect the land was to find a responsible buyer, something that may not happen if the town simply seeks the highest purchase price. "That's something we thought long and hard about," Bowen-Smythe said.

For the past several months the park has been the scene of bitter public debate following the arrest of 23 gay men on charges ranging from public lewdness to sodomy.

Three weeks ago, Board of Selectman Chairman Paul Stanwood was found there beaten to death. After that, the park was closed to the public.

A half hour after he filed his story, Quinn headed to the basement pressroom in anticipation of that day's run—something his father had done every day he'd worked, Monday through Saturday, without exception. Nothing went out the door without Jake's okay.

Quinn wasn't exactly a detail man. That morning was the first time he'd actually stood around, waiting for the presses to start. Usually he left that to Blythe, who prided herself on catching as many of his typos as possible. In fact, when the head pressman saw Quinn coming down the stairs with her, he nearly choked on the cigarette he shouldn't have been smoking inside the building.

"Johnny, I was beginning to think you forgot we existed down here," Bernie Stone said, still gasping.

"Now, you know that isn't true," Quinn said.

"Does he?" Blythe asked in a sharp tone.

"He sure as hell should," Quinn answered.

Blythe didn't looked convinced. "Your father paid a little more attention to things," she reminded him for perhaps the thousandth time.

"So I've been told."

Meanwhile, Stoney was grinning and walking back toward the press, where his crew was adjusting plates and jogging giant paper rolls that webbed the length of the eight units. Bells clanged, and the line hummed and lurched in stops and starts until the first wet copies flew through the folder into the waiting flyboy's hands.

The kid passed one each to Quinn and Blythe, who checked the date on the front page, the folios, and each headline and cutline.

"Everything okay?" Stoney asked.

"Everything's great," Quinn said.

"Blythe?" Stoney asked, as though Quinn hadn't said anything.

The old woman nodded patiently.

Satisfied, Stoney signaled his crew and they turned the press up to full speed and got things moving. Soon the whole room was shaking as the cylinders rolled over and over, printing copy

after copy

after copy

after copy, as the pressman checked the pages and adjusted the ink, and the flyboy bundled and tossed fifty at a time on a chute, where they tumbled on a conveyor belt and through the back door. Outside, drivers were lined along the building in minivans, beaters, hatchbacks and anything else that would run. Fourteen thousand papers would print in an hour and an army of carriers would make sure they were delivered to three out of five Georges County homes and every store from Rockland to Belfast.

"Jesus Christmas!" Stoney shouted over the clanging folder as he walked away from the third press unit and shook his head. He was reading the lead article—not just checking the ink—and pointing to the quote where Bowen-Smythe made his guarantee.

Blythe had been just as surprised. Moving close enough so she was shouting into his ear to be heard over the machinery, she told Quinn, "They're burying their heads in the sand."

He agreed.

"And to think Seth played a part in it," she said, holding a copy of the wet early edition in front of her.

"So how's this gonna go over?" Quinn asked.

She peered over her copy toward Stoney, who was still reading the story and pointing out its contents to a member of his crew.

"Well, I better see what our boy has to say," Quinn muttered to Blythe, who was busy gathering a handful of papers to pass out to the newsroom. Then he quickly went to the top of the stairs and through the steel doors that abruptly shut the noise and clatter behind him.

HE HADN'T REALIZED HOW loud the pressroom had been until he crossed the soft carpet of the advertising department and a tall, thin ad assistant looked up—annoyed—before she saw who it was and quickly smiled.

"Good afternoon, Mr. Quinn," she said.

"Is he in?" Quinn pointed toward Seth's door.

"On the phone," she explained.

Quinn kept walking, right into his cousin's office, and took a seat in a leather chair. Seth had a nice setup: built-in mahogany bookshelves, Winslow Homer prints on the paneled wall and the antique time clock from the days of the *Weekly Pilot.* It was the same office Quinn's grandfather once occupied.

"Ever hear of knocking?" Seth asked once he hung up.

Quinn handed him a smeared early edition.

Seth looked at the stain in his hand and frowned. "Did you have to give me this particular copy?" he asked.

"Just read it."

Seth did. Twice. If the story bothered him, he showed no sign.

"Did you have anything to do with this?" Quinn asked.

"It was already in motion before I volunteered to become a selectman." Seth reached for a tissue with his fingertips.

"So do you have a problem with it?"

"No."

"So what's the park worth?" Quinn asked.

"Millions. Last week an acre lot went for half a million on Brewer's Island."

"That's insane."

"That's the market." Seth sounded bored. "Prices have doubled in the past three years. The whole state's that way. Given the interest rates, people consider real estate a smart investment—much better than the stock market—or for that matter, a family newspaper."

It was an old argument. Shortly after Jake's funeral, they discussed their options, and Seth and their attorney wanted to sell the paper. Quinn and Aunt Blythe didn't. Since Quinn controlled ninety percent of the company, that ended the discussion. "I told you before, a newspaper stands for something," Quinn said, and he was prepared to make the argument all over again.

"Of course it does. But when you let the financial performance slide, you put everything at risk and every employee's well-being on the line."

"Oh, come on," Quinn said. "You don't give a shit about our employees."

"Why, because I don't play softball with them or bowl in the company league?" Seth bent forward in his chair and raised his voice. "Is that what you're talking about?"

"You don't even speak to half of them."

"So what? You're going to slap their backs all the way to the unemployment line. No matter how much fun and games you try to make it, this is still a business. Just like a bank. Just like a pizza shop. Just like any other member of the chamber of commerce." As if to prove this, Seth pointed to a sepia print on his wall that showed a horse leaping from a high platform before an amazed turn-of-the-century crowd. "Like they say, a picture is worth a thousand words."

The first John Cole—Quinn's great-grandfather—had originally come down from Aroostook County to run a diving stallion attraction at a summer amusement park. The posters he plastered throughout town claimed the horses naturally learned to dive off cliffs into desert oasis pools on their native Arabian Peninsula.

In reality, Cole took worn-out farm nags, bleached them white and trained them to walk up scaffolding to a hot-wired metal platform, where they either took the plunge or got a brutal shock—then took the plunge.

The locals loved it. To spread the word even further—and to battle his critics—Cole formed a weekly newspaper. The sideshow didn't last but the paper did. "And it's just as much a part of the *Pilot*'s history as your framed front page of the Kennedy assassination," Seth said.

"I never said it wasn't."

"Not in so many words. But let's be honest: you don't pay attention to the money end and you ignore me when I try to explain things. You have contempt for any part of the business that isn't the newsroom."

Quinn couldn't argue. That's why he relied on his cousin. No question, Seth knew what he was talking about, which is why Quinn continued to listen when he argued, once again, that it was time to sell.

"Chains are still paying good prices for small community properties like this," Seth added.

"And if I sold, what would happen to you?"

"I'd get by."

"You'd slash and burn everything so they could make their margins," Quinn said.

"I see the big picture, and that's something you better start considering."

Instead, Quinn went back to his office to consider the latest development. The fools on the town board probably thought they were doing the right thing by getting rid of the park. That way they could wash their hands of the problem. They didn't really give a damn about the murder, which was why Angus had been so worked up at the meeting. He'd been right about them all along. And it made Quinn wonder what else the old bastard had been right about and hadn't been able to share.

14.

Angus lived in a wild, Gothic-style home updated with all the extras: a wraparound wooden deck, an in-ground pool and cabana, sauna, giant satellite dish and six-car garage. But his biggest extravagance was his most eccentric. He went all out each year for Halloween and had a crew decorate from top to bottom, with ghosts, goblins and a few busty witches, along with a light and fog show featuring swarming bats. When the neighbors complained, Angus told them to go to hell and kept the lights up year-round—though he never turned them on before October 1. That's when he kicked off his dealership's annual Halloween sale with live television remotes from the front yard.

Yes, he was a character. Quinn still couldn't believe he was stubborn enough to walk out of the hospital. Quinn was even more surprised when Angus answered his own door.

"John-ny!" he said in a slow but upbeat voice. He was still pale and had lost weight but managed to project the same old enthusiasm.

"Why aren't you at Stone Harbor Memorial?"

Angus dismissed the notion with a sour frown.

"I'm serious," Quinn said as he stepped inside. "They have

people who work there called doctors. They've spent years studying the human body so they can help guys like you—no matter how far your head happens to be stuck up your ass."

"Don't shout. The heart attack didn't affect my hearin'."

"Well, something affected you," Quinn said. "I'm just not sure what." He gently put his hand on the older man's shoulder. "But you do look better than the last time I saw you."

Angus shrugged. "I feel bettah."

"And I suppose you've been back to work."

Angus shook his head. "Why scare the customers?" When he laughed at his own joke Quinn knew he really was doing better. "Drink?" Angus added as he shuffled into the kitchen.

"Sure, I'll have a beer," Quinn said, following him.

They sat at the table a few moments, sipping Miller High Lifes. Angus didn't go for fancy microbrews, though he wasn't opposed to chasing the High Life with single malt scotch, a practice he skipped that afternoon in deference to his health, or at least appearances.

"Do you know why they're selling the park?" Quinn finally ventured.

Angus took a raspy breath. "Ask Queen Elizabeth."

"What's she have to do with it?"

"She's the one in real estate," Angus said. "And that's the reason this whole crackdown was orchestrated out of town hall."

Quinn tried to process that. "I don't understand," he said. "The board pulled Sears out of the park."

"Sure, once they got what they wanted: a chance to sell a valuable piece of public property for less than it was worth."

But they couldn't have planned on Paul getting killed. "This all sounds too far-fetched," Quinn said.

"It came straight from Danny Sloan—before his little mishap." Angus got up for two more beers and Quinn wondered when he'd talked with Sloan.

When Angus returned, he asked Quinn what happened to the papers he had at the council meeting.

"They must have gotten lost in the chaos. What were they?"

"Copies of the plans to build a resort." After he explained the details, Angus said a lot of money would be made on side deals. "Check who's buying land. I wouldn't be surprised if my sweet daughter-in-law tipped off her friend Sears."

With a beer halfway to his mouth, Quinn stopped himself. "So how long have you known about them?"

"It doesn't matter."

"Then why do you hate her so much?"

"I don't."

"Oh, come on." Quinn looked at him sideways. "You accuse her of murder and now she's involved with the chief of police and you tell me that doesn't matter."

Angus shook his head and took a long swig from his own can. "I can't blame her for that," he said. "But I don't trust her, either."

Quinn felt like a fool all over again. "So you knew about Paul's other side?"

"A father knows his son," Angus said. "Just like one good friend knows another. Admitting it's different."

"What are you talking about?"

Angus slowly shook his head. "Remember the time you hit him?"

Quinn hadn't thought of that in years.

It happened when they were swimming. He'd dunked

Paul and then Paul dunked him, and when Quinn came up out of the water, Paul grabbed him around the waist. That's when Quinn, for what now seemed like no reason, gave him a bloody nose. Just some roughhousing between teenagers that got out of hand. They never discussed it and it never happened again.

"He told me," Angus said. "Not that long ago." His voice sounded very weary. "It couldn't have been easy."

"No," Quinn admitted. "It couldn't have been."

"I should have been a better father, but I can't change that now."

Quinn understood.

"Maybe that's why he felt he had to have a perfect family," Angus continued. "Maybe he wanted something he never had."

"Who has a perfect family?" Quinn asked as he refilled his glass.

"Well, your own father knew he'd been hard on you," Angus said. "Jake just didn't know how to undo it."

Quinn considered that while he drained his glass. "So how do I reconcile with a dead father and you with a dead son?" he asked.

The hell if Angus knew.

After yet another beer, this one finished in silence, Quinn stood up. "I better take off. You could probably use some rest."

Angus clasped Quinn's elbow. "Just remember what I said about her."

Quinn said he would.

NOBODY ANSWERED WHEN HE knocked at the Stanwoods'. Unlike his last visit—when the house and grounds had been teeming—the front door was locked and the place was quiet and empty. He walked along the driveway, then into the backyard. A window was open and the curtains rustled in a soft breeze that swept through town like a silent invitation, so he popped the screen and slipped inside, where he landed in a lump on the pine floor. "Damn!" His knee throbbed like it would explode, but he picked himself up and looked around.

The kitchen had seen better days. Smeared plates, glasses and a lonely array of wine bottles lined the counter and sink. The ashtrays were full. The dog dishes were empty. "Anybody home?" he ventured.

Standing perfectly still, he heard music playing softly down the paneled hall, some classical crap with horns and strings and maybe a harp. He followed the sound along a row of pictures: framed shots of Paul and Lizz at the Bay of Fundy when they were teenagers; Diane and Paul at Disney; the whole family together at the San Diego Zoo.

Then there were her magazine covers: a fishing village on the Labrador coast for *Condé Nast Traveler;* a close-up of a weathered lobsterman's face for *Down East;* a kayaker taking on a class V rapid on West Virginia's Gauley River for *National Geographic.* She was good—better than most people in town realized—maybe even better than she realized herself.

As Quinn continued on, the music grew louder with each step until he found the lady of the house huddled under a comforter in an old leather chair.

"Lizz?"

She didn't say anything.

"Hey, you all right?" he said a little more loudly.

She still didn't respond.

"Hey—Lizz!" he practically shouted.

She finally raised her eyes toward him. "Who let you in?" she asked softly.

"I let myself in." He sat down across from her on a footstool. "An old habit, I suppose."

"They can be hard to break." She waved a hand toward an empty wine bottle on the coffee table. "Just look at me."

"I would, if you'd let me."

When she did, he saw that her bruised and swollen face was wet from tears.

It made Quinn feel like he'd been hit himself. "What happened?"

"Funny you should ask." She pulled the blanket back around her. "I've been turning things around in my head and can't come up with the answer."

Gently he asked, "Why didn't you call me?"

"Look where that got me the last time," she said. "You had to run off and tell everyone Al had men in the park the night Paul died. You just couldn't let a small-town cop think for a moment he was smarter than you."

"That doesn't excuse what the son of a bitch did."

She tightened her shoulders and put a hand to her mouth. "It's complicated."

"It's criminal."

"It's a lot of things," she insisted before breaking into more tears. "You don't know the whole story. Your reporter missed it, but the autopsy showed Paul was HIV-positive."

That stopped Quinn cold.

"As you can see, there's a little more to this than meets the eye."

He put his arms around her. "I'm sorry."

"Yeah, well, so am I—about a lot of things."

She was thin and fragile and sobbed quietly as she laid her head on his shoulder. She felt more like the skinny thirteen-year-old who used to stuff newspaper inserts so she could buy school clothes than a respected photographer and owner of an adventure company that guided international expeditions. In many ways, she was still that same embattled little girl.

Back then his father helped her. Quinn had no idea how he could do the same. "Have you been tested?" he asked.

"Not yet."

"Does Sears know?"

She turned to show her full profile. "What do you think?" One eye was completely swollen shut.

"Why'd you ever get involved with that guy?"

She spoke softly and deliberately. "I don't know—because my husband was a faggot. Because I needed to be with someone. Because he was there and nobody else was."

"How could you let him do this?"

"He was angry," she said. "I betrayed his confidence and kept things from him. I may have even infected him."

"He still had no right."

She put a hand to his lips and spoke even more slowly. "None of us ever does."

He took her hand in his. "Did he kill Paul?"

Her face went blank, almost without emotion. "I don't know."

"Doesn't that scare you?" he asked.

"There's not much that scares me anymore," she said. "Paul and I went down this road a long time ago. I tried to pretend otherwise, but after a while, even that wore off. The only thing left was appearances."

"You were never one to worry about appearances."

"Especially now," she said, and then she actually started to laugh. "It's true. I didn't care what people thought. I still don't. Paul was another story."

"You could have divorced him."

"It sounds so easy." She looked up at the ceiling. "But the children didn't know and I didn't want them to and that's only part of the whole mess. At one time he had political aspirations."

"He always told me he wanted to put his family before politics," Quinn said.

"Maybe he did. We would have been the ones who suffered. But who am I kidding? I brought my own baggage to the party. Maybe Angus is right. Maybe I'm not fit to raise my own children."

"Do they know what's going on?"

"Diane does." Lizz lowered her eyes till they met his. "And she hates me for it."

"Does she know about her father?"

"Probably. Even you finally get the picture."

He let that slide. She was in bad shape and he couldn't expect any better treatment. Besides, he wasn't the issue—she was. Quinn stood up and started pacing. "We've got to report this."

"What—that Paul liked men?" she asked.

Quinn spun around and punched the air. "That Sears did this to you."

"I've had more than my share of personal humiliation, thank you very much. I'd like to avoid a second round."

Quinn was seething. "He's a psychopath."

"Well, he can be a bastard," she admitted with a shrug. "I'll give you that."

Quinn started pacing again. "I swear to God I'll kill him."

That made her smile.

"I'm not joking," he said.

"Oh, you have to be. You'd be crazy to try anything."

It was hard to believe: the man had beaten the crap out of her and she was still bragging about him. "You really think a lot of him, don't you?"

She sighed patiently. "John, don't take things personally."

Quinn couldn't help it. He always took things personally. He stopped pacing and looked right at her. "Did you know he's also fucking Sarah Sewell?"

"The odd little reporter you're so infatuated with?" She laughed bitterly at the thought. "It's probably just what she needs."

Quinn resented the implication. "You know, Sarah may be just what he needs. She's young and attractive and won't let anyone push her around."

"Unless they want her crime scene photos and know an easy way to get them."

But no matter how tough a front she put on, he knew his words had gotten to her. And for a moment, he hated her.

And for that same moment, she wasn't so crazy about him. "Now that you know all our dirty secrets, is there anything else?" she asked.

"Angus thinks you're involved in the park sale."

She shook her head. "He'll say anything to make me look bad. He always has. But what I can't believe is that you're taking him seriously."

"I didn't say that."

"You didn't have to," she said quietly.

Behind her, between the bookcases, he saw a giant framed photograph of Diane and Pauly looking happy and carefree on the family's thirty-foot sailboat. "Where are they?" he asked.

"Safe. I'm not going to let them get in the middle of this. They've already been through too much."

Thank God she had some sense left. He started to leave, then stopped himself. He felt guilty for his petty remarks. "Is there anything I can do?"

"There's nothing anyone can do," she said.

Quinn wasn't so sure about that.

OFFICER EARL STUFFLEBEAM WAS at the front desk of the police station, reading that day's newspaper, when Quinn walked in. "Mr. Quinn, I'm still pursuin' some angles on your wife's car," Earl quickly explained as he put down the sports section.

"Thanks, but I have something a little more serious this time—though it may be related."

"What's that?"

"I'd like to report an assault involving the chief and Lizz Stanwood."

"Come again?" Earl asked, like he hadn't quite heard.

Quinn leaned down and looked him in the eye. "Your boss beat up a woman."

"Now hold on just a minute." Earl raised his hands so Quinn wouldn't speak so loudly. "How can you say something like that?"

"I saw her with my own eyes," Quinn said, just as loudly as before. "She told me what happened and I know what he's capable of doing."

Earl seemed confused. "Does she want to fill out a report?"

"She's afraid."

"Then how can you expect anyone to take this seriously?" Earl shook his head. "This all sounds pretty far-fetched." He was looking around as he said this, as if somebody else would be able to confirm his doubts. Since he was the only cop around, he leaned forward and nearly whispered: "When are you saying this happened?"

Sensing that he'd finally gotten somewhere, Quinn finally spoke in a normal tone. "I'm guessing yesterday."

"So you can't really say for sure," Earl said, regaining his confidence.

"No."

"You're aware there's a penalty for filing a false report," Earl said.

"I'm also aware that there's a difference between right and wrong."

Earl quickly looked back down at the box scores on page 2B of the newspaper.

"The fact that this involves the chief shouldn't stop you from doing your job," Quinn said.

"It won't."

Quinn wondered who Earl was trying to convince when he said that. "So where's Sears?" he asked.

"I don't know."

"When he comes back, tell him I'm looking for him."

"Tell him yourself," Sears said when he walked out of his office.

Quinn glanced at Earl, but the younger man turned away, embarrassed that he'd been caught in a lie. Quinn turned back to Sears. "I saw what you did to Lizz," he said.

Sears gave him a knowing grin. "You might want to be a little more specific, 'cause for the last year, I've done quite a few things to her—and believe me, I never had any complaints."

"You beat the crap out of her."

"I think you're mistaken." Sears kept moving toward Quinn in an attempt to intimidate him.

"Don't come any closer, you son of a bitch."

Sears laughed as Quinn stepped back.

Sears shoved him and Earl started to come out from behind the counter. "Guys, let's just calm down," Earl said.

By then Quinn had a look in his eye that made Sears smile. "I talked to your wife again at the park this morning," Sears said, goading him further. "Seems like that cute little Cuban is gettin' lonely."

Quinn put everything into an overhand right without thinking. It knocked Sears back into Earl, who caught him and kept the chief from falling all the way to the floor. Quinn stepped forward, ready to swing again, but Earl put his own body between them.

Sears rubbed his mouth, which covered his hand with blood.

That was nothing, really, compared to Quinn's problem: he'd broken his hand in three places and was cradling his fingers in the crook of his arm and wincing.

The chief sighed. "You hit like a little girl," he said.

"Then you should feel comfortable hitting me back." Now Quinn was holding his right arm and the pain was flowing over him; he thought he'd pass out.

"Earl, take it from here," Sears said as he regained his footing and straightened himself to his full height.

Officer Stufflebeam hesitated.

"Now!" Sears snapped, and Earl did as he was told.

QUINN DIDN'T FARE SO well this time around. Sears was pressing charges and the district attorney was going along.

How could he do anything else? Nobody hits a cop and gets away with it, even if you do own a newspaper and buy ink by the barrel.

Quinn had lost his head and hit the police chief—which may have been justified but didn't make it legal. He was learning that the hard way. The more calls he made, the more impossible the situation seemed. Nobody was willing to make this one go away. Not Bowen-Smythe. Not George Baribou. Seth even laughed in his face and he was family. "John, I'm a selectman—not a miracle worker," he said the next morning.

"You know this is bullshit," Quinn argued.

"I hope so, because the fallout could mean a lot more than you paying a fine and doing community service."

"I know." Adding to his misery, Quinn's right arm would be stuck in a cast from his fingers to his elbow for the next six weeks while his bones healed. He'd have to do everything one-handed—left-handed at that—from typing to tying his shoes and driving.

"Maybe it'll make you think next time," Seth said.

But when Quinn really did think about things, he could only picture Lizz's bruised face. The image haunted him. He knew she needed to be protected—from herself as much as Sears. He just wasn't sure how to do it. And from the annoyed look on Seth's face, he wasn't going to get any help there. "So why do I get the feeling I'm the only one who cares that Paul was killed, another man is in a coma and the cops don't seem to give a damn?"

"Because you take yourself way too seriously," Seth said. "Plenty of people care. They just don't make a circus of it."

"Then why does it seem like they're waiting for the whole thing to blow over?"

"They're letting the police do their job."

His superior tone set Quinn off. "Well, I have news for you and the fools you serve with on the board of selectmen," he snapped. "The police aren't doing their job. And they're not doing their job because of one thing—Alvah Sears. You know why? Because that son of a bitch is involved. He may have even killed Paul. And the only reason Lizz is still alive is because he can use her."

Seth's brow tightened as the words sank in. He paused before bursting out laughing, then asked if Quinn had any other big theories.

"I also know you're going to develop the park from A to Z with condos, boat docks, restaurants, a hotel and a golf course," Quinn said, as though he'd been waiting for the exact question. "So much for this 'environmentally sensitive' crap. You name it, Angus told me. He said you even have three hundred million in financing."

Seth was no longer laughing. "You're out of your mind."

"As you said earlier, that seems to be going around." Quinn stared hard at his cousin and didn't like what he saw. "Jesus, what's wrong with you?"

"I have to live in this town."

"So do I."

Seth rolled his eyes. "Oh, you'll stay a few more months and decide you're too big for Stone Harbor. That's been your problem all along. You think you're better than the rest of us. People know you look down on them."

Quinn was unaffected by the charge, which he knew was at least partially true. "Well, I don't look down on them all."

"You look down on enough of us," Seth said. "This is a quiet town. It's been a quiet town for three hundred years, and no matter how much you try to imagine it any other way, it will never change."

He was right and Quinn knew it. The place had driven him nuts for as long as he could remember. In the twenty-year prediction section of his high school yearbook, Quinn had written that he was going to be "anywhere but Stone Harbor."

Yet there he was, which was quite an irony, one his cousin pressed him on. "Why don't you just sell the paper and leave?" Seth asked. "Go back to Florida. God, I don't think I can take you whining about another winter."

"It's not that simple." Quinn remembered when it had been. Then after Jake died, Paul pressed him to come home.

"So what are you gonna do, just sell the paper and say the hell with everyone who works there?" his friend had asked.

"I left Stone Harbor and the *Pilot* behind a long time ago," Quinn said.

"You may have tried, but you didn't really," Paul said. "And the only way to fix whatever you ran away from is to come back."

Quinn considered that. Hell, he'd done more than consider it. He'd taken the advice and look where it had gotten him. Now he was sitting across from his cousin, considering the opposite advice.

"I get calls from brokers all the time," Seth said. "They're interested. They're willing to connect us with serious buyers who will put serious offers on the table. Instead of losing money every month, you could walk away with a fortune. I could even walk away looking pretty good."

Quinn was shaking his head back and forth. "I can't sell."

"The hell you can't." Seth's cheeks were starting to flush. "Have you been listening to a word I've said?"

"You're the one who should listen: I'm not going to sell the *Pilot*."

"Why not?"

Quinn didn't answer.

"You don't belong here," Seth said. "You never have. That's why you left before and that's why you should leave now."

"It's what my father would have expected."

Seth looked at him more closely. "So you're staying just to prove him wrong? Is that a good enough reason?"

"It's part of it, but far from all of it."

Seth gave a loud sigh. "And God help those of us caught in the fallout as you and Sears fight over a girl."

"That's not what this is about."

"Isn't it?"

"Hardly." Quinn decided to end the conversation before he broke his left fist on Seth's skull.

A MOMENT LATER HE was walking down Front Street's brick sidewalk.

"Mr. John!" a voice boomed out. It was Nate Morrison—lover of women, teller of tales, outdoors columnist for the *Pilot* and registered Maine guide—standing with hands on hips, his shirt open halfway to his navel and an arrowhead dangling from a gold chain on his thick, gray-haired chest.

"Nathan!" Quinn yelled back.

"Well, my Gawd—look at you—still full a piss and vinegar." Nate eyeballed him from head to toe as he approached. "No worse for the wear aftah your recent legal entanglements."

Quinn held up his plastered hand.

Nate's eyes lit up at the sight. "I heard you pasted him a

good one." Nate patted him on the shoulder. "I don't know what he did, but I know he must have had it coming."

Quinn appreciated the vote of confidence. "So where you headed?"

"Mr. Gould and I have a professional engagement."

"I see."

The two men walked together to the water's edge and Nate broke into a wide grin. "There she is!" he thundered.

The *Pot O' Gold* had two decks and was painted the color of its namesake; it was tied to bleached pilings surrounded by seaweed and splinters of wood that slopped in the dark water. Dozens of sailboats were anchored just past the docks, the bare masts wagging back and forth as the hulls rocked in the tide. Stone Harbor had gotten its name from the granite shores that lined its entrance, and farther out, hundreds of seals sunned themselves on the rocks. The air was thick with gulls cawing in the wake of incoming lobster boats.

"This is our third group today," Nate said, nodding toward a mix of potbellied men in NYPD hats and T-shirts, young mothers in Capri pants and their energetic children, along with elderly couples in hats and Windbreakers, khakis and bright white sneakers.

Nate and Ernie went out as many times as the market would bear and charged tourists twelve bucks a pop.

"See any puffins this morning?" Quinn asked.

"Well, now that you mention it . . ."

"I mean real ones."

Nate grinned again and shook his head. Quinn knew that on the rare occasions when the birds were thin on Egg Island and the tourists were thick on the *Pot O' Gold*, Nate wouldn't say anything to detract from the guests' oohs and aahs as the cameras were snapping. He just never had the heart to tell them they were shooting pictures of decoys, which looked identical to the real things, except the wooden birds only had one leg.

"They're awful still," Quinn said the one time he'd witnessed the deception.

"And awful convenient," Nate exclaimed after he collected a few hundred dollars in tips from the grateful photographers who now had another Maine adventure to tell back home.

Quinn, for his part, had experienced enough recent adventures. He turned away from Nate and saw Ernie smiling at the top of the gangplank.

Ernie walked over when he saw him. "My Gawd, it's the light heavyweight champ himself."

Quinn felt his face flush as a few tourists jostled to get a better look.

"Maybe you ought to sign a few autographs," Ernie suggested.

"Come on. If I wanted to be mocked, I'd go back to work and listen to my cousin."

Ernie's jovial nature disappeared. "He's got no room to talk."

Nate muttered in agreement.

Quinn wished he hadn't mentioned Seth, and nodded toward the restaurant to change the subject. "I see your sign's still up."

"Yep. But that's not the big problem anymore. Now they're ticketing everyone who stays in the town lot more'n an hour, which means my customahs."

"Then I guess it's time for a follow-up story."

Ernie agreed. "And then some."

"Been an interestin' summer, that's for sure," Nate said.

"Too interesting," Quinn said. "So what do you think of the town selling the park?"

The guide shrugged. "No matter to me, really. It's a nice piece a land but it's been off limits to hunters since the boys lit out. Now the private owners have gone and posted everythin' around it."

"Who are the private owners?"

"Don't really know. Those woods have always been open, till this spring. I used to go back now and again to gun partridge. But nobody's gonna be doin' much a that anymore—at least not legally."

"So what is it they'll be doing?"

Nate grinned once more and waved good-bye as he climbed onto the boat. "That, my dear John, is somethin' else you should look into."

15.

THE NEXT MORNING JACK was surprised to find his father in the kitchen.

"Hungry?" Quinn asked as he pulled a chair out for him.

"Yep."

"Good, because I've got eggs Benedict with asparagus and Canadian bacon—and sausage." Quinn chuckled as he turned the spattering links with a fork and served his son by carefully balancing a plate on his cast. "This is really the way to start the day."

Jack eyed the heaping food without much enthusiasm.

"What's the problem?" Quinn asked.

"Usually Mom gives me cereal," Jack explained.

"Cereal!" Quinn cried. "I stay home to make you a real breakfast and you're talking about cereal?"

"I was just sayin'..." Jack began, before hesitating.

"...that you couldn't wait to have a great big, home-cooked breakfast," Quinn said.

"No."

"Then what were you saying?"

Jack wasn't sure, so he went for a simpler approach. "I was just sayin' we can't eat if you keep talkin'!"

"Good point." Quinn sat down beside him and they ate in silence, until Maria came in and pulled up a chair of her own.

"Hey—what's cooking, besides a heart attack?" she asked.

"Jack and I are having eggs," Quinn said, a little defensively. "We haven't had eggs in a while." He wasn't sure if the poor kid had even heard of sausage, since Maria was convinced Quinn was going to die of a cardiac-related event and refused to allow unhealthy food in their home. She also hounded him about his diet, lack of exercise and stress level. None of this nagging helped with the stress, but she was concerned—and persistent—and he didn't see any point in arguing.

Jack didn't care. He held up his plate for seconds, which Quinn took as a compliment.

"So these aren't so bad after all," he said.

"Nope." At forty-five pounds, Jack was an eating machine.

"I used to make eggs like this for my father," Quinn said as he carefully ladled out another poached egg. But he decided not to mention that they were supposed to cure the old man's hangovers.

OF COURSE, THOSE WERE the mornings when he'd made it home. On really bad nights Jake would leave the Laughing Gull, stagger back to the office and pass out. In a chair. Under a desk. On the composing room floor. It didn't matter. A few hours later, after a whore's bath in the men's room, a shave and some Aqua Velva, he'd be ready to face the new day with a vengeance—whether or not the new day was ready to face him.

He thought his family didn't know, and whenever his son questioned him, Jake would say he'd been too busy working to come home. "That's because I have a difficult job," he'd say.

"Something you wouldn't understand. You had everything handed to you. You didn't have to come up the way I did."

"But you don't have to stay down in it, either," Quinn answered on a Saturday morning when he'd had it with his father's behavior. Jake had a temper. "An Irish temper," he used to say. On that particular morning, alone in the newsroom, he told his son not to press him.

Quinn was happy to take the challenge. "And is your Irish heritage an excuse for being a slobbering drunk?"

Jake didn't answer. Instead, his overhand left knocked Quinn across a desk into a wastebasket, where he lay crumpled and discarded like yesterday's news.

He was fourteen years old.

Quinn never said another word about the drinking, but never forgot what it was like to be hit in the face by his own father. To make things worse, he lied to his mother about how he'd gotten the black eye. For whatever reason, he always found himself covering up for Jake's behavior, from either embarrassment or pity.

His own son's voice jarred him from the memory. "Aunt Blythe says you look like Grandpa Jake."

"I don't know about that," Quinn said.

"I remember him," Jack insisted, though it wasn't possible.

"You only saw him once," Quinn said.

"He was tall and he called me Big Buddy," Jack said matter-of-factly. "But he died."

"That's right," Maria said. "He had a heart attack."

"He was seventy years old," Quinn insisted. "And it's not like he took very good care of himself."

"No, he didn't," Maria said. "He spent all his time worrying about the *Pilot*—and that's where he died, pounding a fist down on a page-one flat."

"Relax," Quinn said. "We switched to full pagination my first month back, so we don't have any more composing room flats for me to look at, let alone pound my fist on. Unfortunately, the system cost eight hundred and fifty thousand bucks and put us even further in debt."

"See, that's all you do—worry about your newspaper."

"Then stop telling me it's gonna kill me," he said, laughing. "That's just one more thing to worry about."

"This isn't funny."

"I know it's not funny," he said. "It's serious stuff. That's why I'm taking today off."

"And that's supposed to be a big deal?" she asked, though she was actually very glad to hear it. "This is Saturday. Normal people don't work every weekend."

"That just shows I'm turning over a new leaf," Quinn insisted. "Jack and I are going hiking. We aren't even stopping in the office to read the papers."

She raised her eyebrows when he said that. "Make sure you have your cell phone."

"I'm trying to cut down my stress," Quinn said, shaking his head. "A ringing cell phone would only add to it."

She didn't think that was funny, either. "Put it on vibrate."

"I don't know how."

She snatched his phone from the counter, changed the ringer and handed it to him. "Here. Knowing you have this will cut down on *my* stress," she said firmly.

He put an arm around her hip. "Honey, I'm flattered," he said.

"Don't be." She stepped out of his embrace. "I was thinking of Jack." She looked at her son. "Now, don't let your father overdo it."

"Okay."

Finally, she smiled. Jack was so serious-looking when he agreed that she couldn't help herself. "I'll see you boys later." She leaned down to kiss Jack on the cheek. Then she swatted her husband on the behind. "I'm off to run a few errands."

Once she was gone, Quinn turned to their son and smiled. "More eggs?"

Jack nodded eagerly and they both went at them.

When they were finished, Quinn asked if Jack had packed provisions.

"What are provisions?"

"Stuff to eat. Stuff to drink. You get pretty hungry when you're hiking," Quinn said as he scanned the counter for possibilities. "Let's see. These bananas would be good." He tossed them in a backpack, along with six granola bars, then looked in the fridge and found some leftover tamales in a Styrofoam takeout container.

"And this," Jack said, adding a box of bran cereal.

Quinn opened it and tried some. "I can't believe your mother feeds you this." He made a sour face. "This stuff tastes like bark."

"You ever eat bark?" Jack asked, doubtful, but curious nonetheless.

Quinn looked down at the little skeptic. "Of course I've eaten bark," he said. "Plenty of times. Have you?"

"No!"

"Then we better find something more than this, because believe me, you don't wanna eat bark." Quinn started rifling through the cupboards. He didn't even know what half the crap was: muesli, protein powder, soy granules. "When I was your age and your grandfather was mad, he used to make me eat bark, and from the looks of this stuff your mother feeds us, things haven't changed."

"Grandpa Jake never made you eat bark!"

"Oh, yes he did, and unless I chewed very carefully, it could get pretty splintery." Quinn peered in the pack, then added sunscreen, two light jackets and four bottles of water.

"Where's the cell phone?" Jack asked.

"This is about nature, not cell phones."

"Mom said you should take it."

"Well, here's the difference between you and me," Quinn said. "When your mother tells you something, it's an order. When she tells me something, it's an option."

Jack held his finger up to his mouth and smiled. "You better not say that!"

Quinn laughed. He had nothing to worry about: Maria had driven off fifteen minutes earlier.

FOR HER PART, MARIA didn't mean to be such a nag. She just worried about her husband and son and didn't think John worried nearly enough. He went through life without a second thought—head-on and reckless—which often put him at odds with everyone else, especially everyone else in Stone Harbor, with its social cliques, insular traditions and smug attitudes toward anything new or unexpected. Now he'd actually gone and hit someone—the chief of police, no less. Public ridicule was the least of his worries. This time he could go to jail. Maria was at her wit's end.

When she pulled into the parking lot of the Hanaford

Brothers grocery store, an old woman in a Crown Victoria honked at her for taking a spot—one of three available.

Maria shrugged her shoulders. "Sorry!"

Mrs. Liver Spot On Her Wrinkled Forehead displayed typical Yankee friendliness and turned her head as she pulled her car in so crookedly, it took one of the remaining spaces and a foot of the next, which was already filled by an Audi SUV.

Good luck getting out, Maria thought as she switched on her door locks and hurried across the pavement. She noticed Police Chief Al Sears watching from a white Ford Explorer idling in the fire lane.

He waved and smiled.

She meekly waved back. Normally she liked to be noticed. This time she was mortified. The chief was such a nice man and her crazy husband had actually gone and hit him. When John tried to explain why he'd done it, Maria had immediately called Lizz, who said she was fine. Whatever happened between the two men, Lizz explained, had nothing to do with her. The conflict went back years. Maria loved her husband but this was so embarrassing.

It was even worse when Al Sears rolled down his window. "Where's Jack?" he asked.

"Out with his father," Maria said, stumbling over the words. Then she just blurted it out: "I'm sorry John hit you."

"I'm fine," Sears assured her.

"Well, if it's any consolation, he'll be wearing that damn cast for six weeks, which serves him right."

Sears warmed considerably at the news. "So why's he leavin' his beautiful wife all alone on a nice day like this?"

"They're hiking the hills behind Sullivan Park."

"Really?" Sears seemed surprised.

"Believe me, I'll manage without them," she said, smiling. "I have enough errands to last all day."

"Well, I better let you get to them," Sears said. "Enjoy your Saturday." But before he drove away, he allowed himself a long look in his rearview mirror.

At Sullivan Park, Quinn pulled his Volvo wagon to the side of the road at the gate. The No Trespassing sign "issued under the authority of the board of selectmen" was the same as it had been all summer, but the road had been rutted and torn by heavy equipment. The dirt mounds and logs were gone and fresh mud smeared the path. "Well, I'll be damned," he said.

Soon loose gravel was popping under their sneakers as they walked along. It was a pleasant day, full of blue skies, sunshine and birds singing in the trees. When they got to where the flattened bathhouse had stood, the only thing left was a concrete slab, though in the distance, Quinn could see surveyors' flags close to the tree line.

"Why are there flags?" Jack asked as he pulled one up, then punctuated his question by pointing his prize at Quinn and waving it back and forth as though it were a sword.

"They're taking measurements," Quinn said. "They must be building something, so put that back where you found it."

Jack crookedly replaced his flag and tilted his head sideways to see how he'd done.

"Close enough," Quinn said. Jack wasn't sure, but Quinn coaxed him along. "Hey—remember nature?"

"Yep."

"Well, it's right this way."

They took the trail down to the water and walked beside

twisted granite ledges. A few feet away, waves sprayed weathered rocks and bearded seaweed twisted in the current. On-
shore, the low tide left shallow pools of knotted wrack,
rockweed and blue-green algae. Quinn was studying one of
them when Jack tossed what must have been a five-pound
rock into the brackish water.

"Hey!" Quinn shouted. "Watch what you're doing."

Jack laughed and launched another.

"Stop it!"

Before Jack could throw a third, Quinn strained to drop a
small boulder into the pool, soaking them both.

"I can't believe you did that!" Jack shouted.

"Neither can I," Quinn admitted as rings spread along the
water's surface. The big rock had almost slipped out of his bad
hand and onto his toes.

Jack lifted his forearm to his nose. "Now we smell!"

They did, too, like ammonia and slime. "Oh, we'll dry off,"
Quinn insisted.

"We better!"

"Trust me," Quinn said. "We won't melt."

"Look!" Jack said. "Crabs!"

Sure enough, tiny green crabs scuttled through the weedy
brine.

"And a starfish!" Jack said.

It was amazing, the things the little boy noticed. And it
was amazing, the things his father missed, such as the vehicle
that had followed them that morning, then parked near another trail.

MARIA SET THE BAGS on the table and surveyed the damage to the stove and counter, which were stacked with yolky

plates and pans. She sighed. At least they'd given her an esti-
mate for when to have dinner—and time to clean the kitchen
and prepare something nice from the groceries she'd bought.
She planned a cold gazpacho appetizer, a tossed salad and
grilled chicken with avocados and mangoes. It was healthy,
light and simple.

She went to the fridge, opened a bottle of pinot grigio and
poured a glass. The wine was dry and crisp and perfect for a
summer afternoon—or at least the bright, windy day that
passed for one on the coast of Maine.

"Summer's not usually like this," John always insisted
whenever she complained about the cool weather.

She didn't believe him but tried to tell herself not to be so
negative. *You need to relax,* she thought as she sipped her wine.
You should be tired of the tension.

Maybe John was right.

Maybe she got worked up over nothing.

She had another glass of wine and the kitchen no longer
felt as cold and drafty. Her boys would be home soon enough.
In the meantime, she decided to take a little nap, so she curled
up in a comforter on the couch and went to sleep.

"How you holding up?" Quinn asked Jack as they
neared the top of a hill overlooking the harbor. They'd been
hiking, on and off, for quite a while and Quinn didn't want to
overdo it.

"I think this goes to a castle," Jack said, ignoring the question from atop his father's shoulders.

"A castle?"

Jack grinned and nodded as Quinn bent over to let him
slide to the ground.

"Then we better find it," Quinn said, and they followed the worn piles over gentle hills of white birch and spruce.

"It's gonna be right here." Jack ran ahead into an unexpected clearing. The razed trees didn't make sense to either of them, until Quinn saw the freshly graded dirt road. "Hey, more flags," Jack said.

Quinn couldn't believe Jack still had the energy to run to them. Maybe it hadn't been such a good idea to carry him the past few miles. While Jack had his second wind, Quinn was exhausted.

"Look at that!" Jack pointed to a bulldozer. "Can we ride it?"

"We can pretend," Quinn said as he lifted him into the seat. "Just be careful not to pull any levers."

Jack made a rumbling noise and shook in the seat to simulate driving while Quinn surveyed the scene. Hilly islands stretched through the haze all the way to the horizon, where clouds were beginning to gather. Below them, Stone Harbor's white steeples and Wellsen's brick Memorial Hall peeked through green treetops. He had no idea who was cashing in on the location but made a mental note to find out. In the meantime, he looked over at Jack, who was still caught up in the heavy equipment. "Ready to go?" Quinn asked.

"Yeah," Jack said reluctantly. "Too bad we can't take this home."

"What would you do with a bulldozer?"

"I'd bulldoze the garage. The fence. And the neighbors' cat."

"The neighbors' cat?" Quinn asked. "I thought you liked Muffy."

"She makes the backyard smell like pee."

That's when a shot rang out, loud and unexpected. For an instant, Quinn froze as the bullet hit the dozer blade and ricocheted into the trees. Then he grabbed his son and crouched, trying to figure out where it had come from.

"Are they shooting at us?" Jack asked.

"They probably don't know we're here," Quinn lied.

"Hey!" Jack started to shout before Quinn cupped his good hand over his mouth.

"Don't say anything," he whispered.

A second shot rang out.

After that, Quinn picked the little boy up and ran for the path with everything he had. Slipping in the loose dirt, he clung to Jack as a third shot whizzed overhead. In an instant he was up again, determined to gain as much distance as his burning lungs could handle.

At the crest of the hill they were the most exposed, so Quinn tore over the loose rocks and scrub. Soon they were in the slanting light beneath the trees and the cover became thicker and the air cooler. Jack squeezed his father's neck and Quinn stumbled over the roots that split the hardened trail, which dropped and carried them forward with their own momentum. Quinn's left arm felt like it was going to fall off from Jack's weight, and his right arm—heavy and stiff in the cast—wasn't much help. But he kept running and didn't look back.

16.

MARIA WOKE WITH A headache. Her mouth felt sandy and dry from the bottle of wine she'd emptied and her back ached from the well-worn couch. Mother of Christ. She hadn't meant to drink so much. She sat up and let her eyes focus on the sitting room beyond the front staircase. Light split the darkness through the bay window and left a soft glow on the Queen Anne furniture and the framed pictures of her dead in-laws.

Jake Quinn smiled out from a black-and-white print, taken at his desk in the early 1960s, with his trusty Olivetti typewriter in front of him, a cigarette cradled in his left hand and his right fist shaking at the camera. He wore a crew cut, white shirtsleeves and a black tie.

In the other shot, Gwen Quinn was laughing and leaning against a boulder in a loose summer dress, with Penobscot Bay behind her. She was a free spirit who knew how to live, whether that meant spending the spring in Spain or going on a snow-shoeing expedition to Labrador.

It was odd Jake and Gwen weren't pictured together, but what did it matter? They were both dead and gone. Looking at their images a while longer, she saw her husband in both of them: he had Gwen's bright eyes and smile and Jake's size, hard jaw, sharp nose and Irish coloring.

At that moment, Maria felt cold and terribly alone. Shivering, she went to the hall closet and got a sweater, then put the kettle on for tea before she looked at the clock and wondered why John and Jack weren't home.

THE WOODS WERE QUIET and the thick canopy of trees blocked most of the light, but they stayed huddled together. Quinn should have taken the hint when the car tires had been slashed and stayed away from the park, or from whatever he was getting close to there.

He signaled with his good hand for Jack to keep quiet. With eyes wider than ever, his son nodded like he understood and they waited . . . for nothing. After ten minutes that seemed like two days, Quinn finally asked if Jack wanted his jacket.

The little boy shook his head no.

"If you get cold, let me know."

"Okay."

They got up and walked even farther off the trail, careful not to make a sound.

"Did you hear that?" Jack asked.

"Hear what?"

"Listen!"

Quinn froze till they both heard a crash among the nearby bushes.

He spun around, backed up and fell, only to see a moose deliberately wading through the underbrush with no more effort than it took to walk through a flower garden.

Quinn grabbed Jack, and as he pressed against him, they watched the big bull patiently chewing plants and leaves—

completely indifferent to their stares. For a moment it turned its head in their direction before stepping through the branches and disappearing, as if it had never been there at all. Its musky odor lingered while they considered whether to move or wait and see what else would come their way.

"Where are we?" Jack asked.

"Near the coast. We just need to see the bay to get our bearings."

"I don't see water."

"It's out there."

"Can we call Mom?"

"We didn't bring the cell phone."

"I did." Jack fished the phone out of his pocket and held it up in front of his face.

"You're a smart kid," Quinn said gratefully.

Jack dialed the number, but before Maria had a chance to pick up, Quinn covered Jack's mouth since it was suddenly a very a bad time to talk.

"Hello," she said after she'd read the caller ID. "John? Jack? What's going on?"

The call ended.

She immediately dialed the number, to no effect.

Damn. How could they do that to her?

But she didn't stop there. Right away she called Seth, who was dining with his beloved Meredith at the country club. "Something's wrong," she said. "John and Jack went hiking hours ago and now I got a call, but then we lost service."

"They'll call back," Seth said. "It goes in and out in those hills."

"I think they need help."

"Hey, John needs to get outside and relax," Seth said, pretty much ignoring her concern. "He's been under too much stress. The woods will do him good."

"It's been eight hours."

Seth thought about that. "Did they take any food?"

"I don't know."

He told Maria she was worked up over nothing. "John, Paul and Lizz used to backpack all the time. They probably climbed Mt. Katahdin a half dozen times," he said, referring to the state's highest peak. "He can take care of himself in the woods."

Maria wasn't so sure. "I have a bad feeling."

"Don't worry," Seth assured her. "Maybe we can all meet later for a drink."

Disgusted, Maria hung up. She waited fifteen minutes without getting another call, then went back into action.

Sarah Sewell told her she should check the office. "You know he has a habit of showing up and staying for hours," she said.

But they weren't at the *Pilot*.

The police dispatcher told Maria she'd send a cruiser out to see if his Volvo was still in the parking lot.

"Then what?"

"We'll let you know."

The fire dispatcher asked if she'd called the police.

"Yes, I did," she said. "They're checking the parking lot."

"Then we'll find out soon enough."

"To hell with it," Maria said to herself before pulling a business card from her purse. Al Sears's cell phone number was on the back. John could say what he wanted, she wasn't too proud to seek the chief's help.

Sears offered to pick her up at the house, but she declined.

"I'll meet you at the park," she said.

"All right. Make sure you wait for me."

"Where are you?" Maria asked, since he sounded out of breath.

"Outside," he said. "But I'll be there quicker than you can blink."

"Thank you!"

SHE HAD NO IDEA her husband and son were crouched behind a fallen tree, frozen in fear as the sound of cracking twigs grew louder. The shooter was almost there. Quinn couldn't get a look and didn't dare move, so he stayed put with his hands over his son's mouth until the danger passed. They waited a full ten minutes, then began moving in the other direction.

Quinn hadn't seen the bay in a while and they hadn't come across the stone wall, flags or other markings. Instead, they were heading deeper into the trees. More than an hour passed and he was certain they were alone.

"It's getting dark," Jack said.

"We'll have plenty of daylight as soon as we find a clearing."

"We been here a long time."

"I know." Quinn stopped to get his bearings. "It's confusing."

"Call Mom."

Quinn opened the cell phone and handed it to Jack. "I'm afraid this thing needs a charge."

Jack sadly looked at the phone to make sure it was true before quietly putting it in his pocket.

Quinn took off his pack and reached inside for a jacket. "Maybe you better put this on," he said. The temperature had dropped, the wind had picked up and the sky had darkened. "The weather feels like it's about to change."

Quinn leaned against a fallen pine and pulled his son onto his lap. It was dark but not that cold, but they had a long night ahead. "Do you want any more cereal?" he asked.

"It's gone," Jack said. "But we could eat some bark."

"Very funny."

Despite the circumstances, they both laughed after he said it. "You know," Quinn added, "I'd eat some bark if we had any water left."

"It's okay," Jack said as he rested his cheek on Quinn's shoulder. "I know you'll take care of me."

His son still had faith in him, though Quinn couldn't understand why. Soon Jack was asleep inside his father's jacket, which was buttoned over them both. The boy felt small and fragile against him. They were lost and there was no use denying it. Walking around would only reinforce the point. Quinn figured the best thing was to stay warm and dry and wait for daylight.

At least they were safe.

Maria knew they were out there.

The temperature was in the low fifties and they had nothing to worry about—until the rain came. It fell softly at first, just a warning, really, before the drops came harder and started to sound like bullets hitting the rocks and trees. Then it was a total downpour.

17.

"I HAVE HALF A notion to leave the numb shit out there all night," Sears told Earl Stufflebeam. They were standing in the parking lot at Sullivan Park, where a makeshift command center had been formed. The rain showed no sign of letting up, and the muck was ankle-deep and getting worse. "Everyone's goin' through all this trouble because of that fool."

"He could be hurt," Earl said. "And he has a six-year-old with him."

Sears understood. He'd spoken with the mother on the phone and was about to speak with her again. A few yards away, as she shivered in a short jacket, thin jeans and sandals, the chief draped his Gore-Tex raincoat over her shoulders.

"You're very kind," she said.

The headlights from one of the cars caught Sears's smile. "You look like you need it more than me."

"Will you be all right out in this?" she asked.

"I don't plan on bein' out long," Sears said. "Besides, I've nevah been affected much by weathah." He still had on rain pants and a wicking turtleneck.

"My son has asthma," she said. "This could be very dangerous."

"Don't worry." Sears squeezed her shoulder. "I'll find him."

"Thank you."

"You're more than welcome." He lingered a moment on her sad, frightened eyes, then turned to focus on the task at hand. He pulled a two-foot-long, stainless steel Maglite from his belt, snapped on the beam and started walking.

Earl fell in behind.

"Wait here," Sears said flatly.

"Shouldn't we go together?" Earl asked.

"If they're out there, I'll find 'em."

"The volunteer firemen are taking spotting scopes along the construction roads," Earl said hopefully.

"Then our lost little hikers are sure to turn up, one way or another." Sears had no doubt. He'd hunted and roamed the hills since the Sullivan boys farmed the place and had a pretty strong suspicion of where Quinn had gotten turned around. So he followed the only decent trail past the construction road. Chances were that was the route they'd taken.

"*Quinn!*" he shouted, though the sound of his voice was broken by the pounding rain. Sears shined his light back and forth as he made his way down the trail. They couldn't have gotten very far in the loose and unforgiving terrain. Though in that weather, anything could have happened.

QUINN'S LIMBS ACHED AND his feet stung with cold. Jack seemed heavier than ever. They'd been slumped against a downed birch tree, trying to recover. "You warm enough?" Quinn asked.

"I'm all right."

"Can you breathe okay?"

"Yes." To prove his point, Jack took a deep, wheezy breath and his small chest rattled from the effort.

"I have to get you out of here." Quinn figured the best approach was to keep going in one direction, whichever direction that was, so he stepped slowly until he regained circulation in his knees. It was very dark and he was unsure of his footing, but with each step he began to regain his confidence until he stepped into water.

The shock of the frigid stream staggered Quinn, who caught his balance for a second before falling to his hands and knees, which soaked them both.

"*Dad!*" Jack shouted.

"You okay?" Quinn asked.

"I'm wet."

"Me, too." Suddenly they were also very cold.

"How far to the car?" Jack asked.

"We have to be getting close."

"What if we're not?"

"Then we have to keep going." And that's what they did.

THE WAIT WAS ALMOST more than Maria could stand. She was sitting in the chief's SUV with Earl Stufflebeam as the rain came down so hard it sounded like it would tear through the metal roof.

"Is it ever going to let up?" she asked.

"Sure," Earl assured her. "It can't rain this hard for long."

"What if they're out there all night?" Her eyes were wide with fear.

"They won't be." Earl patted her knee, then felt awkward and embarrassed that he had.

She didn't seem to notice. "How do you know anyone will find them before daylight? It's already pitch-black."

"The chief will find 'em," Earl said confidently. "You can take that to the bank." But to himself, Earl had to wonder what was going to happen when he did. Damn. He wished he'd ignored Sears's warning and gone into the woods.

LESS THAN TWO MILES away, Quinn was in water again and Jack was standing on a boulder.

"Dad, come up here," Jack said.

"Just stay put."

"All right." Jack tottered forward a bit before wobbling back on his heels, which put Quinn's heart through his stomach.

"Hold still!" Quinn said as he rushed toward him.

Despite the darkness, he could see Jack trying the cell phone once more. "What are we gonna do?" Jack asked.

"I don't know." Quinn picked him up again.

"Hey—look!" Jack said as a light bounced in the distance.

Quinn watched it come closer, the beam broken and split by the trees. For a moment he wondered if they should take cover, but at that late hour, it had to be someone Maria sent to find them. At least that's what he thought. Or maybe he wasn't even capable of thinking clearly. *"Over here!"* he shouted.

"Who is it?" Jack asked.

"Hey!" Quinn kept shouting. *"Right here!"*

The beam seemed to be going past them.

"Over here!" they both shouted together.

It stopped moving. A flood of light swept in their direction.

"Quinn—is that you?" It was Sears.

"Yes."

"Walk toward me!"

Quinn hesitated. "There's a stream out there somewhere." He could hear the rushing water, though the sound was mixed with the hard rain.

"I'm on dry ground," Sears said. "Come on!"

Quinn tried. That's when the footing gave way and the current knocked them into the dark, swirling water. The cold gripped them and they struggled to breathe as their heads bobbed up and down. Quinn cradled Jack to protect him from the rocks and limbs. His jacket was being shredded until he managed to catch a low-lying branch with his left arm and hang on while Jack clung to him.

"Jesus Christ!" Quinn shouted to Sears. "Why didn't you tell me about the water?"

"I didn't see it!"

Quinn lunged forward against the stream and held out his son. "Take him!"

"All right," Sears said. "Come on, kid!"

Jack wouldn't let go of his father.

"Go with him," Quinn shouted. "Al, get him. Please!"

Sears finally got his hands around Jack and pulled him away.

"*Dad!*" Jack shouted as Quinn fell again, this time in a deep pool.

Fueled by the downpour, the current was deep and powerful. Quinn struggled to breach the surface as his lungs were about to burst. Finally, he did—but only for an instant before going down again. His soaked cast felt like an anchor. Worse, his strength was fading. In the darkness, he had no sense of direction and scraped the bottom. He thought of his son, alone with Sears, and was angry and kicking again. His clothes were heavy and he'd swallowed a lot of water. He was afraid he wouldn't make it when he surfaced one more time, panting and thrashing. *"Hey!"* Quinn shouted.

Sears was walking away with Jack, who was squirming to look back toward his father. Quinn crawled on his knees in rushing water that was now only a foot deep. He pushed himself onto the bank. *"Al!"* he shouted.

Sears turned the light on Quinn, who coughed and gagged and held up his good hand to shield his eyes from the bright beam. "Your pretty wife is worried about the two of you," Sears said. "She told me you left at eleven o'clock this morning. It's pushing ten o'clock at night."

Quinn was too tired to answer.

"We bettah get goin'," Sears said.

"He's hurt!" Jack said as he tried to twist out of Sears's arms.

"I'm okay."

"The firemen have been out here two hours," Sears said. "I don't know if they'll be glad to see you or will wanna wring your neck."

"I don't blame them." Quinn pushed himself to his feet and sloshed forward. "I should have my neck wrung."

Sears thought he'd come pretty close.

"Does my mom know where we're at?" Jack asked.

"She will soon enough," Sears said. Then he asked Jack if he was hungry.

"A little."

He handed him a bag of trail mix and a bottle of water.

Jack thanked him and dug in.

Quinn didn't have the energy to take back his son as they

slogged out of the woods. Sears led the way with Jack in his arms and barely glanced over his shoulder during the next half hour to see if Quinn was keeping up.

When they got back to the parking lot, Maria was talking to a volunteer. Her arms were crossed and she looked more tense than usual. She rushed over when she saw them. "How could you have done this?" she asked Quinn.

"Believe me, it wasn't intentional."

"That doesn't make it any better." She looked down at Jack's bare left foot. "Where's his other sneaker?"

"It fell off," Jack said matter-of-factly.

"John, he's covered with mud."

"It'll wash off."

"No, it won't wash off," she said as she wrapped Jack in a heavy wool blanket one of the firemen had given her. "Not everything washes off, no matter what you seem to think."

18.

QUINN WALKED INTO THE kitchen in a hooded sweat-shirt, sweatpants and bathrobe. His skin was flushed after a long, steaming soak in the tub and his neck was draped in a towel. As he sat down at the table, Maria stared oddly at him.

"What is it?" he wanted to know.

"Your hand," she finally said. "What happened to your cast?"

"I cut it off."

"By yourself?" she asked, eyebrows raised.

"Well, it's not like it was made of titanium," he said, tapping a finger on the oak. "I used a steak knife."

She looked at him in disbelief. "And what do you plan on doing now?"

He stared down at his palm, which was still pale and rotten-smelling, then up at her again. "I didn't mention this earlier," he said quietly, "but the real reason we got lost is that someone was shooting at us."

"Why didn't you tell the police?"

"Because I don't trust them."

She lifted a hand to her cheek and sighed. "Then who do you trust?"

"I trust you," he said. "I trust Seth. And I trust Angus."

"What about Lizz? She called to ask how you and Jack were doing. Do you trust her?"

He carefully chose his words before answering. "I don't trust her judgment."

"But I'm supposed to trust yours?" Maria stood up and went to the stove. "I can't believe you," she said, her voice rising over a whistling tea kettle. "You have something like that happen and keep it to yourself?" She picked up the kettle, then slammed it back down for emphasis. "Think about your son! Think about me!"

"I have been."

"So have I." She calmly turned off the burner, picked the kettle back up and poured two cups of tea. "That's why I'm taking Jack away for a while."

"Good idea!" He was relieved at the thought. "Your mother will be glad to see you."

She slowly shook her head. "I don't want to go that far— unless you come with us."

"You know I can't. Not now."

"That's what I figured." Maria set a cup in front of him, along with a pair of keys. "Lizz said we could use her place in Old Orchard Beach."

He reconsidered his earlier enthusiasm as he picked up the key chain and pictured the small cottage among dozens of others along the southern Maine coast. "So you've been thinking about this for a while?"

"Yes."

He mentally calculated how safe the crowded little resort town would be. "Who else knows about this?"

"Nobody."

"Let's keep it that way," Quinn said. "Everyone can think you're in Miami. It'll be safer."

"What about you?"

"I need to find out who's trying to scare me off."

"What if they want to do more than that?" she asked.

He held up both his hands, then clenched and unclenched them. "Then I guess I better be ready."

THE NEXT MORNING, QUINN still found himself looking over his shoulder—not that he could see much. Fog had socked in the entire coast, and dawn was marked by only a slightly lighter shade of gray. Pulling out of the driveway, he could barely make out a few feet of green grass in the yard; his headlights barely penetrated the rest. Overhead, the occasional streetlight glowed in the mist, offering little in the way of guidance along the pavement below.

Maria and Jack had called from the beach house shortly after midnight, and he hadn't slept since. He was still on edge as he made his way through the quiet streets past the shadows of the navy destroyers along the waterfront. He'd left earlier than normal and had beaten the first-shift traffic into Bliley's Newsstand. Everything felt heavy and cold and he found himself shivering as he opened the door.

"Editor Quinn." Bliley handed over the day's papers, his eyes lingering on Quinn's bruised face.

"Thanks." Quinn left without the usual chitchat.

A few blocks later, he mounted the creaking *Pilot* stairs. Inside, his steps echoed across the floor until he flicked on the bank of newsroom lights. The electric hum did little to reassure him as he sat at his desk. No matter how hard he tried, he couldn't concentrate on the *Globe*. He could only wonder who'd shot at them in the park. Was it Sears? Bowen-Smythe? Someone else? The possibilities ran through his head.

An hour later, Sarah came in and went straight to work. In fact, nobody said a word about the day before. Instead, the staff quietly put the newspaper together, then drifted out once the presses were shaking the ancient floors.

Quinn used that as a cue to take a walk. As he strolled down Front Street, every face that appeared through the sifting fog became a question mark.

Eli Povich stood like a scarecrow in a tailored suit in front of his store.

Selectman George Baribou stepped out of his law office and smiled.

A volunteer fireman nodded in passing.

They all looked at Quinn, but he didn't know what they saw. That also went for a burly pair of shipbuilders in hard hats and a handful of Wellsen students bouncing off one another, laughing and joking past him. Tourists and locals alike crowded the sidewalk, and he felt boxed in and agitated until he stepped inside Becky's Seafood Shack and was nearly drowned by the warm, thick air.

Despite the lunchtime crowd, Ernie spotted him immediately and came over.

Quinn was relieved to see him.

"Found out somethin' very interestin' about our favorite selectman," Ernie said. "And once you write about it, signs and parking spots are gonna be the least of his worries."

"Is that so?" Quinn asked as Ernie walked him to a corner booth.

"Since the learned professor is so concerned with our business, we thought it was time somebody started lookin' into his."

"So what'd you find out?"

"Better ask him," Ernie said, pointing to the corner booth, where Angus was sitting with his elbows on the table and his hands knitted together.

Quinn sat down across from him. The older man was still pale but the spark was back in his eyes. "You look better every time I see you," Quinn said.

"And you look as bad as expected."

Quinn's bruised face was suddenly red.

"I heard what happened," Angus explained. "Word gets around."

Quinn wondered how much of it had gotten around. "So who was shooting at us?" he asked.

"My daughter-in-law."

Quinn laughed, though he wasn't sure if it was from nerves or the crazy theory.

"I wouldn't be laughing if I was you," Angus said. "She killed Paul and now she may have her hands on something that makes her even more dangerous."

"You mean the business she built for the past ten years?"

"I'm talkin' about land."

"Well, you own half the friggin' town," Quinn said. "That should make you the most dangerous man in Georges County."

"Some people think I am." Angus was dead serious. "Hell, I bought property before it was fashionable. And I paid taxes on it. That's different than the games goin' on—like sellin' a park meant for everyone to enjoy. I didn't expect much from your cousin, but I expected more than this. He listens to the wrong people."

"He just wants to avoid controversy."

"Well, he'll have it soon enough," Angus said. "Turns out

he and little 'Lizabeth could make a helluva lot of money outta that sale."

"How?"

Angus told him.

REAL ESTATE CONFLICT UNCOVERED
By John Quinn
Pilot Staff

Acting Board of Selectman Chairman Bryan Bowen-Smythe, the late Paul Stanwood and Seth Quinn, the man who replaced him on the board, bought undeveloped land around Sullivan Park two months before plans were announced to sell the 200-acre oceanfront property.

Records at the Georges County Clerk's office show Stanwood purchased 100 acres for $850,000. Bowen-Smythe bought 50 acres for $500,000. Quinn paid $400,000 for 40 acres.

Three weeks ago, Stanwood was found brutally beaten to death in the park.

Quinn, the general manager of this newspaper, dismissed any potential conflict of interest. "It's a small town," he said. "It would be hard to find a plot of land that wasn't next to a parcel owned by someone you know. It's really nothing more than that and I hope you don't try to make it into anything else."

The largest private landowner with property abutting the park is Stanwood's estate. His wife, Lizz, is expected to get the property, though his father, Angus Stanwood, is contesting the will. Angus Stanwood has owned 50 acres near the park since 1973, when he paid $25,000 for it.

"I don't exactly know what's going on, but something stinks," Angus said. "And I'll donate every last foot of my property to the Nature Conservancy before I become part of their shenanigans."

Lizz Stanwood and Bowen-Smythe couldn't be reached for comment.

In fact, she couldn't be found. Quinn had even stopped at the Stanwoods' but nobody was home. By the looks of things, nobody had been there in a while. The yard was overgrown and a week's worth of *Stone Harbor Pilot*s were piled in front of the door. The mailbox was brimming with bills and magazines and mounds of mail.

None of the neighbors had seen Lizz, so he called her sister in New Jersey. They hadn't talked since Paul's funeral.

She had cousins in Bangor, but they weren't close.

He even went back to the office and called Sears.

"I wish I knew where she was," the big cop said. "You're not the only one who wants to talk to her."

That surprised Quinn. "How about her kids?"

"No sign of them, either."

"Does she have a lawyer?"

"George Baribou has handled Rock Coast for years," Sears said matter-of-factly. "You might wanna try him. Right now he's meetin' with a friend a yours, the district attorney."

"Why?"

Sears laughed, then paused a moment before explaining. "Because she's strong as a horse and had a motive to kill her husband."

"She isn't the only one."

"What's that s'posed to mean?" Sears quickly asked, annoyed as usual by Quinn.

"It means I wonder why she took off, unless she was afraid of somebody."

"Oh, you can wonder," Sears said. "Maybe you can even ask her. It's only a matter of time before I find her."

"Then what?"

"We'll talk . . . among other things." Sears laughed again. "Oh, I could tell you stories that'd make your head spin."

Quinn was sure of it. "Just like the time you beat her to shit."

The chief's voice grew more serious. "I'll tell you what," he said flatly. "I make an arrest, I'll call you. In the meantime, stay outta my way."

Quinn still kept calling Lizz.

"It's me again . . . If you won't talk to me, can you at least call somebody else? A lot of people can help. Maria. Earl Stufflebeam. Hell, Angus would even pitch in if you told him what was really going on. You just need to let us know where you are. For God's sake, will you pick up the phone?"

Of course, she couldn't. She didn't have her cell anymore and each time Quinn left a message, Sears listened to every word, then erased it. Despite what he'd told Quinn, the chief knew exactly where Lizz was, every minute of the day. He made sure of it, not that it was difficult. She'd been going along with anything he'd wanted for a while.

At times, even Sears was surprised at how compliant she'd become. "So did you really slash that asshole's tires?" he finally asked that evening as he was dressing to go out.

"Yes."

The big cop laughed and checked his black shirt in the mirror over his dresser before deciding another color would better highlight his pecs. "Earl's pretty certain you did, and it's only a matter of time till he charges you. Hell, you can't keep hidin' here."

"I'm not hiding," Lizz insisted.

"You haven't gone anywhere in days."

"I haven't felt like it." In fact, she hadn't felt like doing much at all, which is why she was still in the T-shirt and sweatpants she'd slept in the night before, though evening was already approaching.

"Well, what's it gonna look like if you get arrested and it turns out you been stayin' with me?" He checked his profile in the mirror again. That was it. He was going with the light blue because of the way it matched his eyes.

"How could things look any worse than they do now?" she asked.

Sears turned to face her and, still smiling, said, "You don't wanna find out."

He was right: she didn't want to find out, which was why she stopped talking until he began to hum a little tune. Since he was in a good mood, she decided to press him. "So does anyone else know I fired those shots?"

"There's no danger a your boy Quinn figurin' it out," Sears said, slowly and deliberately. "He'll believe anything he's told—and people have been tellin' him a lotta things. I'd be more worried about Sarah Sewell. If anyone's capable of puttin' two and two together, it's her."

"You're sure?"

"Absolutely," Sears said, and Lizz didn't like the knowing grin on his face. "Funny, but I haven't talked to Sarah in a while."

The bastard. Lizz was certain that was about to change.

• • •

"So how is it?" Aunt Blythe asked, nodding toward her nephew's plate.

"Great," Quinn mumbled as he forced himself to swallow yet another bite of her tuna casserole. His aunt was nice enough to cook him dinner; he could be nice enough to pretend what she'd made was edible.

"You were never a very good liar, John," she said. "Your eyes always give you away."

"Sorry."

Blythe shrugged and drank from her wineglass. "I think all those years of smoking killed my taste buds," she admitted. "But it does make cooking for yourself easier."

"The wine is excellent," he offered. It was a sauvignon blanc.

Her face puckered over her dentures into a prunish smile. "That, my dear boy, is something I've never skimped on."

For that, Quinn was grateful. He was on his third glass. "So what have you heard about Lizz Stanwood?"

Blythe's eyes looked even larger than before behind her thick, round glasses. "The poor girl has had her share of problems."

"Angus thinks she was the one shooting at me."

"She competes in skeet," Blythe said. "If it was her, she was only trying to scare you away from something."

Quinn was annoyed by her nonchalance. "Aren't you a helluva comfort?"

Blythe savored a solid gulp of wine. "I do what I can."

Quinn thought about what she'd said.

"So how long is Maria staying in OOB?" Blythe asked.

"I'm not sure," Quinn said uncomfortably. "How'd you know she was there?"

She shook her head. "It's a small town."

"So plenty of people have been talking about it?"

"I'm afraid so."

He sighed and took a deep breath. He should have expected as much. Hell, his wife and son were staying at a cottage Lizz Stanwood owned, supposedly for their own protection. Yet he had no idea where Lizz was, or what her role had been in the events of the past few weeks. He also had no way of knowing how much danger Maria and Jack faced. He just knew he had to talk to them right away.

19.

SITTING ON THE CHEAP bed in a hoodie and tights, Maria Quinn stared out the cottage's second-story window. She wondered if leaving Stone Harbor had been a mistake. After all, she and Jack could have stayed with John. Despite the risk, there would have been fewer worries. But taking flight had become a habit. In the past five years they'd lived in twelve different places, an assortment of apartments, condos, beach houses and for several stretches, hotels and motels. She was tired of moving, or running, or whatever it was they always did, yet there she was again. Their son deserved better.

Jack couldn't understand anything that was happening. "When are we gonna go home?" he'd asked her.

"I'm not sure."

"Is it 'cause Dad and me got lost?"

Maria picked her son up and hugged him. "Not at all. We just needed a vacation."

"From Dad?"

"From Stone Harbor," she said. "Maybe your father can come down in a few days." Not that he would. But she kept that to herself in the hope that wishing might actually make it come true. She wanted her family to be together. She wanted a normal life without fear and constant worry. Yet that's all she could do.

She watched the ocean waves peel and break across the empty beach. The rhythm was soothing, almost hypnotic. She was drawn to the sound, which under any other circumstances would have been reassuring. The mix of tide and sand and starry night was fresh and clean. Maine was a beautiful place. Maria understood her husband's need to return. She just couldn't understand how things had gone so wrong.

Then the sound of the unfamiliar phone startled her.

It was John.

"You know, it's awfully late," she said softly into the receiver on the bed stand.

"Well, I was hoping it wasn't too late," he said. "I don't like being away from you and Jack."

She looked down at their little boy, who was still breathing deeply and steadily. "Right now he's asleep. But he misses you."

"So how's OOB?"

"Overrun with old men from Quebec. Many are quite full of themselves—as full as their tight little Speedos." She giggled. "So don't be surprised if you have unexpected competition. Remember, they now sell a thing called Viagra."

Quinn groaned. "I'm not sure this was such a good idea."

"Does the thought of suddenly virile old men competing for my affections worry you?" she teased.

"No."

She sounded disappointed. "So where are you?"

"At the paper. I can't stand an empty house."

"Yet an empty office is all right?"

He looked around. Except for the glow from his computer screen, the newsroom was dark and quiet. "To tell you the truth, you don't notice it as much," he said. "The house is like a morgue."

"John, that house has felt like a morgue for a while."

"Then we can move."

"Away from Stone Harbor?" she asked hopefully. In the pause that followed, she could hear the hum of the small fan in his computer.

Finally, he answered. "I was thinking of something out of town on the water."

"We need to go farther than that," she said. "Do you want to become your father? A stinking rummy who cares more about the *Pilot* than his own family? Just look at you. You're there at eleven o'clock at night."

"I'm too wound up to sleep." That's when he told her Lizz had disappeared. "Angus says it's because she's mixed up in a crazy real estate deal."

"He'll say anything to make her look bad," Maria said. "Especially now, when she's at such a vulnerable place."

"She made things harder for herself," Quinn said, thinking back on the unpleasant things he'd learned over the past few days. "She used to be a strong person. Now she's a doormat."

"That's harsh."

"You never knew her like I did."

"No, I didn't." Maria paused a long moment, then asked the question that had been on her mind forever. "Was there ever anything between the two of you?"

"No." He said it too quickly.

"Really?"

"Okay, we kissed in the second grade, but that hardly counts." At least that's what he said, though no matter how flip he tried to sound, his throat tightened when the words came out. "Why do you ask?"

"I don't know." Maria suddenly felt foolish for bringing it up. "In some ways I've always been a little jealous," she admitted. "You shared a lot together. Things I only know second-hand."

"Trust me. Stories get better over time."

"It doesn't help that she's tall and beautiful."

"And crazy," Quinn added. "Don't forget the crazy part."

"She isn't crazy."

"Look, I don't even know if I can believe anything she tells me anymore."

Maria hesitated a moment, then finally asked, "Can I believe what you tell me?"

"What do you think?"

"I think you're lying," she said quietly, without much emotion. "I think there was something between you and Lizz. I've always thought that."

"Yes, there was," he finally admitted.

"I see." She sounded farther away than ever.

Quinn told Maria it was long before he'd met her.

"That doesn't make it any easier."

He wondered how long this had been bothering her. "There's nothing between us now."

"I hope not."

He considered her reaction. "That's not really the answer I was looking for."

"Well, that's life, John. It's not a fairy tale."

Her words stung more than he could have ever imagined. This wasn't what he wanted. This wasn't anything he saw coming. "So how's this one gonna end?"

"You tell me," she said. "You're the one who writes the stories."

That was true. Yet after they hung up, he was beginning to wonder if anyone read them anymore. Even if they did, nothing changed. People were dead, and for what?

A piece of land and a bit of money.

Quinn looked at the newsroom clock. It was eleven thirty—long past the time to go home—only he didn't want to be alone in an empty house. So he decided to go next door.

THE LAUGHING GULL WAS long and narrow and filled with the smell of smoke and stale beer. Pool balls cracked and a Red Sox game played on three giant TV screens, though the announcers were drowned out by the sound of the jukebox. The Gull hadn't changed over the years, except that more names and numbers had been carved into its wooden walls.

After his second drink, Quinn noticed the redhead from Bowen-Smythe's class at a table with some of her friends, so he went over and asked where the professor was.

"You mean Bryan?" Julie Chapman shouted over a Sheryl Crow song.

"Yeah, him," Quinn shouted back. "Does he come here often?"

"Does the sun rise in the east?"

"I guess that means he'll show up," Quinn said. "Hey— what are you drinking, Coronas?"

"And shots," a blonde named Sandi added.

"Tequila, I'm guessing."

"You would be guessing correctly," Sandi told him.

Her pals cheered like they'd already had a few and soon the waitress delivered more. Julie moved to make room for Quinn and patted his knee when he sat down beside her. "Here's to our new friend," she said.

"Yeah," Quinn agreed. "Here's to me."

They drank up, then had another.

"Should you girls be out on a school night?" Quinn asked after he bought round three.

"Does your wife know you're drinking with women young enough to be your daughters?" Julie asked right back.

"God, I hope not." He thought of Maria and Jack and asked himself what he was doing. He should have been home in bed.

Julie snapped her fingers in front of Quinn's face. "Hey— why so quiet all of a sudden?"

Her friends thought that was hysterical.

So did the newest addition to the gathering: "The editor, at a loss for words?"

"Bryan!" Julie shouted as she pulled Quinn closer to make room for another body.

Bowen-Smythe nodded. "Looks like everyone's had plenty to drink." He tried to act indignant but couldn't help laughing at the scene he'd stumbled onto. "Oh, hell. This round's on me. Shots and chasers for everyone."

The girls hooted, Quinn shook his head and before he had a chance to say "Cuervo Gold," Bowen-Smythe had his arm around Julie like they were long-lost . . . friends?

"I was afraid something happened to you," she told him. "You never know around here."

"Oh, we probably have the safest town in Maine," Bowen-Smythe insisted.

"Tell it to that Sloan guy," Sandi said.

"That happened out in the country," Bowen-Smythe said. "It wasn't in Stone Harbor."

"He still got stomped and another guy's dead—all in a month," Julie said. "It's crazy. I don't know if my parents would approve of my living here if they knew how dangerous it was."

Sandi leaned forward and put her drunken, smiling face in front of everyone at the table. "It's still the *prettiest* town in Maine!" she shouted, quoting from the signs at the entrance to the town limits. Then she howled, as if that were the *funniest* thing ever.

They all joined in the laughter, except Bowen-Smythe. "I guess I'm a little behind," he said, "but I don't see what's funny about violence."

"Nothing," Sandi said. "But your top is hysterical!"

Bowen-Smythe looked down at himself. In honor of Corona night, he'd worn a particularly festive Mexican wedding shirt he'd picked up years earlier in Acapulco.

"Jesus, I don't get out enough," Quinn said.

Bowen-Smythe stood up. "Some of us probably get out too much," he said. "Excuse me."

Quinn followed him into the men's room.

"What the hell are you doing out there?" Bowen-Smythe asked while they stood side by side at the urinals.

"Me? I'm just having a few drinks. What's your excuse?"

"I didn't know I needed one."

"I guess not. If you can use your position to become a real estate speculator, I guess you can get away with anything."

"The town attorney doesn't have a problem with my investments," Bowen-Smythe said evenly.

"You appointed the little weasel!"

"I also appointed your cousin Seth to the board," Bowen-Smythe countered. "Surely you trust his judgment. Paul Stanwood did."

At least Quinn had in the past; he wasn't so sure anymore. He wasn't sure of anything. Mostly, he was just dizzy.

"My God, look at you." Bowen-Smythe sounded disgusted.

Quinn stood in front of the bathroom mirror. No question he'd seen better days. He needed a shave, his shirt was rumpled and his eyes were red with spiderwebbed veins. "So why do you think Paul's dead?" he asked.

"Because there's a lot of hate in the world."

"Did the land have anything to do with it?"

"Paul didn't deserve to die, let alone die the way he did, but I hardly think it's because a few people bought property. In case you hadn't noticed, real estate has been a hot commodity. Maybe that's something you should consider."

"What's that supposed to mean?"

"It means we have nothing else to talk about." The professor went out the restroom door, said his good-byes and headed into the night.

"What's with him?" Julie asked when Quinn walked back to the table.

"I don't know," Quinn said. "I can't figure him out."

"He's usually a lot more fun," Julie said.

"And he has a cute ass for an old guy," Sandi added.

"Sure," Quinn said. "When he doesn't have a stick up it."

"He can get into moods," Julie admitted. "And he has a temper you wouldn't believe."

"Really?"

"Oh, yeah," her friends agreed.

Quinn also found out Bowen-Smythe was unhappy in his marriage and that he'd been telling them it would be his last semester at Wellsen. Quinn bought them another round and tried to decide what to do next. He'd had too many Coronas to drive. The last thing he needed was to get pulled over by Sears or one of the boys—his blood alcohol (and lime) content would have been off the charts, so he stumbled next door to the paper, something his own father had done thousands of times under similar circumstances.

He sat down on the front steps and thought for a moment. Thank God he wasn't like the old man. Quinn stood up and took a deep breath. The night air felt soft and fresh after the smoke and grime of the Laughing Gull. It was only midnight and he wasn't that bad. So he had six beers? That was nothing on a summer evening. It's not like he knocked down shot after shot—just a few tequilas to amuse the girls.

Looking back, the evening seemed like a hazy dream. It was only fifteen minutes after closing and Front Street was quiet and tucked in. The Gull and Wellsen House were shut up tight. So was the pizza shop and diner.

That left the *Pilot* as his only option. He wasn't tired and figured somebody would be inside: the sports editor reading the wires, the cleaning crew, or maybe a sales rep making long-distance calls on the company dime. To his surprise, the place was dark and quiet, just like the rest of the block. Since Tuesday night offered no other prospects, Quinn climbed the steps and rattled open the door. It was unlocked—nothing unusual in the Prettiest Town in Maine—but he still made sure to turn the antique tumblers into place behind him. Too many weird things had been happening.

He looked around carefully: the front desk was safe and sound. So was the advertising department, where a half dozen desks lined the walls, punctuated with tacked-up notes, Caribbean travel posters and a giant white board thermometer with sales figures and ever-distant goals. The mercury for August was closer to $100,000 than the $400,000 goal.

Quinn finished the beer he'd carried out of the bar and took the squeaky wooden stairs to the second floor. He missed a few and caught his balance on the railing. He didn't care. Nobody saw. The landing was dark but he continued on without further incident.

When he hit the light in his office, he found Lizz Stanwood behind his desk. She was wearing a light, low-cut summer dress and her hands were folded together with her chin resting on them.

"Surprised?" she asked.

"Yes."

"This town's full of them." She sat up and took a drink from a small bottle of Southern Comfort, then tilted it his way.

"No, thanks," he said.

"You always were a straight shooter, weren't you, Johnny?" she said. "At least that's what you wanted everyone to believe." She took another drink. "You know, Paul believed that, right till the end."

"Why wouldn't he?"

She let her cheek slide to the desktop, then laughed. The

bruises were lighter, but her face looked more weathered than he remembered. "Sure you don't want a shot?" she asked, peeking up at him. "But the question is, which one?" She pointed to the bottle, then at the chrome-plated Glock 9 mm she'd been covering up.

"I'll take the Comfort," he said.

"What little there is left." She pushed herself back up and slid the bottle toward him. He couldn't help noticing she was braless.

Quinn took a stained coffee cup from a shelf and poured himself three fingers.

"You won't catch anything from the bottle." She motioned with the gun. "Besides, you've got more pressing concerns."

"One of them is you." He tilted the cup toward her.

"How sweet. Most people have given up on me."

Whatever she was thinking, he decided to play along. "Well, I'm not most people."

"You certainly aren't," she said. "You were the first boy I ever kissed."

"I know." It had been in the closet of Miss Middleton's second-grade class, during recess. He panicked when she slipped him the tongue, before she ran outside triumphantly to a playground full of laughter. Turns out she'd acted on a dare and every other kid had been in on it.

He was hoping she was out of surprises when she leaned forward. "Maybe you'll also be the last," she said, "depending how you play your cards."

"Can't we talk about this?"

"I've talked enough already. That's all anybody wants to do is talk. They talk about me and Al. They talk about you. They still keep talking about Paul, even though the poor boy's dead and gone. But nobody wants to listen. They just keep talking."

"Why haven't you told me what's going on with the real estate deal?"

"How could I, after what happened between us?" She took another drink, then stared at him as she wiped her mouth with one hand, as though trying to get rid of an awful taste. "You're ashamed to have fucked me, aren't you?" And there it was, finally out in the open, after all those years.

"It shouldn't have happened."

She slowly—barely—shook her head sideways. "Well, you really know how to make a girl feel special."

"I betrayed a friend."

"We were twenty-one years old. There were no marriage vows or children. We were all just starting out. But you didn't have the guts to finish."

It happened just after his graduation from Miami, when Paul was off on a canoe trip to the Allagash. Quinn and Lizz had teamed up on a *Yankee* magazine story about a haunted bed-and-breakfast in Bar Harbor. On a lark, they spent the night. That's when things took an unexpected turn.

"It's a helluva thing," Quinn had said the next morning.

"It is." With her head nestled on his chest, she'd slowly run a hand along his cheek. "And it's always been there between us."

He couldn't deny it, and for the next ten days, didn't try. But Quinn left home for good before Paul returned. A few months later, Paul and Lizz eloped.

"You never told him about us, did you?" Lizz asked, her face full of hostility.

Quinn looked at the floor. "No."

"Well, I did." Lizz waited for a reaction.

It never came. He was still digesting the fact that Paul had known the secret and never seemed to care. "When did he find out?"

"I told him when your father died," she said. "It was when Paul got the idea that he should convince you to come back home."

"Didn't you want me around?"

"I wanted to hurt him as badly as he hurt me," she said.

"I should have told him myself. Years ago."

"Oh, don't worry," she said. "He kept plenty of secrets from you." She grinned crazily. "So in a way, we're no better than he was."

"I never said I was better than anyone."

"You never had to. It was written all over your face and in the tone of your voice when you talked to people."

That's when he wondered if she hated him. "I thought I was doing the right thing," he explained.

"You ran away," she said, her eyes suddenly full of sorrow. "And what I want to know is if you ever regretted it."

"Yes, I regretted it," he admitted. "I regretted it every day for years. Then I met Maria. What happened between us was fifteen years ago."

"Now Paul's gone and she's gone, and we're still here."

"I'm sorry."

She laughed bitterly. "I figured you would be."

They looked at each other as her gun hand slowly floated back and forth. "I hope the safety's on that thing," Quinn said.

She turned the gun over in her hand and checked. "Oh, don't you know?" she asked, pointing it at him again. "Glocks don't have safeties."

"Jesus Christ," he whispered.

"Aren't I a mess?" She laughed. "That's why you preferred running away, Paul preferred men and Al prefers your little reporter. Nobody prefers me, and now you're looking at me like I'm nuts and you have no idea if I'll actually pull the trigger."

He held out his hand. "You can still trust me."

"Last time I did, I got the crap beat out of me."

"I won't let him hurt you again," Quinn said. "You can stay with us."

She silently mouthed laughter, as much from the booze as anything he'd said. "Wouldn't that make a household?"

"We're friends."

She looked at him with bleary eyes and squinted, as if trying to see him more clearly. "Were you really my husband's friend?" she asked, almost desperately.

"Yes." Quinn refilled his cup.

"Some people think that's why he's dead."

Quinn couldn't believe it. "Why's that?"

"They prefer to keep lower profiles," she said. "Especially when it comes to their business transactions. Take Bryan Bowen-Smythe. He doesn't want anyone writing about Sullivan Park, or even thinking about it."

"He did seem a little uptight when I mentioned it earlier," Quinn said.

She laughed. "If you really want to get him going, tell him you know about Mystic Development, the group that's prepared to pay twenty million dollars for the park so they can develop it with a luxury hotel, a private golf course and a marina."

"And then Bowen-Smythe can cash in on the nearby land he picked up for a song," Quinn said.

Lizz tilted her head and studied him, then poked at the air with the gun. "You seem pretty calm."

"That's not how I feel, so don't do anything stupid. Especially while you're pointing that thing at me."

"This?" She'd looked as if it were the first time she'd seen the pistol and gently caressed the barrel with her long, tanned fingers. "Oh, Johnny, you crack me up."

"Sometimes it's even intentional. So come on. Give me the gun."

She smiled impishly, then bowed her head and slowly licked the length of the barrel. Her lips were full and sensual; finally she smiled, cocked the hammer and shoved the muzzle in her mouth.

He took a step toward her. "Lizz, don't!"

She slowly began bobbing her head up and down its length.

"Stop it!" Quinn said.

That just made her go faster. Soon she was putting her whole body into it.

"Damn it, give me the gun!"

She stopped and looked very surprised. "Afraid it's gonna go off?" she asked.

"Yes."

"Isn't that what's supposed to happen?"

"No."

"I guess you're not as much fun as you used to be." She let her arm fall slack and that's when he moved. He tried to push the gun down and away from them both, but she had surprising strength, and for a moment he wasn't sure he could control her because of his weak hand. Then the gun went off, burning his face from the flash and bursting his ear with a sound that didn't seem to stop.

20.

Sarah Sewell had been lying around the trailer in a camisole and panties, watching Hitchcock's *The Birds* for the second time that night and probably the hundredth time in her life when the call came over the scanner.

No problem.

She was always good to go, with a bag on the table with two Nikons, a flashgun, a variety of lenses, lipstick, a cell phone and a handheld police scanner that was usually squawking.

She threw on a raincoat and was gone.

Ginny had been sound asleep on the couch, but a second after her daughter slammed the door to their 1984 Lincoln Continental, she was behind the wheel and grinding the ignition. It took a moment before the engine rattled and rolled to life. Then Ginny put the car in gear and floored it, suddenly shaking the assortment of pink flamingos, birdbaths and out-of-season Christmas lights that lined the fence of their small lot.

The neighbors would bitch, since none of them liked being jarred out of bed by the Dingbatmobile, no matter how much they enjoyed the news stories that followed. The girls were too focused on the task at hand to care, which meant a hard right onto Mulberry Lane, a left on Maine Street, a blind eye to the first two red lights, and a power slide onto Front Street; trees and ditches and white picket fences came along the roadside while the dashboard scanner—in addition to Sarah's handheld one—howled *"Proceed with caution, proceed with caution!"*

A storm had come off the bay in hard waves that slapped the dirty streets and sagging rooftops of the north-end tenements stacked along the narrow streets. That patch of town would never make a postcard, no matter how hard the developers tried. Broken tree limbs covered the sidewalks and the gutters were overflowing, but Ginny didn't think of letting off the gas. She raced through the downpour with her wipers on high as water sprayed her floorboard and rain pinged the car roof.

"Jeesum!" Sarah put a hand to the roof to keep her head from going through it as the car bounced on the uneven brick.

"Hang on!" Ginny hit the brakes and lurched hard into the wheel before they smacked the granite curbing in front of the newspaper office and spilled sideways in the front seat. Sarah had her door open and was out and running before her mother had a chance to caution her. Not that it would have done any good. She never listened to anyone, from her boss to her friends on the police force, though they all had a grudging admiration for her hardheaded determination.

Less than four minutes after hearing that night's call, Sarah ran squarely into Police Chief Al Sears on the *Pilot*'s steps. He wrapped his arms around her on impact so she wouldn't fall over. That still didn't keep her from dropping her purse and camera bag, along with most of the contents.

She struggled to get out of his grip. "Let go of me!"

"I did that once and I'm not gonna do it again," he said.

"My mother's in the car."

"That's a good place for her."

"I mean it."

Sears dropped his hands to his side but didn't step back. Sarah did—in a hurry. As she scrambled to gather her gear, Sears held a palm up. "There's been a shooting," he said patiently. "So don't do anything rash."

"Well, I have a key to the building," Sarah said. "So don't piss me off."

UPSTAIRS, THE BULLET HAD shattered and sprayed glass out into the newsroom. The gun's echo was still ringing in Quinn's ear, but things were finally starting to speed up to normal, or as close to normal as they were going to get, given the circumstances.

He felt his wet cheek. "I don't believe this." He checked his fingers. Thank God it was only sweat and not blood. His ear was still attached, though his whole body was drenched in perspiration. Quinn slumped against the wall as Lizz got to her knees, then fell on him. Her lungs were heaving and she was crying and limply holding the gun.

When he suddenly gripped it, she resisted.

That's when he put his shoulder into her chest and knocked her onto her back. The Glock dropped onto the worn carpet and he held both her wrists. "Now, you have to understand," he said in an ever-so-calm voice. "I am really through fucking around."

She nodded like she understood.

"Now, we're gonna clean up this mess and you're coming home with me," he said. "And this whole evening will be another one of our little secrets."

"All right," she said, wincing, which made him realize how tightly he was holding her wrists. But when he relaxed his grip, she smiled and moved beneath him in a way he hadn't expected.

Jesus.

She kissed him and arched her back. Things that had been building for months were about to erupt when he let go of her arms and sat back, away from her.

"Don't be shy." She was laughing and unbuttoning her dress when they heard a voice:

"Busted!"

Quinn turned and there was Sears, with Sarah right behind him. "Looks like somebody got caught with his hand in the cookie jar," Sears said.

Quinn backed up like he really had been shot. "Who let you in?" he asked.

"Sarah," Sears answered. "We got a call about gunplay." He shook his head and laughed. "But maybe it's a sexual assault."

"Maybe it's none of your business," Quinn said as Lizz pulled her top together to cover herself.

"Anything she does is my business," Sears said.

"I wanted him to stop," Lizz insisted.

"You what?" Quinn asked.

"I kissed him on the cheek—out of friendship—and he took it the wrong way," she nervously added. "He tried to rape me."

"You came here with a gun!" Quinn shouted at the crazy bitch. "How do you explain that?"

She had her hands over her eyes like she was trying to block out the memory.

"Well?" Quinn pressed. "Try lying your way out of that one."

"My husband has been killed," she said. "I have good reason to be afraid. And I have a permit."

"You're both drunk," Sarah said.

"It's more like shitfaced." Sears walked over to Quinn, who was starting to stand up. "Give me the gun."

"So what happened?" Sarah asked.

"It went off a few minutes ago," Lizz said. "I'm not sure how."

"That's what happens when you pull the trigger," Sears said. He thought it was all so funny, he had to sit down at one of the desks. "We have a helluva mess, now, don't we?" By then sirens were blaring and the red lights from patrol cars were flashing through the second-floor window, over the walls and across the ceiling.

Lizz wouldn't look directly at Sears. Instead, she walked to him with her head down and put her arm around his waist.

"Nothing's happening without our lawyers," Quinn said. He was irritated at how quickly she had run to Sears. "So everyone just sit tight and get comfortable."

"There's no need for that," Sears said as he took the pistol from Quinn and put it in his belt. "I'll just drive her home and we'll file this under lesson learned. We know it was all a mistake. We learned from it and won't let it happen again."

"She's not going with you," Quinn said.

"Yes, she is," Sears said, this time like he really meant it.

"I'm fine," Lizz said quietly. Her eyes were filled with tears and she seemed like a different person. "I really am."

"She just threatened to kill herself," Quinn said. "I want her to go to the hospital."

"I'll take care of it," Sears said as he walked her toward the stairs.

Lizz didn't say another word. It was amazing the control Sears had over her.

Sarah stepped toward Quinn. "Aren't you going to do anything?"

"I'm not sure there's anything I can do," Quinn said. Then he turned his back to her and tried to make sense of the shattered glass that had rained down on the worn and filthy newsroom carpeting. Lizz may have been a flake, but she didn't kill him when she had the chance. There was no way she killed her husband.

21.

Quinn nearly banged the front door apart in the still-early morning hours. Once Seth put on a robe and stumbled down the stairs, he switched on the porch light and cracked it as far as the chain allowed.

"Can I come in?" Quinn said.

"You have to be kidding."

"Then will you come out?"

"Sorry." Seth pulled the silk fabric tight against the damp air. "This is the best you'll do till I slam it in your face."

Quinn told him what happened.

Seth listened without interrupting. After his cousin was finished, he unlatched the chain and led Quinn into his kitchen. "So what set her off?" he asked when they sat down at the table.

"She said Paul was dead because he was close to me. She said too many people wanted to keep things quiet. She said a lot of what Angus has been saying all along—that Bowen-Smythe wants to whitewash everything about the park. It has something to do with a land deal."

"And you believe them?"

"Why else would you fuckers buy land near the park?"

254

Seth's mouth fell open in surprise. "Then you're as crazy as they are," he said once he regained his composure.

"I don't think Angus is crazy," Quinn said. "And something made Lizz that way."

"Try raising a family in a small town when you're married to a queer."

That nearly set Quinn off, but he stopped himself from exploding and spoke very slowly. "I meant since then."

"Isn't that enough?"

"No, it isn't." Quinn leaned forward and looked Seth in the eye. "So why did you buy land near the park?"

Seth shrugged like it was no big deal. "It was just an opportunity that presented itself—nothing like the conspiracy Angus makes it out to be. Land came up from an estate and we paid fair market value. That's all."

"Why wasn't it listed?"

"Paul helped the owner with some tax trouble last fall and was able to get his bill reduced. He was a sick man who needed a break or he'd have to sell. His heirs were grateful the liens were gone."

"Where'd you get four hundred thousand dollars?" Quinn asked.

"The bank."

"And they lent you the money—just like that."

"Why not? They lent you thirteen million so you could pay your taxes."

"I put a newspaper and printing company up as collateral," Quinn said.

Seth wasn't impressed. "That can't match land in a rising market."

Quinn wanted to throw up. Even his own cousin was trying to make a quick buck buying and selling the town. But that wasn't all. "So why is everyone protecting Sears?"

"They're not."

"Like hell. Now the son of a bitch has taken Lizz and I suppose you won't do anything about that, either."

"She fired a gun in your office," Seth said. "She should spend the night in jail, if not a lot more time than that. She's the one you should worry about. Not Al."

Quinn didn't believe that. "Nobody got hurt. She doesn't have it in her."

Seth slowly shook his head. "How would you know what anybody really has in them?"

"I don't, but I've got more questions than ever about your buddy Bryan Bowen-Smythe. Angus said Paul had something serious on the professor."

Seth pushed his hands in the air wearily. "Angus says a lot of things."

"And most of them turn out to be true."

Seth seemed to consider this. "Well, Bryan has developed a paranoid curiosity about the investigation. He asks a lot of questions but never offers any suggestions."

"What's his attitude toward Sears?"

"The guy makes him nervous." Seth paused a moment, like he wanted to say more. "Look—I'll try to find out what's going on."

Quinn was relieved. "Thanks." He needed all the help he could get.

As he walked to his car, the wind gently pushed the tree branches overhead and a cool spray kissed the neighborhood rooftops, a calm reminder of the gales that had blown through Stone Harbor. The temperature was already dropping each night, hinting at what the change of seasons would bring.

It had been a helluva month.

Paul was dead and somebody knew all about it.

Bowen-Smythe's routine had grown thin.

Lizz was involved, but he didn't know how. So was Sears.

Seth knew more than he was saying. That much was certain.

All for a real estate deal?

That's what didn't make sense. Then again, maybe the whole thing was just the pretext for the petty shit that floated to the surface. Quinn was exhausted by the time he walked into his own living room, and the only thing on his mind was his couch. He was out the instant he hit it. He didn't even move in his sleep. It was as though he'd turned to concrete.

No thoughts.

No dreams.

No distractions.

Only sleep—a deep trance that felt like it would never end.

WHEN HE OPENED HIS eyes to the gray light of the living room, his back hurt like hell, which shouldn't have surprised him. Maria had complained for months that they needed a new couch. He was finally starting to see her point.

The DVD player beneath the television read 10:00 p.m. He had slept fourteen hours and his mouth was parched, so he went to the fridge and drained a Geary's. He went slower with the second but was still groggy as he picked up the kitchen phone and dialed Maria's cell. He hadn't talked to her or Jack in a while and wanted something good to come out of the day he'd missed.

The phone hummed.

It hummed again.

It hummed a third time.

On the fourth hum she said, *"Hey!"*

"Where've you been?" he asked.

"This is Maria," she continued right over him. *"If you leave a message, I'll get right back to you."*

"Damn!" He slammed the phone shut, then immediately picked up and called again.

She still wasn't there.

That time he left a message: "It's John. Where are you guys? I'm getting a little worried." He paced with a beer in his hand and a knot in his stomach—and hoped she'd get right back to him—before he finally gave up and turned on CNN. No use worrying, he told himself. That never solved anything.

Oh, the hell with that. He turned off the TV and quickly left Maria three more messages. He had no idea why they hadn't been answered. Maybe she and Jack were asleep. He just hoped they were safe.

That's when he heard a ring.

Damn. He didn't know where he'd left his own cell phone, though the sound was coming from the bedroom. He checked the dresser. He checked his closet. He checked three suit jackets, two pants pockets and a pair of shorts.

He finally found it ringing on the floor next to their bed.

When Quinn answered, nobody was there—though a signal indicated a voice mail. Actually, four of them. That's when he realized his own phone was still in his pocket. The other one belonged to Maria.

How could she have left it at home?

MARIA WAS THINKING THE same thing. "We really need to call your father," she told Jack.

They were walking away from the boardwalk, and the darkness was edged with an electric glow. The smell of greasy pizza and cotton candy and suntan lotion hung everywhere, punctuated by the fading sounds of kids screaming on amusement park rides, the muffler of a motorcycle burping over idling car engines, frenzied video games with electric bells and boings. When the other noises faded with the slap of each sandaled step on the brick sidewalk, all that was left was the steady surge—as regular as breathing—of the waves lapping the sand beach.

Jack took a deep breath and smelled the sea. They continued walking.

A few blocks away, the hotels and condominiums gave way to rows of cottages. The beach house where they were staying was empty and dark, save the occasional neon flash from the boardwalk on its white exterior. During one of those electric bursts Maria saw a shadow in the front window and froze.

Somebody was inside.

She quickly took Jack by the hand and turned around. "Come on," she said. "I don't feel like turning in."

He didn't mind. Jack was happy to return to the arcades and rides, and for once, as he plunged ahead—pulling her by the arm—his mother wasn't trying to hold him back. Instead, she moved right along, which made him squeal with laughter.

Maria didn't feel the same way. She was panicked and scared, especially when she heard the beach house's screen door screech open. By the time it slammed shut, they were on to the main street and, a moment later, among the amusement rides.

"Let's go on this." Jack pointed to the Ferris wheel.

"Sure," Maria said as she fumbled with her wallet at the ticket booth.

"And some ice cream," Jack pressed, since she was suddenly so accommodating.

"Maybe later."

"Okay."

Maria fidgeted in line, waiting for the operator to load the people ahead of them, two at a time, stopping and going and laughing and joking until she just wanted to scream. Instead, she pulled her hoodie over her head and got Jack's Red Sox cap from her daypack and put it on him.

Finally they were on board. A few passengers later, they were gently swinging in the open air, and after another lift, they were above the town with a view of the lights below, and out beyond the pier, the dark water of Casco Bay.

Then they stopped; she had a good look at the beach house and noticed a black Lexus a block from its driveway. At that moment, she believed everything her husband had said about the police chief.

And the worst part was that Al Sears was there. Somewhere.

22.

Seth was in the newsroom looking for Quinn. He figured his cousin would be at work, but the place was empty—even though every newsroom computer and light was still on, as if electricity were free and the staff didn't have a care in the world.

What could he expect?

They behaved like children in *Romper Room*. To prove his point, the back corner that housed the sports department had a full-size hockey net, pucks from every school in the Eastern Conference, a goalie mask and an autographed Paul Kariya jersey, all part of a shrine to the University of Maine Black Bears. A Nerf basketball hoop hung from another wall, along with a whiteboard full of standings from their daily games of horse.

Newsroom types had a way of making the business unbearable, with their breathless empathy, their oblivion to the bottom line and their go-go-go enthusiasm for every wild rumor that came their way. Even John fell into it. He'd gone as far as asking Bowen-Smythe a lot of questions about Sullivan Park, questions that sounded more like accusations by the time they got back to Seth:

"When did you know the development company was interested in the land?"

"What did Paul think?"

"Did the deal have anything to do with Seth being named to the board of selectmen?"

The arrogant bastard thought he could make the world a better place, but he only hurt the newspaper. The just-completed audit confirmed everything Seth tried to tell him, not that he would change. Just like Paul Stanwood, self-preservation had never been his strong suit.

Seth walked to John's office at the front of the room and noticed the message light on his phone. He knew every security code in the building and punched it in.

Quinn had two voice mails.

The first was a reporter in South Carolina with information on Mystic Development.

"John, nobody's heard of the company, but I checked with a friend in the secretary of state's office in Columbia. They were just incorporated this month. Let me know if I can do anything else."

The second call nearly made Seth's heart stop.

"John, this is Bryan Bowen-Smythe. We really need to talk. It's very important, so call me as soon as you can. It would be better if we met somewhere private."

Seth couldn't believe the professor's desperate tone. He imagined a similar call the night Paul Stanwood had been killed, which is why he had to get to his cousin before Bowen-Smythe did.

WHEN THE RIDE WAS over Jack ran ahead of Maria to the Tilt-A-Whirl.

"Oh, no, honey. Not this one."

"Come on!" He tugged on her arm and she gave in.

"All right," she said, since the line was moving quickly. Before she knew it they were sitting on the hard seat and the teenage operator clanged down the safety bar that locked them in place.

When she looked up, Sears was standing beyond the fence, smiling.

Rather than make eye contact, she looked away as the metal floor began to rise and roll and spin their car. When she looked again, he was gone.

Easy does it, she thought as the ride gained speed. *Just keep breathing.* She figured it wouldn't be so bad. It was just a ride—a ride for children, at that. Then the speed increased and the car creaked and jerked in a half circle and jolted back again in the other direction, knocking them against the metal that held them in place as Jack squealed in delight. The floor moved faster, and before she knew it, they were spinning completely around.

Jack had no idea how upset she was, which was a good thing. She wasn't really sure herself. She just knew that with someone waiting in the cottage, she and Jack had to flee.

As the ride continued to spin, she briefly saw that Sears had his hands on the chain-link fence surrounding the ride and was staring at them. The spinning began to have its effect, so she closed her eyes tightly. Things were going even more quickly; Jack was still squealing and she was gritting her teeth, hoping the ride would end. But it continued on, over and around, and she was getting nauseous. Once she opened her eyes, Sears had moved again. By the time it was over she really had to throw up.

The bar rose automatically, but Maria didn't move.

"Mom, are you okay?" Jack asked.

She nodded and tried to stand. "Yes." But she felt horrible and listed to one side as she took Jack by the hand and moved toward the entrance line.

"The other way, ma'am," the operator told her, but she ignored him and stumbled through the entrance, away from Sears past a line of customers who either laughed or complained—some did both.

Maria stumbled down the stairs onto the street. "Mom?" Jack asked, but she ignored his question and stepped into a dark arcade, which was filled with rat-tat-tats from video machine guns, only to notice, outside against the bright signs and lights, Al Sears hurrying past them.

Maria snatched her son's hand and went in the opposite direction, down the busy walkway toward the beach house. "Come on, run!" she told Jack, though she still felt awful.

A few minutes later, she was backing up her BMW before Jack had snapped on his seat belt and was soon idling in traffic, impatient to leave town.

"Where we goin'?" Jack asked.

"Home."

He took the answer in stride, as the pace of the traffic picked up along Saco Avenue and the BMW approached I-95.

"What about our stuff?" Jack asked.

"We can get it another time."

"Are we comin' back?"

She didn't answer. She was too busy deciding which way she was going to turn: north toward Stone Harbor or south, away from it all.

•   •   •

"Something's up with Bryan," Seth said when he finally reached Quinn on the phone.

"Well, it's gonna have to wait."

"I'm not sure it can." Seth was frantic. "He has a town cell phone and I checked the records. Turns out he's the one who made the 911 call to the police the night Paul was killed."

Quinn pictured the nervous professor. "Then the little bastard knows who did it."

"Or he did it himself," Seth said.

Quinn had been skeptical that Bowen-Smythe had it in him, but maybe he'd been wrong. "No wonder he thinks Sears is doing a good job on the investigation. The dumb shit has no idea he's involved."

"We really need to talk," Seth pleaded. "About a lot of things. I'm here at work. Where are you?"

"On my way to OOB." Seth sounded unglued and Quinn was hoping his cell phone reception would start to fade.

"Why do you need to go to there?"

"That's where Jack and Maria have been staying all week."

"I thought they were in Miami."

"We figured everyone would," Quinn said. "That was the whole idea. They're at a place Lizz Stanwood owns."

"Then Sears knows," Seth said. "And I'm guessing Bowen-Smythe does, too."

"I have to get to them."

"Please, avoid Sears and Bowen-Smythe," Seth begged. "No matter what they say. I don't trust either of them anymore." His voice was full of fear.

"All right," Quinn lied. "I won't go near them."

• • •

THOSE TWO HAD OTHER ideas. The professor had hooked up with the chief, and they were trying to figure out their next move.

"I'm tellin' you," Sears said into his phone. "I couldn't find her."

"How hard could it be?" Bowen-Smythe asked. "You have the damn address and a key to the cottage."

The chief didn't appreciate the criticism. "They weren't there. I went inside and waited a couple hours. Then I looked all over the beach and boardwalk." Sears didn't bother to mention that he'd seen them both.

It was the second time that day he'd been made a fool. The first was when he'd gotten into his Lexus and found a small gift neatly wrapped, with a bow on top and a note that read: "Been looking for something?"

Inside he'd found the dope and pipe he'd planted in the silver BMW. Now this.

"So you have no idea where they are," Bowen-Smythe pressed.

Sears hesitated.

"Well, don't worry. I've got a call in to Quinn," Bowen-Smythe said. "That should take care of everything—one way or the other."

MARIA FINALLY FOUND A pay phone at a truck stop and quickly punched in John's number. He needed to know what was going on. "Hey, it's me," she said when he picked up on the fourth ring.

"Where are you?"

"On I-95," she said. "I couldn't take it anymore."

"Well, don't worry. I'm on my way."

"Stay put. We're just north of Augusta, less than an hour away."

"All right," he said, relieved they were both safe.

"So where are you?" she asked.

"Just outside Stone Harbor."

"Meet me at home."

When he hesitated, she knew what he was thinking. He was going to stop in at the damn newspaper. What she didn't realize was that he planned to find out everything Seth knew, even if he had to beat it out of him. "Just make it quick," she said. "I don't want to go home to an empty house."

"I'll be there before you are," he said.

"Is that a promise?"

"Yes."

"All right." For once, she believed him. "You know I love you."

"I love you, too."

23.

"Are Maria and Jack finally coming home?" Seth asked when Quinn found him in the newsroom, of all places.

"Yeah, they just called and they're on the way," Quinn said. "So what the hell's going on?"

Seth sighed, like he was finally letting something out that he'd been holding in too long. "I was afraid Bowen-Smythe and Sears were going to kill you."

"Why?" Quinn's face grew even more puzzled when he realized Seth was carrying two large cans. "What are you doing?"

"I need to take some of this cleaner home," Seth said absently.

"So what's so urgent that you need to talk to me?" Quinn asked.

Seth's face fell into a frown. "The bank's about to foreclose," he said. "The last audit gives them no choice."

Just like that. "I never figured things would come to this," Quinn said, and he really hadn't. He'd come home to run the family business and he'd run it into the ground. "I should have listened to you."

Seth smiled a cold smile. "That's never been your strong suit. You're just like Uncle Jake."

This time Quinn didn't wince at the comparison. It just didn't matter anymore. "So how do you think he would have handled this?" he asked.

Seth shrugged. "I thought I understood him, then he died and I realized I had him all wrong."

"You sound bitter."

"I am."

"Hell, I don't blame you." Quinn should have handled things differently. So many people could have. In a way, Seth was a casualty in a war he had no part in starting. Quinn and his father had been too stubborn to pick up the phone and put their differences behind them. Instead, Jake entrusted more and more of the business to Seth, who never complained—until it sunk in that he was doomed to remain hired help.

"Is that what made you go in on the land deal?" Quinn asked.

"Sure."

"So why is Paul dead?"

"It was a matter of principle," Seth said, as though he were talking to someone who would never get the obvious. "Paul changed his mind at the last minute, which was easy enough for him. He could afford to back out."

"And the rest of you couldn't?"

"That's why I turned to plan B," Seth said. "I knew Paul had been playing a dangerous game and figured I could blackmail him. But things went too far. Once I started with that flashlight, I couldn't stop."

"What flashlight?"

That's when Seth pulled out the Maglite. He swung fast and hard and caught Quinn on the side of the head, which put him down and out.

Seth didn't waste any time after that. He wasn't going to make the same mistake he had with Danny Sloan and leave another victim alive. And this time, instead of going after a source who talked too much, Seth was going to the root of all his problems.

Gleefully, he picked up the cans and soaked the wooden staircase with accelerant, then the newsroom carpeting and the piles of paper on Quinn's desk. He thought of hitting the arrogant bastard one more time to save him the horror of being burned alive, but figured he wasn't worth the effort.

None of them were.

"Ah, justice," he said as he went to the corner of the sports department and looked down at the cans of industrial solvent used to clean the presses. He read the label, which said it was highly flammable. "I guess it's time for a good cleaning." He threw what was left of the can on the hockey net, the autographed Paul Kariya jersey and the shrine of souvenir press passes. He even picked up their Nerf basketball and wiped it along a particularly wet spot on a desk.

Perfect.

He lit it, then chanted, "He *shoots* . . . he *scores!*" as he tossed the burning ball into the corner and in his best sportscaster voice shouted, "That's what I call *lighting things up!*"

He had everything in place to make it look like Quinn had committed suicide.

Any evidence linking Seth to the crime was gone, including the pictures taken by that fool Sarah Sewell. He'd seen to that. The newspaper's grim financial picture had been painted and everyone knew John had grown disillusioned with Stone Harbor. It looked like his wife and son had left him. Why not end it all at once? The coup de grâce was the e-mailed suicide note sent from Quinn's computer.

> *Maria,*
>
> *I'm sorry for everything. I never expected things with Paul would get so out of control, but just couldn't take his constant criticism. I never meant to kill him, but when I learned what he put Lizz through, I can't say I'm sorry. Looking back, he was right about one thing. I screwed the* Pilot *up more than anyone could have imagined, but that's nothing compared to my personal life. I've failed as a father and can only hope Jack will understand when he's older.*
>
>

Love,

John
>

Seth laughed out loud. The critics were going to eat up that final touch. Of course, he also made sure to wipe down the Maglite and add Quinn's prints before leaving it in the Volvo's glove compartment. Once Sears and the gang saw the car on the sidewalk, they'd be sure to check inside.

Seth was still laughing as he shut the car door and began trotting down the street. The whole thing had been more of a rush than he expected, and he was half tempted to double back to the scene to watch the *Pilot* burn against the backdrop of a small, clueless town that would be quick to pass judgment on his feckless cousin. Seth didn't give a shit about the paper. His new game was real estate. The only thing left to take care of was Maria and Jack. But what the hell. He knew where they were heading.

24.

MARIA WASN'T REALLY SURPRISED to come back to an eerily quiet house. The garage was empty, the lights were out and from the looks of things, her husband hadn't been there in a while. Despite all the promises in the world, some things would never change. And to think, on the way into town, she had an urge to drop by the *Pilot* to make sure John had really left, then thought better of the idea. The last thing she'd wanted to do was sit around the newsroom with Jack while her husband promised "just five more minutes" that were sure to turn into another hour at his keyboard.

They could hear sirens wailing in the distance, and when a car rolled to a stop in front of the driveway, Maria hurried through the falling rain to the driver's-side window.

It was Seth.

"Where's John?" she asked.

"Where else?" Seth replied with a shrug.

She was furious. "Of all times for him to leave the two of us waiting . . ."

"That's why I'm here."

That didn't make sense to her. "What's going on?" she asked. "Why all the sirens?"

"We need to get out of here," Seth said. "You made a big mistake coming back. It's just not safe."

Maria got in the passenger seat, next to Seth, and Jack climbed in back. "You know, John should have come himself," she complained.

"Oh, don't be too hard on him," Seth said. "Sometimes he just can't drag himself away from work."

THIS TIME HE WAS trying. As the fire raged, Quinn stretched his shirt to cover his mouth and nose. He tried to shield his eyes from the smoke as he crawled along the floor, since the building was fully engulfed. The flames reflected off his office glass, and he could feel the heat bearing down as the walls cracked and the ceiling blackened.

His forehead was bleeding and he was groggy, but he knew enough to put one foot in front of the other. "Come on!" he told himself. "You have to get moving." He could hear sirens and taste ash as he managed to cross the newsroom.

The heat was almost more than he could take. Plastic computer shells were melting and burning embers fell everywhere. He winced in pain as something scalded his back and caused him to roll over like a dog in grass to put it out. In a panic, he tore up a piece of the worn carpeting. Shreds of it stayed stuck to the floor but he managed to get enough to wrap around himself as he stood up and ran for the stairs, which he stumbled down, retching and gagging. He was halfway down when they started to give. He crashed through the splintered boards and his momentum carried him forward.

The floor was smoldering, and overhead, the ancient sprinkler system sputtered and moaned before dropping on top of desks and chairs that were already burning. Quinn hoped the floor wasn't next. The charts, graphs and travel posters that lined the ad department desks were nothing more than charred remains. By the time he staggered out the front door, flames were roaring from the windows.

Sarah Sewell was in the middle of the unfolding chaos, taking pictures of everything:

The volunteers spilling out of the fire trucks.

Paramedics running up to Quinn.

Hoses blasting spray against the blaze.

The heat from the building came in waves and Quinn thought he was going to pass out as he stumbled forward. The next thing he knew, he was lying down and gasping in an oxygen mask as the scene around him continued to unfold.

A power transformer near the building exploded.

Fire trucks and police cruisers continued to arrive.

Finally, a volunteer grabbed Sarah by the arm and dragged her back from the building.

Quinn wondered where she thought the shots were going to be published. The *Stone Harbor Pilot* was just about gone, and he couldn't help thinking that the story had broken at a perfect time for their news cycle.

Maybe it was for the best that Sarah hadn't realized the scope of the situation. She had a sentimental attachment to the place. So did he. Six months earlier, he'd come home to make an honest living in the same fashion his family had for generations.

Now this.

Half of Front Street was out on the sidewalks. The drunks from the Gull had been rousted, then reassured the bar was in no danger, thanks to the alley separating them from the *Pilot*, along with the thousands of pounds of water that were being pumped out each second by the giant hook-and-ladder truck that swung into action. Despite their best efforts, the fire department didn't have a chance to save the upper floors.

As Sarah continued shooting, Quinn had a pretty good view of the scene before him. Flames and heat pushed the gawking crowd back across the street, but the cops couldn't keep them moving. A few kept trying to get as close as possible. Finally the firefighters let the hoses loose, scattering the fools, who shoved and climbed over one another to get away. Nobody was arrested. The fire raged on. Occasional blasts erupted from the basement pressroom.

Quinn thought of his father, grandfather and great-grandfather before him. Three generations had run the family business, and this was going to be his legacy. He could imagine his father's reaction. Only this time, Quinn didn't have a snotty comeback.

Then he thought of Seth.

The little fucker was going to pay. Quinn ripped off the oxygen mask and started running, propelled by anger and rage until, just beyond the crowd, he was stopped by the unexpected presence of Police Chief Alvah Sears.

"Hold it right there, Quinn."

"Alvah, I don't have the time for this."

"Make time." Sears stiff-armed Quinn in the chest.

"Seth set the building on fire," Quinn said quickly. "He killed Paul. He may be after my family."

"And I'm s'posed to believe you?"

"Look, I need to find him!"

"Well, I tried findin' your wife and son for their own protection," Sears said. "But since I wasn't able to do that, the least I can do for their sake is to make sure you stay outta trouble for the rest of the night." Sears emphasized that last point by planting a palm hard on Quinn's shoulder.

Quinn knocked the cop's hand away. "You don't wanna do this."

"Oh, really?" Sears asked as he did it again, only this time he knotted Quinn's shirt in his fist.

Quinn gripped Sears's hand tightly, then swung his opposite forearm across the cop's elbow, shattering it. As Sears's face twisted in agony, Quinn pulled hard on his wrist, causing him to scream in pain. Quinn buried a fist in his solar plexus, then hit him in the throat, and finally, as Sears doubled over, he grabbed his shoulders and kneed him in the stomach.

Sears fell to the ground like a sack of shit.

While he lay crumpled in a ball, Quinn opened the door to the police cruiser and popped the trunk. As Sears forced himself to his hands and knees, Quinn helped him up, then grabbed him by the back of the belt, shoved him hard into the trunk and slammed it shut.

"You done it now, Quinn," Sears rasped from inside.

"I haven't even begun." Quinn got behind the wheel, turned the ignition and raced away, determined to find Seth.

25.

"It's starting to rain pretty hard out there," Maria said.

Seth could tell that from her shirt, which was damp and clung to her skin. He couldn't keep his eyes off her chest.

"Anything wrong?" she asked.

He lifted his eyes to hers. No question—she'd caught him—but he didn't care.

"Do you know Al Sears was in OOB?" she asked.

Seth's eyes widened. "Did he see you?"

"No."

"Thank God."

Maria and Jack were still drenched, but Seth had turned the heat on and she was finally warming up.

"Is that better?" he asked.

"Yes," she lied. Maria wished they hadn't gotten in the car. Seth was making her nervous. She wasn't sure why, but she sensed something was very wrong.

"Don't worry." It was as though he'd read her mind.

"I need to use this." She nodded down at his cell phone, which was lying between the seats. "John's probably worried to death."

"Fair enough." He wheeled into an empty lot behind an auto parts store. "I just wanna stop a second." He pushed the phone back, out of her reach. "Relax." He shut off the car's ignition, raised the tilted steering wheel and turned to her. "Don't you think it's time we got comfortable?"

This was too much and Maria was ready to scream. "I think it's time you told me what's really going on."

Seth laughed. "Don't you trust me?"

"No."

"Isn't it a little late for that?"

His phone rang and he snapped it open. "Hello," he said in an entirely different voice, one of a friendly salesman.

"I'm calling from hell," Quinn said. "And I want you to join me."

Seth swallowed his surprise. "Well, I already have a little company."

"They have nothing to do with this," Quinn said.

"Oh, that's where you're wrong," Seth said.

"Don't make things worse for yourself," Quinn said. "The cops are already looking for you."

"Really?" Seth asked. "My guess is you're too arrogant to tell Sears what happened and the cops don't even know."

"Don't bet on it."

Seth turned and looked at Maria and Jack. "If we're betting, the stakes are pretty high."

"If anything happens, you're dead," Quinn said.

"John, please. If anything happens, they're dead. So meet me at the Baxter Bridge in twenty minutes. And by God, you better be alone or they're both going for their last swim."

26.

THE BAXTER BRIDGE ROSE out of the sifting fog like a silent green monster reaching across the Penobscot River. Its upper deck carried Route 1's traffic, though the railroad below hadn't seen a train in years. The whole structure was complicated by a midsection that rose and lowered twice a day so ships could pass beneath.

The railway entrance was fenced off, which never kept teenagers from using the tracks as a drinking spot. The river looked calm and tranquil, but its volume and flow could carry away the strongest swimmer, and every few years disaster struck.

One of Quinn's classmates died there the summer before ninth grade. It had taken two weeks to find him—once the gases expanded enough to carry his body to the surface. When the cops finally made the recovery on a Sunday afternoon, Jake headed to the scene and Quinn tagged along.

The rubbery corpse was stretched on a gurney, and Jake took pictures like there was nothing to it. "Once you get a good look at death," he told his squeamish son, "you learn to appreciate life."

Quinn didn't argue. He was too busy throwing up.

Quinn could still picture the bloated remains. And before he knew it, he was running toward his wife and son. A rusted chain-link fence stood between them, but he was up and almost over it when he caught his pant leg and slipped, head-first, onto the rotting planks and cinders. Shit. He got right up, muddy and bleeding, and went forward, leaving pieces of khaki and skin behind.

At least he was moving. His legs were burning by the time he reached the wet wooden ties. His lungs were tightening and his head felt light. He listened for voices but could only hear the soft rain against the steady pounding of steel from the yard a half mile away.

His chest was heaving as he looked down through the railroad ties. The black water was rising. That's when he heard voices—Maria's, high and excited, Seth's low and firm. They weren't in sight as he adjusted his steps to the space of the planks, going slowly at first, then picking up the pace as he got used to the clipped cadence.

He didn't feel anything but adrenaline.

"Who's there?" Maria's voice echoed in the darkness.

Quinn could tell she was scared but he couldn't move any faster. "Stay away from her!" Quinn shouted. "I swear to God, Seth, you better not do anything crazy!"

Then everything was quiet, except Quinn's pounding heart as he pushed on, desperate, till he was stopped by Maria's scream. Quinn hesitated a moment as he saw Seth pick his son up with one arm and feign like he was going to throw him off the bridge.

"Well, well, well," Seth said when Quinn appeared. "Looks like you're just in time."

"Put him down!"

"Or what?"

"He's a little boy," Quinn said. "He's your own cousin."

"So now family ties suddenly mean something," Seth said. "Funny how they didn't a few hours ago."

Maria moved toward Seth and was stopped when he leveled a pistol at her face. "Now take a step back," he said, "or this little boy's gonna have a mommy without a face."

"Seth, your problem is with me!" Quinn said as he stepped closer.

"It always has been."

"I'm sorry to hear that."

"I doubt it. But here's what I propose." Seth put down Jack, who ran to his mother. "You jump off this bridge and everything's forgiven. I'll even let the little wife and son walk away from here."

"And if I don't?"

"Then you watch them die, knowing you could have prevented it."

But Quinn wasn't taking any chances. He burst forward and before Seth had a chance to raise the gun again, Quinn buried his shoulder into Seth's chest and took them both over the side of the bridge, where they fell—screaming—into the darkness.

Maria and Jack pressed against the rail and watched the twisting, tangled bodies shrink in size in what seemed like slow motion. Maria held her son, who clung to her leg and turned his head away from the sight.

"Oh, sweet Mary, Mother of God, help him," Maria said.

But it was out of her hands as well.

• • •

BOTH SETH AND QUINN tensed for an impact that didn't seem to come as their stomachs filled their throats and their bodies gained speed—seventy, eighty, ninety miles per hour. Their ears popped from the pressure and Quinn felt a stab between his eyes as blood vessels burst. The two men were dropping at a rate of more than a hundred miles per hour when they hit the Penobscot River.

Seth's body broke the surface and Quinn's shoulder drove through his cousin's neck and face. Seth felt an overwhelming flash of electric pain along the length of his body, then nothing.

At the same time, Quinn's collarbone ground and crunched as his shoulder dislodged. But despite Quinn's horrible pain, Seth's body had absorbed most of the force as they plunged below the cold water, beyond the reach of the moonlight.

Quinn's shoes and shirt were lost on impact and he felt numb everywhere. Still, he could move and managed to separate himself from the limp body that he could already tell was dead. He slowly kicked toward the surface. The current had carried him thirty yards south of the bridge and he wasn't able to use his right arm, which dangled limply at his side. He was disoriented and weak and was pushed slowly by the big river till he finally breached the surface and gasped a desperate breath before sinking again into the dark water.

He was even weaker but stroked with one arm and kicked with both bare feet. Once he reached the surface, he turned his aching body ninety degrees toward the shore and kicked again with everything he had left.

The flames from the newspaper lit the horizon and he thought of Maria and Jack, who were running toward him. He concentrated on reaching solid ground but wasn't sure if he could, and that's when his feet hit the rocky bottom. Coughing and retching, he finally made it.

He could hear them calling and that was all that mattered.

EPILOGUE

THE EARLY MORNING NEWS began with live coverage by *Action News* reporter Chip Hess and footage of Seth's bagged body being loaded into an ambulance: "Controversial cop Al Sears solves a Stone Harbor homicide—and if I know anything about the chief, he won't apologize for his take-no-prisoners approach."

"That's for sure," the beautiful anchor agreed from the studio, before throwing it back to the early morning scene at the river.

"This is Chip Hess in downtown Stone Harbor, *live,* to get the public's reaction to news that the general manager torched the *Stone Harbor Pilot* after killing one man and botching a murder attempt on his *own cousin!*"

"That's just so hard to believe," the anchor said as she shook her head in a practiced move that would be repeated throughout the broadcast.

"Residents here are *shocked*!" Chip told her as the station cut to footage of the natives.

The broadcast then jumped to a collage of brief statements from an assortment of residents and tourists in Becky's Seafood Shack, all of whom expressed disbelief at what had happened.

Not Ernie Gould.

"He wasn't really from around here," Ernie said flatly. "He didn't come here till he was in high school." Then he held up his petition for Bryan Bowen-Smythe's removal from the town board, which now had more than three thousand signatures, but the camera quickly cut to a customer before he could explain.

"That youngest Quinn was nothin' but trouble," Nate Morrison added for emphasis.

"Might even be some question about how old Jake Quinn died," a third man insisted, without giving his name. "That's somethin' to be investigated."

Then Chip read a great deal of copy from the *Pilot*'s coverage of the land deal, an old TV trick. The talking heads would put a reporter on location, get a few live shots, then hope nobody noticed they'd lifted the local newspaper's work.

The story stretched beyond the Portland stations. Al Sears was being lauded across New England as a small-town hero who hadn't rested till he found his friend's killer. The chief made no attempt to dispute the reports. Sears said he was just doing his job. He failed to mention that he'd been doing it from inside the locked trunk of his police cruiser, which was just as well for everyone involved.

The *Pilot* eventually managed to come up with its own coverage—at nine o'clock that evening, which didn't stop every issue that hit the streets from selling out, even though the number of single copies had been pushed from three thousand to five thousand, along with the usual eleven thousand home subscribers.

Readers just couldn't get enough of the story.

NEWSPAPER GENERAL MANAGER
CHARGED WITH MURDER
By Sarah Sewell
Pilot Staff

Police say the general manager of this newspaper murdered one man and attempted to kill another—his own cousin—before he died after a struggle and fall from the Baxter Bridge.

Seth Quinn beat Paul Stanwood to death in the early hours of May 13 because Stanwood wouldn't cooperate in a real estate deal, according to a confession he made to his cousin, *Pilot* owner John Quinn. Seth Quinn had conspired to sell Sullivan Park—a public landmark—to a holding company that planned to develop the land as a gated community, complete with a 36-hole private golf course and marina.

He brokered the deal with a Malaysian firm looking to expand its U.S. real estate holdings and was expected to make several million dollars for his efforts. Things began to unravel when Stanwood threatened to go public with the entire scheme . . .

Then there was Sarah's money shot. It was a great photo, one that would probably win an award, which was important to a kid just starting out. Razor-sharp and tightly cropped, the picture captured the grim expression on Quinn's haggard face as he staggered out of the burning building. The Associated Press was happy to transmit it across the country, since it wasn't often that one family member burned down another's newspaper.

Quinn had to admit, the whole experience gave him a new

perspective on what he did for a living. He tried to explain it all in a front-page note.

PILOT TEMPORARILY PRINTED IN BANGOR
BY JOHN QUINN
Editor & Publisher

BANGOR—A fire never stopped the Stone Harbor Pilot in the past and it certainly won't today.

In 1895, a blaze leveled most of the downtown area, including the original newspaper building, which was made entirely of wood. My great-grandfather, John Cole Sr., built a new office a block away on Front Street.

Most of that brick building still stands, minus $1 million in damages after my late cousin tried to burn us down. Luckily, the damage spared most of our production facilities, which should be back online within a few weeks.

In the meantime, the *Bangor Daily News* is helping out by printing our paper. We've set up temporary offices over the Magic Muffin Bakery.

We've also gotten some help from an old friend. Angus Stanwood has made a substantial investment in this newspaper to help us through this difficult time. With his help, I'm confident about the future.

The *Stone Harbor Pilot* has been in business for 128 years and we're not going anywhere. So stop in if you get a chance. Even though our circumstances have changed, our mission has stayed the same: to tell it like it is and to let the chips fall where they may.

"This time they fell pretty hard," Maria said as she put the paper on the nightstand and curled into her husband's arms.

"Sometimes that happens." Quinn could just imagine what his father would have said. Jake would have found a way to blame him for allowing Seth to kill Paul, then burn down the family business. But he finally realized it was time to stop worrying about what his father would have thought.

"Do you think any of it made a difference?" she asked.

He didn't really know. Seth was dead, but that didn't bring Paul back. Nothing would. His friend was still gone and the best he could do was try to help Lizz and the kids. She'd gone into detox and was seeing a counselor, which was a start. She'd also taken out an order of protection against Sears, who would lose his job if he violated it.

The land deal wasn't going anywhere, but that wouldn't stop other deals and developments that were changing the coast forever. Yet he'd gotten to the truth in that one instance, or as much of the truth as possible, no matter how uncomfortable it had made some people.

"Well?" Maria pressed. "When we came back here, you wanted to make a difference. Have you?"

"I don't know, but it was worth trying—even at this price." And it had been one helluva price. He'd been forced to kill his own cousin—a cousin he'd loved and treated like a brother. Sure, brothers could be hard on each other, but what had changed Seth?

That was something Quinn would never really know, though it was obvious he could have handled things differently. They all could have, starting with Quinn's father and ending with him. But they all paid for their mistakes.

"So how much more are you willing to pay?" she asked.

"Whatever it takes. And what about you?"

It was Maria's turn to think. She'd never really liked Maine, or maybe it was just life in a small town. Treachery and murder didn't change things for the better. But she was tired, and after all the time and distance, she finally realized that any place was what you made it.

"Well?" Quinn wanted to know.

"I guess I'm willing to stick it out here."

"Anything else you're willing to do?"

"That depends what you have in mind."

He showed her and she tilted her head back and mouthed a silent moan as he laughed.

"Hey," she said. "Don't stop now!"

He didn't. Stopping was the farthest thing from his mind, until the phone rang and her expression changed.

"Don't worry," he said after the second ring. "It can wait."

Maria put a finger to his lips and he stopped talking, but his smile got bigger and bigger, and at that point in time, he didn't want to think of anything else.

How *The Way Life Should Be* Got Published

Gather.com is the social networking site where adults connect around shared interests ranging from travel to cooking and politics to parenting. On Gather.com, you'll find an engaged community of book lovers and writers who read and publish some of the highest-quality user-generated content online. Special groups offer author advice, book reviews, insiders' publishing information, and a virtual writing workshop, all for free.

Leveraging the strength of its members, Gather.com launched the groundbreaking First Chapters Writing Competition in January 2007. The prize: a first-time fiction author would receive a publishing contract with the Touchstone imprint of Simon & Schuster. Over 2,600 Gather.com members submitted manuscripts to be evaluated and voted on by their peers, who narrowed the entries to five finalists. The quality of the submissions was so high that Simon & Schuster published two novels, one of which you're reading today. Join the online discussion about *The Way Life Should Be* at http://waylife shouldbe.gather.com. You can find the other winning novel, *Fire Bell in the Night* by Geoffrey S. Edwards, wherever books are sold.

If you want to influence the next books that get published, visit http://firstchapters.gather.com. Upcoming First Chapters competitions will focus on the romance and mystery genres, launching fall 2007. Join the conversation around the latest novels and cast your vote for the next bestseller at http://www.gather.com.

Congratulations to Terry Shaw from the following Gather.com members:

Stephen Prosapio

Sheila D.

Ty T.

Ann B.

Nana to Seven cutie pies

Karen Dabney

Beth H.

Trish A.

Michelle C.

George Corneliussen

Trudy P.

Judi F.

Terry Wilson-Malam

K. B.

Julie G.

Eric D. Goodman

Kerry Dexter

Samantha B.

Lori F.

Sandra D.

Geoffrey E.

Susan J.

Pat S.

Kathryn Esplin-Oleski

Deb H.

Tom M.

Arlene H.

Jessie Voigts

Andy Z.

Sonia M.

Robin "Buffy's Stunt
    Double" D.
Christine Zibas
Geeta M.
Kathleen L.
Katrina Hall
Sylvia R. C.
James R.
G Photog
C. A.
Elinor D.
Lum P.
Katie S.
Steve H.
Kate K.
Loretta N.
Judi J.
Jennifer S.
Charlene Sharp
Latasha W.
Aurora D.
Katie O.
Mae W.
Michael DeFilippo
Diana B.
Noble Collins
Karen R.
Genevieve S.
Lynn P.
Jessica B.
Ann B.

Marge H.
Becky S.
Anthony Samuel P.
Annie M.
Patti C.
Rae A.
Amy B.
Ms. Meacham: Money
    Maven
Pippa W.
Carla J.
Karen S.
Linda R.
Cathy P.
Beverly Meyers
Kathryn S.
A.C.S.
Yolanda H.
Bruce L.
Cara V.
CL C.
Cindy the Anti-Trite
Catherine B.
Susan Marie
Lisa B.
Jasmin J.
Venessa G.
Thom T.
Gail S.
Lisa M.
Sandra D.

Marsha F.

Clellie T.

Debbie G.

Loretta G.

J.K. Sather

Scott M.

Val Fox, VP marketing at
    Gather.com

Ruthe M.

Edward Nudelman

Jennifer B.

Kristen C.

Cathie A.

Judith W.

Jennifer D.

Cee D.

Jim L.

Ron Booser

Sherri M.

Dave S.

Andy Anderson

Elena Dorothy Bowman

Roy W.

Michael H.

Rand P.

A. C.

Barbara S.

Dawn K.

Deb D.

Andrew Madrid

Terry B.

Londa H.

Jen A.

Jak J.

Linda R.

Alyson W.

Bob Cornell